Prai.

MW01265052

"This book has someti.

and the paranormal collide with a serial killer to make one exciting story. Throw in lots of sex, and what more could a reader ask for?" –Romantic Times Magazine

"I can describe this book in one word. Fabulous! Jake and Allison played well off of each other. The sexual tension in the book you could cut it with a knife. I am surprised that this book did not burst into flames. The killer was written so well that you could almost imagine being at the crime scene yourself. Sloan McBride has a new fan and I cannot wait to read another one of her books." –Megan, Bitten by Books

"Sloan McBride captures readers from the first page and holds them in thrall for the remainder of this fantastic story. I loved how the story opens with us receiving a glimpse of how the killer works. Her writing rivets us as we transition to the other players' points of view. She keeps us guessing as we draw ever closer to finding out the identity of The Surgeon and how everyone seems to fit into this puzzle. *TOGETHER IN DARKNESS* is an awesome, romantic suspense. I was impressed with Ms. McBride's work and will certainly look forward to her other tales."—Melissa, Novel Talk

"Fantastic. Together in Darkness is the first book I've read by Sloan McBride and I was highly impressed. This thoroughly entertaining novel kept me engrossed and turning the pages until the very end. The characters, both primary and secondary, drew me in with interesting dialogue and lively banter that gave you a good idea of their individual personalities and motivations. The relationship between Allison and Jake grew at a steady pace and was believable. They didn't act on their attraction for each other straight away and the love scenes were well written and sensual. I would love to see romantic suspense stories with the secondary characters featured. They interested me, I feel they deserve it. I didn't foresee who the killer was until the author wanted me to and that intrigued and surprised me. Twists and turns woven through the story added a lot of tension that at times had me holding my breath. Want an exciting novel to read? This is a book for you."—Abi, The Romance Studio

Other Books by Sloan McBride

Highland Stone (The Talisman Trilogy)

Dangerous Heat (Men of Fire Trilogy)

The Fury (A Time Walker Novel)

The Treasure (A Time Walker Novel)

Author's Note

I would like to take this time to thank Lt. Joe Aiello from the Gloucester, Massachusetts Police Department, who helped me with the accuracy of the police procedures and policies, and with factual information regarding the City of Gloucester for the writing of this book.

I would also like to thank those friends who read the story and gave me critical input. As always, a big hug goes out to my family for their support.

Together in Darkness
By
Sloan McBride
www.sloanmcbride.com

This is a work of fiction. Although Gloucester, Massachusetts and some of the businesses and landmarks herein mentioned are factual, all characters and events portrayed in this work are from the Author's imagination. Any resemblance to living persons, places or events is merely coincidence.

CHAPTER ONE

The musty scent of out-of-season clothes pressed close; surrounded him with barely enough room to breathe, let alone move. He'd been inside the dark closet for hours while the party raged, venturing out once to grab a plate of food and a beer. Now he pressed his ear to the cool paneled door to hear what they were saying.

He smirked.

One tall, voluptuous brunette had come on to him at the food table. Smiling, he'd raised his left hand flashing the gold wedding band he used at times. "Married, baby," he'd said with a thick Cajun accent. It amused him to mingle with the unsuspecting. Still, his legs were cramping. Changes in the observation stage would have to be made next time to avoid the discomfort.

Calculated. Precise. That's how his plans were laid out. It had taken time to learn, a lot of trial and error.

"I know it's been rough lately and I've been working a lot, but you know I'm doing it for us. Twenty-four is a good age for new beginnings," he heard his target's boyfriend say.

That's what he thinks.

"I'll see you in the morning."

"Okay."

Moments ago the music had ceased. Laughter and birthday platitudes in a jumble of voices faded as partiers left. The door closing and silence indicated—he hoped—the last of the guests were gone. As the dead bolt slid home and the foyer light switched off, he blew a deep, anticipatory breath. It was almost time. She mounted the stairs above his head; the sound of running water assured he could safely leave his hiding place. Upstairs he watched her prepare for bed. She brushed her teeth, rinsed with mouthwash and wandered into the absurdly feminine bedroom, brushing her long hair. The curves of her body beckoned him.

He moved quickly, a silent shadow. Grasping the young woman around the waist he slipped a hand over her mouth. He tumbled them onto the bed stretching across her prone body as she struggled. She was stronger than her slight build led him to believe. Her elbow slammed into his chest and it hurt. "Bitch!" He slapped her hard.

He wrapped his fingers around her slender neck and squeezed. He wouldn't let her suffer long. Frantically, her fingers attempted to gain a hold, nails sliding over the backs of his hands, but to no avail. Bit by bit, he applied more pressure, until the fight drained out of her along with the oxygen. Her thrashing lost vigor, her body lost strength. Her fingers trailed from around his wrists. A familiar adrenaline rush crashed through him at the end when the prey gave up to the darkness.

"Twenty-four won't be a good age after all," he whispered.

Pressing his lips to hers he inhaled the final gasp and stayed there a moment longer.

The kiss of death.

He stood and moved slowly down her body, his hands caressing her breasts and flat stomach, luxuriating in the softness. He straightened her legs and tugged the flowery nightshirt lower to cover the tops of her tanned thighs. The glowing red numbers on the bedside clock read 2:10 a.m.

He slipped out of his leather jacket and folded it neatly over the vanity chair, brushing a non-existent speck from his clean white t-shirt before heading back to the bed where she waited. Carefully, he pulled the shiny straight razor freshly sharpened for this occasion from his jean pocket and opened it with a click.

He slit the garment down the center. Now that her bronzed skin was exposed, he paused, studying her, and moved the auburn hair out of her face. God, she was beautiful, probably as beautiful on the inside.

The razor sliced easily through the skin and underlying tissue, but thick muscle took a moment to carve through. The flaps of skin formed a jagged 'x' across her abdomen and, when peeled back, made it easy for the organs to be removed. Coddling each piece protectively like a newborn infant, he laid them gently on her chest, pausing every time to inhale the sweet smell of blood coating his hands.

He stood back to admire his work, a grin twitched at the corner of his mouth. So many times he'd read the stories about Jack the Ripper and how the cunning devil cut open harlots in White Chapel. It pleased him to repeat the procedure of such a famous mastermind.

Red Rover, Red Rover, send Jakey right over.

He suppressed the laughter and dipped a forefinger into the pool of dark red blood settling in her abdominal cavity. On the bare wall above the headboard, he meticulously spelled out his message—*To FBI Agent Jake Austin. One for the money.*

Satisfied, he walked into the bathroom to wash the blood from his skin. He smiled at his reflection. Picking up the razor from the side of the sink, he ran the blade under the sparkling flow several times, then dried it and his gloved hands on a fluffy pink towel before sliding it into his pocket. He noticed a red splotch on his jeans. "Dammit." Ruining his jeans hadn't been in the plan. He punched the mirror shattering it, leaving his reflection fractured. Leashing the rage, he exited the room. He'd have to burn the clothes.

In the big, airy kitchen, he snagged a piece of birthday cake from the box she'd left on the bar. "Yum. Chocolate, my favorite."

He paused at the French doors to zip his jacket over the blood-stained t-shirt and left, humming as he moved across the lawn within the comforting shadows.

In that instant, the fine hairs on the nape of his neck stood on end. He sensed a womanly presence, sweet and... familiar. He stopped at the gate and inhaled, trying to draw her closer, but she was gone. He looked at the house once more, and opened the gate. Without a doubt, his next destination would bring new, exciting developments.

CHAPTER TWO

Allison Brody couldn't stop smiling. Her latest window masterpiece for R&N's department store displayed old school days, which was relevant since school would be starting again soon. Complete joy filled her the day she'd found the antique desk in the storage room. That had immediately sent her on the quest for school supplies and new school clothes to feature in the display. Borrowing a blackboard from the custodian at Fuller Elementary School was the piece-dé-résistance.

She stretched and groaned. Her limbs ached and a huge knot had settled between her shoulder blades. It was perfect; nothing more could be done. She stashed the tools, turned off the lights, and headed for the door.

The night wind briskly whipped around the buildings and slapped at her, bringing shivers and a runny nose. Fall would soon be making its presence known in the North Shore fishing village of Gloucester, Massachusetts. Taking one last look in the store's window she noticed two things reflected in the glass: how the streetlights glittered in the night sky like diamonds on black velvet, and how her hair had escaped the misshaped bun and spiked in several places.

"Warm cocoa and soft bed here I come," she mumbled and headed for the car.

Normally Allison loved the night, but something seemed off.

A tickling unease crawled along her skin.

The car's engine rumbled to life and she flipped on the heater waiting for the air to turn warm. As she reached for a tissue to blow her nose, a sudden stab of pain pierced her skull then eased, leaving a dull throb at the base. *You're just tired.*

Trying to ignore the unusual headache and what it might mean, Allison searched the sky for a glimpse of the moon, but moving clouds hid it. Her brother would laugh and tease her about being lunar motivated, then make smarmy comments about her new hairdo. Nick wouldn't see any of it though, because he'd been away on some geological exploration for a while.

****

Allison pulled up in front of the quaint Colonial two-story house. Home, sweet, home.

She hung her coat and scarf then headed for the kitchen where she booted up her laptop, put a kettle of water on to boil, and grabbed a mug from the cupboard. When the kettle tooted, she filled the cup with instant cocoa and hot water, and threw some tiny marshmallows in for good measure. No email messages from Nick. She sighed with disappointment.

She took her cocoa and dragged her body up the staircase. Peeling off her clothes, she pulled her favorite gown over her head and climbed into the soft bed, her eyes closing the minute her head hit the pillow in spite of the persistent throb.

Cuddled on her side, Allison dreamed of white sandy beaches, palm trees swaying in the wind, and Alex.

Alex.

He strolled toward her with a big smile. His deliciously toned body tanned from head to toe and she could see every inch of that body...almost. His fingers caressed her cheek and the scene changed to a different place altogether. A young woman came into a room brushing her hair. The images flashed forward in a blur and Allison found herself standing over the mutilated body of the same woman, writing something on the wall in the victim's blood.

Allison's eyes flew open, scanned, searched settling on familiar furniture. Wincing, she looked at the clock where bright red numbers shone 2:10 a.m. The pounding in her head had escalated.

It was a dream. She squeezed her eyes closed, ignoring how it upped the pressure of the headache, and whispered, "Please."

As she drifted back to sleep the two dreams converged. *Alex's smiling face turned ugly and the woman's silent scream echoed in her head. "Alex, what's happening?"*

"*I miss you.*"

Allison bolted upright, again gasping for breath. It was 5:58 a.m. and the sun crested the horizon. She staggered into the bathroom, bent over the sink, and splashed cold water on her face. Several deep breaths later, Allison raised her head. A man's reflection stared back at her in the shattered mirror. She screamed and spun away. When she ventured a second look, she saw only her disheveled image.

Not again.

She couldn't rid herself of the chills or the memory of those black, soulless eyes.

Downstairs she made her morning tea, hoping that would take care of the cold sensation hovering beneath her skin. She flipped on the television for some noise. "This breaking story in from…."

Allison barely heard the anchorwoman on the news. Her hands lay flat against the countertop, her eyes open, but seeing nothing around her. A strange tunnel-vision had her in its spell. It pulled her in at a frightening pace. Suddenly, she found herself in a car speeding down a highway. Rock-n-roll blasted on the radio and the hands that felt like hers, but weren't, tapped the beat on the steering wheel. The white lines on the road rushed past.

A shrill sound like the whine of an engine brought Allison back to her kitchen. The news had ended and another show played. Bile rose and burned her throat. Shaken, she ran to the roll-top desk in the office and tore through some papers until she found a business card for Paul Kincaid, M.D., Psychiatrist. She turned it over to where he'd written his cell number.

Her fingers trembled as she punched in the numbers. "Paul, it's Allison Brody."

"Allison? This is an early surprise."

"Um, I know it's early and I'm sorry but I need to make an appointment."

"My door is always open. What's happened?"

She tucked the phone against her shoulder and rubbed her hands together in an attempt to stop the shaking. "The visions have started again."

CHAPTER THREE

Jake Austin stood with hands flat against the shower wall, head hung forward while the hot water pounded his neck and back. The sun just touched the horizon, but he'd already been awake for four hours. Gruesome images flashing through his mind assured him of many more sleepless nights. The shower spray tapped on the vinyl curtain until the flow turned cold. Sighing, he twisted the knobs to turn off the water.

He flung the curtain open, grabbed a towel to buff his hair, and wrapped it around his waist. He swiped a hand across the mirror to get rid of the moisture.

Grave. Yeah, that was the perfect word for his reflection. Hard eyes stared back, the pupils dilated so big the irises disappeared. Some freakish side effect of his ability to seep into depraved minds, unsure of what he'd find and not always confident he'd come out again as himself. Things he'd seen changed people— changed him.

His team had just come off a month-long investigation in Louisiana. The bayou was not the best place to find a killer who tortured victims then left the remains for the gators. Tired in no way covered how he felt.

He stretched experimentally. Every inch of him ached as though he'd been trampled by an elephant. Okay, a herd of elephants. He needed more sleep, but the nightmares deprived him of that privilege.

Throwing on blue jeans and a polo shirt, Jake headed downstairs to get coffee. Even before he'd taken the first sip his cell phone rang.

"Austin."

"Jake, you need to get in here. We're wheels up in two hours."

"Where to?"

"New York."

****

Jake strolled into the boardroom where the team discussed cases, and examined evidence and clues, trying to catch the human filth that crawled out of the woodwork every minute of every day. His colleagues had already arrived. They stopped talking when he walked in.

As usual, Peter Carmichael, the special agent in charge stood at the head of the table. His blond hair ruffled as if he'd run fingers through it, tugged on it, or hadn't bothered to comb it before leaving his apartment.

"What's the sitch?" Jake finally said.

Peter waved to a vacant chair at the table. "Have a seat, Jake."

Jake had a feeling the floor was about to drop out.

Peter glanced around the room. "We received a call about four this morning from a homicide detective in Schenectady, New York. A woman's body was found by her boyfriend when he came home from a late shift at work."

"Is she another in a string of homicides in the area?" Margo Sullivan asked, as she pushed her glasses up.

"Not that we know of."

Genevieve Tobias said, "Did something come up on NCIC that links this murder to others in another state?"

"No, Tobias."

From his slouched position in the chair to Jake's right Dr. Zach Quincy, the forensic pathologist, chimed in. "So why did you get me out of a nice warm bed to drag my ass to New York when we just got home?"

"There was a message printed on the wall in the victim's blood." Peter's gaze passed to each member and landed on Jake. "It said, To FBI Agent Jake Austin. One for the money."

Jake's stomach did a flip-flop. "What?"

With her big blue eyes, Margo looked at Jake. "Are you

okay?"

Jake picked up a pencil from the table and began spinning it through his fingers. "I need to see the scene."

Peter nodded. "My thoughts exactly. Let's grab our gear. The plane should be fueled and waiting."

During the flight, Jake studied information on the victim. Digital images of the body, the message, and the scene flooded the computer screen. He had no ties to the woman or her family. The message gave no indication why he had been named or what his role was. Of course, he'd wait until he walked the house to make any judgments.

Quincy plopped into the seat next to him. The nevo glasses framed intelligent eyes that saw things others missed. He possessed quick wit and was career-minded, although to look at him most of the time you'd never know it.

The doc looked as shitty as Jake felt. "Anything?"

"Nothing that stands out."

Ticking in the back of his mind something about the body bothered him, but he couldn't put a finger on it.

"Curious."

Jake stared at the girl in the pictures. She looked like she was sleeping, but as his gaze scanned the rest of the body, the picture exploded with gore and the macabre.

****

Emergency and police vehicles blocked Rochester Drive when they arrived. Jake could tell the detective greeting them wasn't pleased to see federal agents, but they were used to that sentiment.

"Hello, Detective Johnson," Peter said as he held his ID up with one hand and extended the other. "I'm Special Agent Peter Carmichael. This is my team."

Johnson nodded their direction. "Is one of you Austin?"

Jake moved forward. "That would be me, detective."

"What's this about, Austin?" Johnson's manner projected authority.

"I'm not really sure yet, but I'd like to take a look at the crime scene."

The detective gave Jake the once over. "Come on."

The forensic guys were finishing up. Jake stopped for shoe covers to prevent contamination of the scene. He took a pair of surgical gloves and snapped them on. Peter did the same. Tobias and Quincy went to chat with the forensic crew.

Jake and Peter followed the detective through the front door, up the stairs, down the hall to the bedroom.

"Any prints?"

"Several. She'd had a birthday party from the looks of it."

Jake walked to the foot of the bed and stared at the wall above the headboard. There, written in the young woman's blood, was his name. An odd sensation dashed across his shoulders and down his spine. At the same time he heard an unusual humming in his head.

As the humming faded, he caught something Johnson was telling Peter.

"… an arrow on the wall in the victim's blood pointing to the DVD player. There was a DVD in the machine."

This drew Jake's attention. "What DVD?"

"*The Perfect Storm.*"

He frowned in concentration, all the cylinders kicking in. He'd heard the title before. Hadn't there been a movie out a few years ago? What did it have to do with this victim?

Jake scanned the scene until it became etched in his memory. Inch by inch, he walked the path the killer had taken, the bedroom, the bathroom, the kitchen. He stared at the chocolate birthday cake. A vague sense of déjá vu stole over him, but vanished quickly. As he stared outside at the yard, he saw a dusky form casually stroll through the gate and disappear like a wisp of smoke. A memory trace.

"It looks like the perp hid in the downstairs closet, and believe it or not, came out to get food and beer. We found the plate with crumbs and an empty beer bottle in the closet. Ballsy," Johnson commented.

Jake said, "Let me guess. No prints."

"Right, but they are checking for DNA from the lip of the bottle. Maybe we'll get something."

"What about the party guests?" Peter asked.

"The boyfriend gave us names of everyone he could remember being there. We already have people contacting them for questioning. We have the preliminary details loaded in NCIC. We're waiting to see if it flags anything."

The computerized index of criminal justice information available to all agencies worked twenty-four/seven, three hundred sixty-five days a year. If there were any unsolved cases floating around with similarities, it would find them.

Peter shook Johnson's hand. "Thanks for calling us, detective. We'd appreciate being kept in the loop on this one."

"Sure thing."

Climbing into the rental car with the rest of the team, Jake grabbed the phone on his belt and punched in the number of the biggest information-seeking geek he knew, who also happened to be a federal agent that worked with the team. "Linc, I need you to find out all you can about the movie, *The Perfect Storm*." The man on the other end of the line grumbled.

"Okay, get some coffee and call me back."

"It looks as though forensics did an efficient job," Tobias offered. "I didn't see anything at the scene that I hadn't seen in the photographs." With her keen eye and cameras, Tobias picked up images at crime scenes which gave new meaning to still photography.

"Tobias is right," Jake said. "The only new information we've gotten is the DVD in the machine. Good police work by the detectives not putting that information out there."

From his place in the backseat, Quincy said, "I need to examine the body."

Peter nodded. "We're headed to the morgue. I'll talk to the coroner to make arrangements for you to sit in on the autopsy when we get there."

"Wake me when we get there," Quincy mumbled, as he slouched in the seat and closed his eyes.

"I'd like your preliminary profile by the time we board the plane again, Jake."

Jake's cell phone shrilled. "Talk to me, Linc."

"*The Perfect Storm* is a book and movie based on a true story of the Andrea Gale, a fishing vessel lost in a freak storm in 1991."

"Where?"

"Gloucester, Massachusetts."

"Thanks." Jake glanced at Peter.

"So, what do we have?"

He relayed the information. "I need some time to analyze everything we've learned this morning."

"I'll drop you off at the airport. While we talk to the doctor about the autopsy, you can do your thing."

Jake nodded.

A few hours ago Jake had been begging for sleep. Now, he was too amped. He stared out the window seeing the landscape as nothing but a blur. Like a virtual tour, the crime scene replayed in his mind as he tried to figure out what bothered him about the victim's body.

CHAPTER FOUR

"Allison, it's a pleasure to see you again," Paul said, moving toward her.

"I wish it were under different circumstances."

It felt strange being here and not seeing the warm smile and kind eyes of Dr. Lomax. She was nineteen years old and unsure of her sanity the first time she'd come to this office. Dr. Lomax helped her realize only she could take control of her life and move past the tragedy. A few years ago her old friend from college, Paul Kincaid, took over Dr. Lomax's practice.

He smiled. "Come, sit down. If I weren't a professional, I'd say I'm crushed." He sat down. "Now, tell me what has upset you."

Allison sat stiff-backed in the soft leather chair, her hands clasped in her lap to keep them from shaking. What could she tell him?

She looked around the office, taking a moment to calm down. Paul had painted the room, filling it with beautiful fall tones, and replaced the worn desk with a rich, cherry-colored one. The bookcase was only a quarter full, where Dr. Lomax had kept it overflowing.

Allison gathered her nerve. "I've been having strange visions—I mean dreams." She licked her lips. "Violent nightmares."

Paul nodded and made notes. "How long have you been having these dreams?"

"Not long. They started a couple of days ago." This time.

"The anniversary of your parents' death is coming up." Paul's powerful brown eyes filled with compassion, making Allison want to cry. "Have you been thinking about that day and what happened?"

"They aren't dreams about my parents, Paul—I mean, doctor. It's more like I'm in someone else's head."

"You're outside yourself." Paul leaned forward, elbows on the desk and fingers steepled in front of him. "What is that telling you?"

Allison shook her head. "I don't know." That she'd lost her mind—again.

"It's been a long time, Allison. Ten years. Perhaps issues that were left unresolved are surfacing."

She knew she shouldn't feel uneasy speaking of her parents' death and these visions to Paul. "I'm not broken, doctor." She gritted her teeth and examined her nails. "I have a nice home, a good job. My life is fine."

"Now you're getting defensive." His smile patronized her. "I'm offering you a possibility. You have obviously tried to move on from the tragedy."

Allison sighed. "I know. I'm sorry. I haven't slept well since these vi—dreams started."

"I'm glad you decided to come in and talk. Has anything happened recently out of the ordinary besides the dreams?"

"No, nothing."

"I assume you are still working at R&N's department store, doing the window designs."

"Yes."

"I read in the newspaper the other day that a fatal accident occurred close to the store, at a nearby intersection."

Allison stared out the window. "I saw them loading a body into the ambulance that night as I passed on my way to work."

Again Paul's warm eyes met hers. "Don't you think it could have stirred something in you? A memory perhaps that in turn started these nightmares."

"I don't know. Maybe." She fidgeted with the purse strap, not wanting to look at him. Let him believe what he liked.

"Allison, I believe it is very likely. I can tell you're apprehensive and hesitant. Why don't you think about what I said? We'll make another appointment for you to come back in a couple of days." Paul pulled out a scrip pad. "I'm going to write you a prescription for a sleep aid to get you through the night."

Gathering her purse, she rose.

"We'll talk a little more about your dreams."

Allison tried to smile. "Thank you." She clutched the scrip he gave her.

Paul followed her to the door and opened it. "Laura, please make a new appointment for Ms. Brody," he called to his secretary.

"Yes, doctor."

Paul grabbed her hand before she could move away. "Good-bye, Allison."

The contact was brief. Warm fuzzies tap-danced along her arm, up her shoulders and across before fading. A picture of Paul flashed in her mind. His perfect white teeth gleamed from a full-lipped smile, and his eyes were smoky and amorous.

She quickly opened the door and rushed away. In the background she heard the secretary calling her name, but she didn't slow down.

Seeing Paul had been a mistake. *I need fresh air to clear my head.* Allison unlocked the car, clicked the seat belt, and started the car.

"That is not all you need."

Allison screamed and slammed her foot on the brake. A car honked as it passed. The voice behind her went on.

"I see your driving has not improved so much."

Allison cringed. Her great-grandmother was in the back seat.

"Hello, Yanni." This wasn't good. Allison had first seen her great-grandmother when she'd turned thirteen. It had been ten years since she saw her last.

"I have always been here, little one. You chose not to see me."

"You're dead, Yanni, a ghost. Choosing to block you out of my life was part of my healing process."

Allison pulled into traffic and drove home as quickly as the speed limit allowed.

"So many things have changed. Everything goes so fast."

Not everything changes, Allison thought as she passed the

fisherman's statue and the quiet waters of the inlet. She glanced at the small woman peering through the window, her dark curls partially hidden under a colorful kerchief and a bright yellow, silk blouse brightening her bronzed skin. "It's been a long time."

"Longer for you than me. Something bad is coming. *Waffedi.*"

Waffedi meant bad in the Romani language. Allison wondered what her grandmother knew, but when she turned to ask, Yanni was gone. Puzzled and a little frightened, Allison hurried home to her sanctuary and solitude.

That evening, Paul called.

"Allison, I needed to talk to you."

"It couldn't have waited until...." She'd forgotten to make another appointment. Oh, who was she kidding? She hadn't planned to go back.

"No. After we spoke today, after seeing you again, I realized that I couldn't be your psychiatrist."

"What? Why?"

"We were friends—are friends—and when we dated in college, certainly you knew I had deep feelings for you."

"Paul, I—"

"I know your parents died and there were so many reasons after that. We drifted apart. But seeing you today made me realize that I still have feelings for you. It wouldn't be the best for either of us if you were my patient."

She had come to the same conclusion. "I don't know what to say."

"I spoke with Dr. Tim Stone today and briefed him on your situation. He would be happy to talk with you. If you're willing that is." He paused. "Have dinner with me."

Dinner? With Paul Kincaid? She had fond memories of their time together during the college days. His wit, his charm, his fabulous kissing ability. But, public places, lots of people, not really her thing anymore.

"It will do you good to get out. You work late hours, spend too much time alone, and now you're not sleeping well. You need to be around people, even if it's only for a little while."

She'd known Paul had wanted to be more than friends back then. It certainly wouldn't hurt to have dinner with him. Or would it? Would he analyze every word, every movement? Would he read something into her slightest hesitation?

"I'll leave my shrink cap at home," he said, almost as if he'd read her thoughts. "I promise."

"Okay, dinner." Allison sighed.

"I'll pick you up tomorrow around eight."

In front of the full-length mirror, Allison studied the dress she'd chosen to wear for dinner the next night, holding it up to her body. It had been years since she'd been out to dinner, much less on a date.

"He cannot help you, *tarno luludi.*"

Allison jumped, startled by the voice, and tripped when she turned around. It had been a long time since she'd been called *tarno luludi*, little flower. Yanni stood in the doorway. Her flowing multi-colored skirt went all the way to the floor. When she moved, the bracelets jangled. At the moment, her arms were folded and she frowned.

"I suppose you already know what's going on."

"I know that your powers have suddenly burst free after years of confinement and neglect."

"You helped me confine them, as I recall." The night her parents died. The night she'd sworn never again to use her gifts.

Yanni sat on the corner of the bed. "Kincaid does not understand your abilities."

"He's a friend, someone to talk to."

"He is a head doctor." Yanni pursed her lips. "You can talk to me."

"Sure, that would help. Then everyone would know I'd lost my mind." Allison sighed. "I need conversation with a living, breathing body. A person I can see and others can see too."

"Humph. 'Tis not so important for those like us."

"Says you," Allison mumbled. "I still don't want this. I've been doing great without it."

"Bah! You have no life." Yanni spread her arms wide and turned in a circle. "You close yourself away; work late at night, and avoid people."

"I'm stronger alone." Allison murmured.

Yanni's eyes softened. "You have no idea how strong you can be. Your visions are only the beginning."

"I don't like these visions. This man frightens me."

"You are linked with him," Yanni said matter-of-factly.

Allison fiddled with the sugilite pendant she wore. "But why now? Why someone like him?"

"Questions, questions. Can you not just accept that you are blessed and embrace it?"

"Cursed!" Allison fumed. "I saw my parents die. That's no blessing."

"It was meant to be."

Allison winked back the hot sting of tears.

"You have gypsy blood flowing through your veins. Although Christina loved my son very much, your mother's choice not to embrace his heritage played a role in their deaths. She would not believe."

Yanni moved to Allison's side. "It was not your fault."

"I should have told her I had a vision that night."

"It would have made no difference."

"I should have talked to Daddy or told Nick to pretend to be sick or something, anything. I let them drive off."

Yes, they drove away. In her mind's eye Allison saw her mother laughing and the twinkle in her father's eyes. He had a quick wit. Allison's smile withered.

A light drizzle, slick roads.

Keith went around the curve into a head-on collision. The car flew over the edge and down the embankment. They died instantly.

Allison threw up her hands. "I can't do this, Yanni." She left the room, but Yanni followed.

"The time is coming when you will have no choice," Yanni whispered, and then disappeared.

Allison only relaxed after she sat on her favorite comfy chair with legs curled under her, holding a nice warm cup of tea. But soon the pressure built, shooting pains behind her left eye. She set her cup down and massaged her temples. It didn't help. Sluggishly, she padded to the kitchen for migraine pills.

As she filled a glass with water, sharp, jabbing pangs speared her brain. She became disoriented. Places she recognized flashed like a slideshow—Gloucester High School, St. Joseph's Chapel and R&N's department store. The glass fell from nerveless fingers and burst into tiny fragments.

Ferocious tremors.

A young woman's face appeared behind Allison's closed eyes. A jagged piece of paper with notes scribbled on it flashed by.

"Oh, God no!" The killer's next victim.

CHAPTER FIVE

Jake arrived in the town of Gloucester in the early evening after sitting through what seemed like hours of debate amongst the team. Margo used her magic fingers and her laptop to confirm that no recent murders had been reported in Gloucester. Despite any sensible argument given, Jake had pushed Peter to let him travel to the small inlet town. He offered no reasonable logic as to why he should go other than his gut told him he needed to be there. Peter relinquished with the stipulation that Jake check in regularly. With some bizarre glee Margo accepted the laborious chore of going through Jake's case files to find any similarities to the present case.

His suit looked as though he'd slept in it. There had been no time to change. He'd made flight arrangements, and gone from the jet to a commercial airliner for the immediate trip to Gloucester.

He parked the plain black rental car in front of a local restaurant on Main Street, secured his gun in its holster, and grabbed his jacket to walk the block to the police station. The lobby was nondescript. Jake picked up the black phone on the wall, and buzzed the desk officer asking to speak with the lead detective.

A haggard-looking man, slightly graying and a little overweight, appeared several minutes later. "Hello," he said sticking out his hand. "I'm Detective Bill Lancaster. How can I help you?"

"Jake Austin, FBI." He shook Lancaster's hand and showed his identification. "If we can speak in private, I'll explain why I'm here," Jake offered.

"Follow me."

Jake followed the older man to a conference room, and Lancaster motioned for him to sit.

"My team was called to Schenectady this morning, to the scene of a murder."

"Okay." Lancaster dropped into the chair opposite him, eyebrows raised expectantly.

"There was little evidence, but one thing we found was a movie in the DVD player, *The Perfect Storm*. Do you know it?"

"Sure. My wife read the book when it came out. The guy who wrote it spent months here doing research."

"It may be nothing. We wanted to let you know this guy might be planning something that involves your town."

Lancaster put his forearms on the table and leaned forward. "Can I do anything to help?"

"Here's my cell number. I'll be in town for a couple of days. I'd appreciate a call if anything suspicious happens."

Lancaster took the card and slid it into his shirt pocket. "The last murder we had here was a year and a half ago. I hope your guy takes a different route."

"Me too."

Lancaster opened the conference room door.

"No need to show me out, detective. I'll find the way." Jake inclined his head and left.

Driving around town, he saw a sign for the Stern Trawler, which boasted both food and lodging.

He parked and strode to the brick building's brightly painted front door and went inside. A few people sat at the bar, while a fair-haired woman with a pleasant smile wiped the counter. He took a seat on one of the open bar stools.

"What can I get ya?" she said.

"Samuel Adams."

The wet rag slapped against the bar as she grabbed a bottle and flipped the cap to set it in front of him.

Jake took a swig of the brew, letting an appreciative moan escape. "I saw on your sign that you offer lodging."

"We do," she replied, adding a nice smile.

Looking over the bottle he said, "Do you have anything

available?"

"Actually, sweetie, one room recently opened up. Normally, during prime fishing season, we're full."

"I'd like to grab it."

She threw him a suggestive grin. "Is the room all you're looking for?"

Jake winked. "I'm afraid so."

"Pity," she sighed.

"What do I owe you?"

"How long you figure on stayin'?"

"A couple of days."

He watched as the woman moved efficiently, arranging glasses, and calling out orders. She'd most likely be a wealth of information about people in this area—someone who knows everyone. It would be worth looking into, tomorrow.

A few minutes passed when the woman brought him a bowl of chowder and told him the room would be ready in a short while.

"Can I ask you a couple of questions?"

"Are you a cop?"

"Worse. I'm a federal agent."

"Do you want another beer?"

"No thanks."

She frowned. "Go ahead with your questions."

"Have you seen anything or anyone unusual in the last day or so? Someone who looks like he doesn't belong?"

"Describe unusual. This time of year we get guys showing up trying to get spots on the fishing boats. A lot of them have been coming here for years, but others are new."

"Nothing strange or out of place then?"

"Not that I could tell."

"Okay. Thanks for giving me your time."

"My pleasure," she said and hurried off to help new arrivals.

Jake settled into a room with two double beds. He dropped his knapsack on one and his body on the other. Sheer exhaustion took over and begged him for sleep. *Sleep.* He didn't sleep much. The borders between dreams and the real world got lost sometimes.

CHAPTER SIX

Jake woke to the noise of fishermen getting ready for another long day. The hustle and bustle on the docks outside created a sort of tempo. He dragged his still-clothed body off the bed and flipped open his suitcase to pull out some fresh, albeit wrinkled, clothes.

He had the water running while he shaved, but could hear the television outside the bathroom door. He'd switched it on for the latest local news. As the anchorwoman presented details of a murder, Jake nicked himself with the razor and swore under his breath. He wiped the trickle of blood with a towel and threw it in the sink as he left the room to hear the rest of the broadcast.

Anger bubbled in him as he listened to the sketchy details of the crime. Fingers ran through his damp hair. He hated being right. Hurriedly pulling on clothes and hooking his belt, Jake grabbed his suit coat and headed out the door.

He programmed the street name in the GPS so it didn't take long to arrive at the scene. The officer held him outside the crime tape.

Lancaster came out of the house. "I'll take care of it, officer."

The officer quickly nodded and walked away.

"I asked you to call me. I need to walk the scene. Now."

Lancaster rubbed his chin, as if thinking it over. "No one gets near the scene until Crime Prevention and Control is done. That could be another couple of hours."

Jake considered rushing the police line and tearing into the house, but common sense prevailed. "Please describe the scene to me."

As the detective read the notes he'd made, Jake compared them to the scene in Schenectady. There were too many similarities for this to be coincidence. The last thing the detective told him confirmed this to be the work of the same killer.

"The message was written in the victim's blood on the wall. It said, To FBI Agent Jake Austin: Two for the Show."

Jake clenched his teeth as his eyes scanned the growing crowd for anyone taking too deep an interest. He saw nothing more than gawkers.

"Seems you forgot to mention this had something to do with you," Lancaster said.

"On-going investigation, detective. You know I can't divulge everything about the case."

"It's a relevant piece of information."

"Excuse me for a minute, please." Jake pulled out his cell phone and pressed three.

"Carmichael."

"Peter, there's been a murder in Gloucester. The information Detective Lancaster provided leads me to believe it's the same killer we had in Schenectady."

"Was there a message?"

He repeated the note. "It's a kid's rhyme, but I can't remember all of it."

"I'll have Linc run it. Have you walked the scene?"

"No." He glanced at the other man. "The detective won't let me in until forensics is finished. It could be a while."

"I'm going to call the police chief and see if I can get them to cooperate. I'll send Quincy out to help you. And just so you know, a call came in checking your credentials."

"I'm sure it was Lancaster." He went up another notch in Jake's book.

"Keep me posted."

"Will do." Jake hung up and scanned the crowd once more.

Detective Lancaster strolled toward him.

"Another member of my team will be coming. He is a forensic pathologist and will need to examine the remains of the victim. Can you get that cleared with your superiors?"

"Sure. Anything else?"

Jake glanced at the house. "I need to get in there as soon as possible."

****

The day had dragged for Allison. She tried to sketch her latest ideas, but kept breaking the tips of the pencils. She dug out old magazines and notes to generate ideas for window displays, anything to engage her mind and steer away from the visions. Not even fashion distracted her thoughts. Maybe a stroll would clear her mind.

The setting sun cast a topaz glow in the sky and dimly lit the boardwalk that crossed over the small inlet. Her house sat in a cove against a backdrop of dense pine trees. She let her thoughts ride the wind. The sensation calmed her erratic nerves.

As the sun dropped below the horizon, she closed her eyes. The salty breeze smoothed her hair from her cheeks. A deep cleansing breath to refocus her center left her sated.

A stirring male voice in her mind whispered. "*The sunsets are beautiful here. Fate draws us together again.*"

Her eyes opened searching the boardwalk for the man who toyed with her sanity. She didn't see him. She knew she wouldn't. A frown wrinkled her forehead. What did he mean about fate?

The dark lilac pendant hanging around her neck glowed in the fading light. Allison wrapped her fingers around the stone and let its warmth radiate through her body to stem the chill.

"Your powers are growing."

Allison whirled to see Yanni smiling at her. "Don't look so pleased."

Yanni shook her head as if understanding her displeasure, but not liking it.

"How can I stop it from happening?" There had to be a way. Allison tried to dislodge the feeling of violation he'd left behind.

"You cannot," Yanni said sadly. "He is right. You are destined."

"No! I'm going to have to work harder to suppress the visions." Her not so relaxing walk over, Allison headed for the house. What had fate dealt her this time?

The grandfather clock in the hall chimed six when Allison opened the front door.

"Wow!" Paul's reaction confirmed that Allison made the right choice to wear the soft green sleeveless dress. "You're beautiful."

He pulled a single rose from behind his back and presented it with a flourish. "For you."

She stood speechless, staring at the flower.

"Are you going to take it?" He looked confused, worried, his hand still outstretched.

"Oh, sorry," she said, taking the bloom from him. "Yes, let me put it in water."

Allison hurried to the kitchen, filled a small crystal vase that had belonged to her mother, clipped the end of the stem, and set the flower gently inside. It looked lonely on her dining room table.

"Are you ready?"

She grabbed a beaded purse from the entryway table and dropped her keys inside. "Okay."

Paul briefly held her hand as she got into the car. His thoughts weren't intrusive, just worrisome.

At Rotinni's restaurant they were escorted directly to a quiet table. Paul must have requested it when he made the reservation. It was away from the majority of patrons and eased her nerves. The classical music, soft lighting, and pleasant aromas brought back fond memories.

After they ordered, Paul asked her to dance.

"Let's sit for a while."

"Come on, Allison. One dance, while we're waiting for dinner." He stood and held out his hand.

Inside, she silently screamed no. Her shields were weak from years of non-use. She'd been practicing being able to withstand a brief touch without having a full melt down, she didn't think she could pull off an entire dance.

Paul smiled. "One dance won't hurt you."

Little did he know how wrong that statement could be. Sometimes when she touched people all manner of visions flashed through her head, some good, some not so good. She had no control over what happened which is why she kept her distance from people. "Okay." She stood and took the offered hand.

Paul glided her across the floor and Allison concentrated so hard on shielding herself that a headache formed.

"Where are you?"

Paul's voice permeated her thoughts. "Sorry. I was remembering." And doing an amazing job of preventing weird sensations and unwanted visions from bombarding her.

"Remembering?"

"I used to come here with my parents."

"I'm sorry. Does it bother you being here?"

She pulled back to look into his eyes. "No. Why would you think that?"

"Well, you have been having nightmares."

She shook her head. "These are wonderful memories."

"Okay."

"You don't believe I have visions, do you?"

"I think you believe they're visions." Worse, he was slipping into doctor mode.

"But?"

"Allison, I honestly think it's your mind we're dealing with, not some paranormal phenomenon."

She stiffened slightly, but couldn't blame him. He was a psychiatrist. She'd dealt with this sentiment—all her life.

"How about we drop it for now, and enjoy the evening."

"Yes, of course."

When the music stopped, he kissed her hand and led her back to the table. Just as they sat, the salads arrived and they talked of lighter things, moving from subject to subject easily. Paul made her laugh and did a good job of cracking the wall she'd erected ages ago making her wonder if she'd been out of touch for too long.

They stayed at the restaurant until almost midnight, listening to music and talking about college. She drank too much wine but had a wonderful time.

On the drive home Paul asked, "Are you going to talk to Dr. Stone?"

"I—"

"Please do, Allison." He took one of her hands between both of his.

Because she'd relaxed with the help of the wine, a slideshow involving Paul played through her mind. He was younger and she was there. These were memories from when they'd dated.

"He's a good doctor and you need to talk to someone. It will help."

She dropped her head, letting hair hide her face, not wanting to make a promise she wouldn't keep.

He raised her head until their eyes met. "Think about it." He waited a moment, but she said nothing. With a sigh, Paul kissed her cheek and left.

Blurry images of Paul paraded through her thoughts. She blamed the wine. Allison locked the house and made her way up the steps to the bedroom praying for sleep.

Two hours later, still awake, she peered at the clock. 3:17 a.m. "Nanna used to say, 'Hot milk puts you right to sleep.'"

Shoving bare feet into blue fuzzy slippers, Allison trudged down to the kitchen. Yanking the refrigerator open, she moved things to reach the milk. She filled a mug and placed it in the microwave. "I hope this works, Nanna."

"My *chai* had remedies for everything. My daughter was special."

"Quit doing that." Allison held a fist against her chest.

"Doing what?" The old woman looked surprised.

"Scaring the begeezus out of me," Allison snapped, waiting impatiently for the milk. It probably wouldn't help now.

"Sorry, 'twas not my intention."

Allison leaned against a cabinet and closed her eyes. "I don't suppose you'd go away and leave me alone."

"Did you not miss me even a little in the years since you saw me last?"

Allison looked at the petite woman. She hadn't changed. Yanni had been a great comfort after she'd gotten over the initial shock of talking to a dead relative. Yanni told Allison wonderful stories of gypsy life. How the family never stayed in one place very long, and were blamed if something happened, whether they were in the vicinity of not.

Her powers were frightening, and Yanni had helped her cope with uncertainty. Her dad hadn't balked when Allison discussed Yanni. She learned never to speak of it around her mom.

She sighed. "I did, Yanni. I'm happy to see you."

The microwave dinged and Allison retrieved her mug, careful not to slosh the hot liquid. "Is there anything in the cards that says this will blow over?"

"*Chavvi*, my girl." Yanni shook her head. "You were so

distraught over your parents' death that I agreed to help you subdue your powers. That time has long passed. You must prepare for the force that is coming."

"Do you really think I'd be treated or looked at any differently now by people?"

"Rest, little one. We will talk again." Yanni disappeared with the blink of an eye.

Later that night, Allison's white-knuckled fingers gripped the bed sheet. A hand that wasn't hers held a small black book with names and numbers written in it. He turned the key and an engine purred to life. She sensed his appreciation for the finely tuned vehicle. He drove around familiar neighborhoods in Gloucester, the business district and the wharf.

Searching.

He studied the victims, learning about them without their knowledge. From behind trees, a black-gloved hand marked down a young woman's height, hair color, date and time, and then the number seven. She drove a minivan and had children with her. It looked like a birthday party with bright-colored balloons and presents. Unloading the small bundles took moments, a knock on the door, a smile, a wave, and back into the minivan. The watcher followed the van to a small Inn perched on the cliffs overlooking the ocean. A well-dressed man sat on the balcony and rose at her approach with a huge smile on his face. The woman kissed his cheek, her hand lingered on his shoulder.

Allison's head pushed hard against the pillow.

Rage filled the watcher's mind.

Birthday parties and celebrating another year of life seemed foolish to him when the harlot would be dead soon. His gloved fingers gripped the wheel before releasing it to find the notebook.

His mind full of hate, lust, and death reached Allison so easily. Her damp skin chilled. A lifetime of images flashed through her mind. Two little boys playing hide and seek in an overgrown meadow. One finding a dead deer nature's scavengers had been at. He crawled close to the carcass, fascinated by the image. A rustling sound nearby forced him back into hiding, but his eyes remained on the lifeless creature.

Allison awoke, rolled to the edge of the bed, and threw up in the waste can.

CHAPTER SEVEN

On the fourth ring Jake picked up. "Austin."

"This is Detective Lancaster from the Gloucester P.D."

"Hello, detective."

"We need to talk."

Jake sighed. "I'll be there shortly."

Lancaster stared blankly at gruesome photographs spread over a table in the small airless room when Jake walked in.

He lost count of how many dead bodies he'd seen. From fits of rage, jealousy, love, crazies, and for no apparent reason at all, people killed. It seemed even in this quiet burb strong emotions had pushed someone to do the unthinkable—take another life.

"Have a seat," Lancaster said without looking up.

Jake moved further into the room and sat in an empty chair across the table.

"So explain to me again why you came here?"

"A lead."

Lancaster nodded. "From a murder in New York."

"Schenectady."

"And why are you alone?"

Jake's brow hiked. "What's this about?"

"Just answer the question."

"I'm following this lead. Part of the team got called to another case."

"And you have no idea why your name is being left at the murder scenes?"

Jake leaned back and crossed his arms. "Is this an interrogation, detective?"

Lancaster leaned back too. "Do you object to answering a few questions?"

"Of course not, but I haven't been read my rights."

"Do I need to read your rights to ask some questions?"

"You damn well do if I'm under arrest."

"Should I consider you a suspect?"

"Do you have anything that's led you to the conclusion that I am a suspect?"

"I think I'm entitled to some suspicions after you show up here telling me there will be a murder committed and then it happens."

"Good point. Ask away."

"I contacted the people in Schenectady. Talked with a Detective Johnson."

"And?"

"He confirmed your story."

"So what now?"

Lancaster tossed a file on the table in front of him. "Here's the report."

Jake didn't touch it. "Let me guess. All the fingerprints your people found belonged to the victim, and members of the household. No other prints, no signs of forced entry, and no witness who heard or saw anything because it happened so late at night."

Lancaster grimaced, rubbing his hands over his face. "He did a number on that poor woman's body. Carved it up and pulled out her insides." Jake could see the memory of what Lancaster had seen clearly shown on his face.

Jake cocked his head as he viewed the photographs. There was something eerily familiar about the scene. A slow burn started in the pit of his stomach as realization dawned. "He's a fan of Jack the Ripper," Jake solemnly replied. That's why the first female's body had disturbed him. There would be more bodies. He'd seen this before in books.

"Some asshole reporter in New York has dubbed the killer the Surgeon," Lancaster informed him.

Jake scoured the report then microscopically examined the

pictures. A second young woman dead. Her innocent blood used to scratch out the next line of the rhyme. He scowled, closing the folder with a snap.

The detective studied him. "From your expression, I'd say it looks familiar."

"Yes." Jake stared at the closed file. The pictures made him feel dirty and disgusted at the same time.

"What's our next step?"

Jake focused on the other man. "I'll move on to the next town or city as soon as I find the clue."

"Clue?" Lancaster pulled the file back towards him.

"At the Schenectady kill, he left something to let me know his next destination."

Suspiciously, Lancaster said, "Why?"

"Obviously he and I are on a journey, but only he knows the final destination and why he's bringing me along."

Lancaster shook his head and let out a weary sigh.

"I'd like to stay for a while to examine the photographs more closely and compare them to the others on my computer."

"Sure. Do you need anything? You look a little dragged out."

Dragged out didn't begin to cover it. "Some coffee if you have it."

"I'll send some in."

Jake trekked back to his car to retrieve his laptop.

****

The bright morning sun had moved as the hours ticked away. Lancaster stuck his head in the room. "Find anything?"

Jake's eyes felt gritty. "No."

"How 'bout I take you for some lunch?"

Jake stretched his arms overhead and leaned back in the padded chair that had molded to his ass. "I could eat. Lord knows I need to move around."

They walked across the street to Cameron's Restaurant. Lancaster slid into one side of the booth and ordered iced tea and the special. Jake asked for strong black coffee and a piece of apple pie. Lancaster shot him a strange look.

"What?"

"None of my business."

"Come on, detective. You strike me as the kind of person who is straight-forward, not much gets past you, and you know more than you let on. What's on your mind?"

"You show up on my doorstep just hours before a murder, spend more hours cramped in a tiny room searching for a clue you haven't found." Lancaster stirred sweetener into his tea. "And I'd really like to know why you're here without a partner or a team. Not to mention this killer keeps leaving you insidious messages in the victims' blood. I don't think I need to tell you this is a bit out of the ordinary." He took a drink and added more sugar. "You've sucked down at least two pots of black coffee today at the station, and yet, you only order a piece of pie."

"Strange things happen. You know that. Besides I've had a lot on my mind. Yesterday morning I looked forward to sleep and time off after finishing a long case in a swamp. I get a phone call, we fly to New York, and suddenly I find myself named in a killer's message." He shrugged and ate a bite of pie. "And, I like pie. Besides, I ate a sandwich earlier out of the vending machine."

The two men sat quietly and ate. Jake finished long before the other man, and restlessness nagged at him. "So how long have you been a detective?"

"Twenty years," Lancaster said through a mouthful of roast beef. "I worked in New York City for fifteen. As the crimes became more violent and bizarre, my wife gave me an ultimatum, so we moved here where I took a mundane position."

Jake nodded. "So she's happier since you moved here?"

"Seems to be." The other man put another forkful of beef into his mouth. "There aren't many murders here. She sleeps better."

"Are you happier?"

"Odd question," Lancaster chuckled. "I am."

"You're lucky."

"I think so too."

Jake took a last drink of coffee and pushed the empty pie plate away. "Uh, thanks for not arresting me today."

"I had to ask."

"I wouldn't have expected anything different. You were doing your job. Normally, when we go into a local county or community investigating a case, we get shunned in some ways."

"But have you ever had this kind of situation? Where the killer names you personally?"

Jake frowned. "No. This is a new one."

"Well, we have very little to go on. Any ideas you can offer?"

Jake's arms rested on the table. "We or I have not been called in to help."

"Hell, we're on the same damn side, aren't we?" The detective wiped his mouth with a napkin.

"Sometimes people forget that."

"Well not that it'll make you any happier, but you were discussed at length among the others in the department."

Jake's eyebrow cocked. "What's the verdict?"

"Based on your current look," the detective skimmed his suit. "It's a toss up between burnout or that you really love your job. Either way, none of them would be particularly happy to be in your shoes."

Lancaster's face flushed, as if he was ashamed of spreading gossip. Jake's lips curved slightly. "Okay, let's go with those."

Lancaster paid the check and they merged onto the sidewalk.

"I'm going to head back to the Trawler," Jake told the other man. "I need a break."

"All right." Lancaster unhooked the sunglasses from his shirt. "I'll be watching you, and I'm still questioning this situation."

"Duly noted. Detective," Jake called as the other man strolled away. "Do you think I could visit the crime scene? I might see something your people missed."

Lancaster kept walking but called over his shoulder. "I'll see what I can arrange."

****

With trembling fingers, Allison pressed the two on her cell. After the first ring, she slammed the phone shut. She didn't want to worry Nick, but she needed to talk to someone. Rubbing her hands over her face, she paced the small entry hall before trying again.

"Nick?"

"Ali, is that you?" Her brother's voice held surprise, and she pictured him, dark hair mussed and torn t-shirt hanging on his slender frame.

"Yeah." She twisted fingers in her hair.

"What's wrong?"

The concern in his voice steadied her, and without hesitation she said, "I'm having visions again."

Nick had always accepted her gifts as a family trait. "I thought you blocked those." He'd known how much she hated being a freak.

"I did. At least I'd thought I'd never have to deal with them again," she said with a groan. "These visions are different though. I'm in his head, Nick. I see horrible things."

There was a moment of silence. "Who?"

"The killer."

"What killer?" He sounded utterly confused. "What the hell does a killer have to do with you?"

"I'm not sure. But, something's happened."

"Are you all right? Have you been threatened?" His worried tone held warmth, inviting her to release frustration in buckets of tears.

A bitter smile curved her lips. "I've seen Yanni too."

"Yanni? Wow, this is serious." He sighed. "Tell the old girl I said hi."

"He's making a list, Nick." She shivered, remembering how he'd watched, how she'd watched.

"You saw it?"

"I've seen him watching them. I've been there."

"Call the police."

It sounded reasonable when Nick said it, but she knew what they would think. "And tell them what?"

Nick didn't have an answer to that because he knew how people had treated her growing up. How the kids at school taunted her. How the cops thought she needed therapy.

"What are you going to do?"

A brisk shiver captured her shoulders. She would do what she'd sworn never again to attempt after her parents' death.

"Ali."

"I think I can help."

"You don't know that for sure. My job is complete. I'll be back in town day after tomorrow. At least wait until I get there and I can go with you."

"I should do this alone. I don't want you under scrutiny as well."

There was a short pause. "You're doing the right thing, but are you sure it's the best thing?"

"No—yes, I have to do something this time," she murmured.

Allison slowly put down the receiver, feeling her life had

taken a sharp turn, a wrong turn.

CHAPTER EIGHT

The victim's house was in a residential area off Myrtle Square. The oak trees were beginning to show fall colors. Lancaster parked in front of the house and got out. He leaned against the tan Crown Victoria, a lit cigarette hanging from his lips. The dents, the cracked taillight, and the missing pieces of side molding gave the car as much character as its driver. "Ready?"

Jake nodded.

They walked up the sidewalk and Lancaster unlocked the door. Jake lifted the crime scene tape and slid under. Inside he breathed deeply and opened his consciousness to the emotions lingering where violence had taken place. Fatigue, joy, excitement, then a sudden jolt—panic, heart hammering, pulses racing and above it all, the lust of the killer.

As the levels rose to near suffocating, Jake opened his eyes.

Lancaster's brow lifted. "Is this how the FBI works a case? I'm not criticizing, mind you, I'm just curious." He grinned.

An easy smile played at the corners of Jake's mouth. He liked the man and sensed a good heart in Lancaster. He shrugged. "Did I forget to mention I'm a profiler? We're a weird breed."

"I'm sure of that." The other man strolled toward the staircase.

As Jake moved forward he could see it all as it had been that night. Careful to stay as close to the killer's path as possible, Jake tuned in to the sounds, sights, smells, all mixed together in a flurry of motion out of control. He moved slowly, sweat beading his forehead and tracking down his back. Deep in the killer's thoughts, anger and fury hammered him mercilessly. Walking the Schenectady scene hadn't overwhelmed him like this one. Years of training his mind to survey, examine, and contemplate logically weren't helping.

Tension and anxiety were all too familiar when he profiled a case. His mind worked through the unforeseen problems, making his head ache. He had a unique ability, a curse, if you will, to get inside the mind of a madman and pull at his deepest secrets and emotions.

Jake ignored Lancaster's watchful eyes as he moved deeper into the house. Wavering as he stood at the foot of the bed, Jake envisioned The Surgeon gleefully dipping his fingers into the victim's blood and scrawling the message on the wall.

Two for the show.

Tangling with the killer's emotions, drowning in them, Jake balled his hands into fists and fought to pull away. He called upon all his mental strength and will to keep from getting lost in the madness.

After wrangling back, Jake wandered the room fingering trinkets and rifling through clothes in search of a hint to the next destination, or some clue as to what would happen next.

Nothing.

Walking down the hall, he glanced at pictures of the family, children in different stages of their lives. Lancaster had advised him the vic's parents were called back from vacation and told their daughter had been murdered in their home. This loving environment now haunted by a gruesome act. Would they continue to live in here?

Upstairs, drops of blood dotted the sink in the bathroom where The Surgeon had cleaned his hands and blade. Black powder coated surfaces, adding to the horror effect.

Jake absorbed every thought and emotion imprinted in the house. He examined the VCR/DVD player, the stereo, the answering machine. He didn't question that the police had done a thorough job he just needed to do it. In the living room, Lancaster waited.

"Well?"

Jake frowned. "Nothing. Something's wrong."

Lancaster tensed. "Wrong? How so?"

Jake raked fingers through his hair. "It's hard to explain. It feels wrong to me—different. I had labeled the clue as part of his M.O., but I didn't find one."

"There's a pretty clear message written on the bedroom wall."

Jake shook his head. "That was to get my attention." He headed toward the front door. "I need to call in." Jake stepped outside and found his phone. He took a couple calming breathes, and rubbed at the incessant tingle on the back of his neck.

"Hi, Jake," Margo said when she picked up.

"Have you found anything in your search?"

"In your old cases, no. However, when I searched for unsolved crimes with similar M.O. over the last five years, I got several hits that were very close. But there were no messages left in the victim's blood. That's new."

"They were practice."

"If it's the same killer. Yes, it looks that way. How goes it on your end?"

"I cased the crime scene."

"Anything?"

"It feels the same as Schenectady, and the message confirms it's the same guy. But no clue."

"I'll fill Peter in."

"Thanks. Call me if you find anything else."

"Will do."

"This doesn't make sense," Jake murmured.

Lancaster who had been standing close by said, "Tell me anything about this makes sense."

"It does to him, detective."

On the return drive Jake appreciated the sight of the picturesque fishing village, wrought with over one hundred eighty years of history. A fisherman statue hailed visitors to come and admire the beauty of the inlet. Tiny boats dotted the horizon. At around eleven, he followed Lancaster through the sparsely furnished lobby of the police station. Jake barely glanced at the brunette sitting on one side of the room until every nerve in his body exploded with sensation.

The desk officer caught Lancaster coming through the inner door. "Bill, the young lady in the lobby has been asking to see you. She insisted on waiting."

"Did she say what for?"

"She asked for the detective working on the murder case."

"Seems to be going around." He turned to Jake. "Why don't you go on back to the conference room? I'll join you in a few minutes."

Jake nodded and glanced at the unknown woman one more time before heading down the hallway.

"I'm Detective Lancaster."

Allison raised her eyes to face him with a tentative smile. "Hello, detective." She rose. "I need to speak with you about the recent murder."

"Yes, ma'am. Do you have some information?"

She fumbled with her purse, silently begging her nerves to settle down. "Is there somewhere we can sit and talk?"

"Okay." Detective Lancaster motioned her to the door and held it open. Carefully avoiding physical contact, she followed him down a slim, dismal hallway.

Allison entered the conference room to find the other man sitting at the table. She stopped short, causing the detective to bump into her. A brief flash of an older woman with a pretty smile went through her mind and then vanished. The detective peered over her shoulder and cleared his throat.

"This is Agent Jake Austin with the FBI. We're working together on this case. I thought it best that he be in on our conversation."

Allison's gaze shifted between the men. The younger man had a vibrant aura, an intensity that shook her already rattled nerves. Dark features so compelling they stole her breath and green eyes so deep in color, they were hypnotic. Dangerous came to mind. "I understand." Did it suddenly get twenty degrees hotter in the room?

The agent got up and gestured to a chair he'd pulled out. "Please have a seat, Miss."

"Brody. My name is Allison Brody."

"Okay, Ms. Brody. What can we do for you?"

He moved back, but didn't sit. She hesitated, distracted by the agent's proximity. "Thank you for seeing me. I—I want to offer my assistance."

"What kind of assistance? Lancaster asked. He took a seat at the end of the long table.

Allison kept her head lowered and clasped her fingers. She'd rehearsed what to say, but now that she was here the words wouldn't come. Deciding to spit out the truth, she said, "I've been having visions of the murder."

A quick look passed between the two men, not totally unexpected. She sensed the strongest doubt in the federal agent. Their combined disbelief ravaged her like a sickness. "Think what you like gentlemen, but it will not change the fact that I have something of value to offer in your search for the killer."

"Not to be disrespectful, ma'am, but I'm sure you understand our skepticism." Lancaster smiled, as if to take the sting from his words.

Allison sighed heavily, far too familiar with the closed minds of people, especially those in the police department. "Yes, detective. I do. It's not the first time I've dealt with it."

In the days that followed her first visions, she had tried to help people. She told Mrs. Gulliver there would be a fire in her house on March seventeenth and not to turn on the stove. Mrs. Gulliver patted her on the head. On March seventeenth, Mrs. Gulliver's stove exploded and her house burnt nearly to the ground. Luckily the woman had managed to escape with minimal injury, but she never spoke to Allison again. The Gulliver fire was the first of many attempts to be a good citizen. All ended in a similar way, leaving many to believe Allison mentally unstable, bizarre, or a criminal.

Austin remained stoically silent, but studied her with cynical eyes. She felt like a freak show. His incessant stare whittled away her resolve.

"What is it you think you've seen?" the detective asked.

She forced herself to go on. "I've had flashes of places I recognize and a—a woman's face."

"What did this woman look like?"

"Reddish hair, brown eyes, young."

Massaging his neck with one hand, Jake Austin finally spoke. "That could describe anyone."

Allison ignored him and spoke directly to Detective Lancaster. "It was here, in Gloucester. I recognized the buildings. I saw things through his eyes."

"Whose eyes?" The agent sounded suspicious, with an undercurrent of anger that sent shudders across her shoulders.

"The killer." She tried to stay calm but dive bombers were crashing into the walls of her stomach. Something about the agent unsettled her. He felt almost familiar.

Austin moved to the windows. "Can you tell us where he is, what he looks like?"

Allison's narrowed gaze settled on him. He didn't trust her. Fine. She frowned. "No. I told you. I see things through his eyes."

"Do you know what his plans are? What direction he's heading? Who his next target is?"

Austin fired off the questions fast. No doubt in an attempt to jar her composure, scare her away.

"He's scouting out his next victim. He records information about each possible target in a notebook. The last woman he watched was a young mother taking a child to a birthday party." Allison's gaze settled on Austin. "I'm assuming he has other women in the book, but I didn't see them. I don't know what his plans are, Agent Austin, but I feel certain one of these women will die if he's not stopped."

"Then I think we'll stick to good old-fashioned police work," the younger man said with a sneer. "You know, looking for leads, evidence, using gut instinct. Dime store palm readers and carnival psychics won't get us any closer to catching this maniac."

His superior attitude and dismissal pissed her off. She clenched her teeth and hands. "I can see you've done real well so far. Third times the charm!"

Austin stiffened, his cool eyes searching her face. His lips tightened to a thin line.

Detective Lancaster cleared his throat. "Ms. Brody, I'd like to thank you for coming to the station and giving us this information."

Startled by her outburst and a little disconcerted, Allison jumped up. "I'm sorry I've taken up your time." While reaching for the door handle, the bulb in the lamp next to her popped. Both men looked from her to the lamp. Allison threw open the door and hurried out before something else exploded.

"Arrogant, jerk." Allison fumed on the walk up the street.

Her gait was sure as she ranted, immune to the stares of a few passers-by. Who cared if she talked to herself? It was a free country. She slowed the pace and concentrated on breathing. "Find your center. Relax." She fingered the smooth stones in her pocket:

blue sapphire for mental toughness, sugilite for courage and conviction, and citrine to keep the feelings flowing.

Her temper gradually subsided enough to think clearly again. The agent's attitude was distracting. She needed to focus. Her skin, juiced by the electricity Austin put off, still tingled.

It happened before. The words of the killer lingered, but what did they mean? She needed a quiet place to recall every word. They meant something, and since the police were no help, she'd have to figure it out herself.

With the top down on her sleek Mustang convertible, Allison headed out of town on Interstate 95 to check out her competitors' work. The black leather seats glistened in the sun and her favorite CD blared tunes on the open road. Focusing on lush scenery and her next window design, colors of cloth and Egyptian props filled her thoughts. She'd use earth tones, bold crimson with royal blue woven in, symbolizing the blood of life in hot desolation. A sarcophagus and various idols placed in strategic positions, so as not to distract from the gowns which would be on display. She continued her calculations, dashing from place to place all afternoon. Her last stop would have to be the hardware store to purchase the necessary supplies to build the sarcophagus.

Allison went immediately to the high school upon her return to Gloucester. She sat in her parked car, bathed by the sun, her reason for doing so unknown. Something compelled her to be here watching the boats in the Blynman Channel.

After fifteen minutes, Allison turned the ignition and shifted to drive. Spasms in her neck warned that someone watched. She stomped on the gas and sped away. Exasperated, Allison rounded the last leg of her tree-covered drive to find Paul Kincaid casually leaning against his car. Although surprised, she greeted him with a friendly smile. "Hello, Paul. To what do I owe the house call?"

He straightened. "On my way home and thought I'd stop by to see how you're doing."

"This isn't on your way home."

He looked at his feet and kicked around the gravel.

"Come on in."

He followed her into the house. An irritating itch between her shoulders said he was staring. She led the way into the kitchen and motioned him to the bar, where gingham-covered stools hid. "Have a seat."

She filled the teapot, put it on the stove and turned. "What do you want, Paul?"

Paul pulled out a stool to sit, laying his keys on the speckled counter. "We haven't spoken since our date and you haven't made the appointment with Dr. Stone's office. I can tell you are still not sleeping well by the smudges under your eyes."

The smile she managed was weak, a tentative lift at the corners. "I thought you weren't going to be my doctor." She leaned against the stove and crossed her arms.

"I'm a concerned friend." Paul sounded more than a little frustrated, and she had a flicker of guilt.

"Did you get the prescription I gave you filled?"

"No." She switched off the burner as the kettle whistled. "I don't want drugs."

"Eventually your body will crumble from exhaustion. Your nerves are shot, and I didn't need an M.D. to diagnose that." He offered a grim smile. "How much longer can you expect to go on like this?"

"As long as I need to," she answered, pouring hot water into two cups.

"It's not healthy. That, I am saying as a doctor."

She handed him a cup, and turned away to get the honey. He leveled his gaze on her face while he drank. Those were doctor's eyes he watched with, scanning, noticing every weakness.

"Your concern is duly noted. If I need anything, you'll be the first one I call."

"And what about Dr. Stone?"

She cradled the cup between her hands welcoming the warmth, and looking deeply into the brown liquid. "I'm not ready to see another doctor, or any doctor for that matter. Right now, I want to be left alone."

But she wasn't alone. She had a killer toying with her mind and she was afraid of where he'd take her next.

CHAPTER NINE

Jake had gone back to his room and tried to catch some sleep. All the details from Schenectady and the Gloucester scenes were cataloged in his brain. They played on an invisible projector whose cord could not be unplugged no matter how hard he tried. Certain things evoked feelings he'd not had in a long while. His suspicions grew and he didn't like where they were leading.

Allison Brody threw another variable into the mix. Jake regretted the way he'd spoken to her, and the snide barb about carnival psychics was uncalled for. Her claims of seeing through the killer's eyes disturbed him. He tried not to believe it, but she knew things. Her description of the women the killer watched and when she said, "Third times the charm."

How did she know that the next would be the third murder? Could she be involved with the killer? He dismissed the thought because if his suspicions were correct, his profile strongly suggested this particular killer worked alone.

"Shit," he muttered. Just what he needed to make this more difficult, a woman.

Luck had a way of screwing with him, so he knew he'd be seeing Allison Brody again. Jake didn't deny the magnetic pull. He chalked it up to the ongoing celibacy, but deep down, he felt a stronger attraction, a familiar similarity.

A muted shrill signaled a call. "Austin."

"Can you come down to the station?"

"Sure, detective. I'm on my way." Sleep was futile anyway.

Lancaster waited by the door holding a strong cup of coffee in one hand and papers in the other.

"Rough day?"

Lancaster grunted. "Meeting with the chief, who'd had a meeting with the mayor. Not the best kind of day."

Jake grinned. "Been there."

"Any new leads or insight to this case?"

"Nope."

The other man snorted. "Nope? Is that your official answer?"

"Unfortunately, it is. Nothing new from Schenectady. Margo found a few similar cases but they don't have the same M.O. so we're not sure if they are connected."

Lancaster grimaced. "We've come up with zilch."

Jake leaned back in the chair. "As much as I am hesitant to buy into the whole carnival sideshow bullshit, I'm sorry to say we might need to take a look at Witchy Woman."

"Allison Brody?"

"I'm keeping all possibilities open at this point. We might need to talk to her again."

"I was thinking the same thing so I ran a check."

Something nagged at Jake. He'd felt a charge the minute she walked into the room, energy so strong his skin prickled. Her shining dark hair shimmered with auburn and those deep brown eyes were like warm chocolate. For an instant, he fell into a scene where she was tight against him, his fingers teased those curly locks, and his tongue explored that sassy mouth. "Hell," he murmured.

"What are you thinking?" Lancaster asked.

Jake wasn't willing to share those particular thoughts with the detective. He ran his hand across a stubbled jaw. "I'm not sure." He looked at the other man. "What information did you get on her?"

The seasoned cop set his cup down with a thump, sloshing coffee on the table. He shuffled the papers. "Her father was CEO at GTT Industries, a family business. Her parents were big into charities, hosting events to raise money for one thing or another." He paused to rub his eyes and sip his java. "About ten years ago, Keith and Christina Brody were killed in a car crash. They were survived by three children: Allison, Nick and Lucy. A newspaper story ran that Allison saw their deaths in a vision." He looked at Jake then went back to reading.

"She's a twenty-eight year old window designer for R&N's department store. It's local. Her family comes from money, but she works anyway."

Jake digested that information as he gazed out the window. The pressure in his head increased with every word. "Interesting."

"The paper ran a bit about the memorial service. Keith and Christina were well-liked in the community."

Jake pulled the copy of the article toward him. A black and white picture of the three children standing next to the graveside lay on top. The boy, about sixteen, stood in the middle with his arms around both sisters. On the right stood a puffy-eyed little girl, Lucy, who clung to her brother, but Jake's gaze rested on the other daughter, a hair taller than her brother, tense and unapproachable. Sorrow-filled eyes sucked Jake in. Even with the boy's arm around her waist, she distanced herself. An unusual reaction, Jake thought, at the funeral of her parents.

"You're scowling."

"Am I?" Jake consciously smoothed the lines from his forehead.

"Mmmm. Any more thoughts on the Brody woman?"

"No." Nothing he wanted to say out loud anyway.

Looking at the picture in Jake's hands Lancaster said, "Slender, but kind of pretty even then."

"Too slim, nervous, and I think more beautiful than pretty," Jake said. Haunted, that would more accurately describe Allison Brody.

"Beautiful, huh?" Lancaster's brow quirked. "So you were paying more attention than you seemed to be. Hmmm."

Turning Lancaster's focus away from Allison, Jake said, "Have we heard anything about the autopsy?"

Lancaster shook his head. "How long has it been since you relaxed, Austin?"

The corner of Jake's mouth lifted. "Too damn long." He breathed deep and rolled his eyes in Lancaster's direction. "The autopsy?"

Lancaster shifted a little uncomfortably. "Okay, okay. Let's take a drive to the morgue."

****

"Hello, Bill," a tall lanky man called as Lancaster came through the swinging doors.

"Hi ya, Steve. How's Elizabeth?"

"Fine, fine," the elderly man replied. "She's just fine. We have the grandchildren visiting, so she's keeping busy."

He reached out his hand, and they shook companionably. Lancaster turned and motioned Jake to step forward.

"Steve, this is Agent Jake Austin, Jake, this is Steve Hallowell, the medical examiner. Jake's helping on this recent homicide. Seems it has the trademark of a killer he's been after."

"Is it the one they are talking about in the papers?" The sixty-something man raised an eyebrow.

"Possibly." Jake confirmed.

"Well, let's go check it out."

They headed toward the cold room, while Lancaster and Hallowell shared pleasantries.

The brightly lit morgue held little more than two tables, a wooden desk, and a chair. Jake hated this part of his job. All morgues felt the same, cold, dead, hopeless.

Dreams ended here. Lives and hope ended here.

The dim gray walls and white ceiling painted a bleak picture. One florescent light flickered occasionally, warning it might desert them at any

moment. But it was the smell he could never get used to, the smell of death. Along the back wall were rows of closed steel drawers housing who knew how many bodies.

One little, two little, three little dead ones, echoed in Jake's mind.

Suddenly, back in the barn on his parents' ranch, he heard the chant and followed the sound. He came upon a small bale of hay with seven dead mouse corpses, their bodies exhibited in a neat row, having been tortured in some fashion. Laughter taunted him.

"Austin."

The sound of his name jerked Jake back to the current surroundings. He realized the two men had spoken to him. "Sorry." He hurried to the table where they stood. A sheet-draped body lay before them.

"You all right?" Lancaster asked.

"Yeah." Jake shook off the uneasiness to focus on the task at hand.

"You're not squeamish, are you?" Hallowell frowned.

"No," Jake stated flatly.

"Okay, let's get started." Hallowell opened the file. "Patricia Gardner, twenty-five years old, very good health."

He removed the sheet to reveal the woman's body. Lancaster looked away for a moment then turned his weary eyes back to the woman's brutalized corpse.

"The bruises around the neck and collapsed trachea suggest strangulation." Hallowell pointed with a pencil.

"He's hands-on." Jake related the fact in a dry monotone.

"With what was left of her insides," the doctor continued, "I could tell she had eaten shortly before being killed."

Lancaster said, "Her husband told me she went out to dinner with girlfriends while he went to a game with some people from work. He claims they do it once a week."

"Same night every week?"

"Yep. Every Tuesday night," Lancaster answered. After a moment, he added, "You don't think he just happened to find her, do you?"

Jake's mind engaged, his thoughts turning over all the reports, the crime scene photos. "No. This UNSUB, unknown subject, is very particular about his victims."

"You'll see here," Hallowell said, pointing to the disemboweled body. "Whoever it is knew his stuff. The cuts are clean. The instrument sharp."

Lancaster turned away from the corpse to face Jake, a little green in the gills. "So there's no doubt this is your man?"

"No." Jake was sure of it, and certain there would be more.

"We're checking out Mr. Gardner's story anyway."

"I'd expect you would." Jake looked up. "Thank you, doctor. We'll be in touch."

"You know where I am," Hallowell replied nodding. "I'll have the full report done by tomorrow."

"Give my best to Elizabeth." Lancaster's color still hadn't returned.

Hallowell waved his hands dismissively as he leaned over Patricia Gardner's remains.

Jake slid into the passenger seat and rested his head back. The pulsing behind his eyes he blamed on the sickly smells in the morgue.

****

Allison wandered out the back door and down toward the cove. A slight breeze ruffled her hair and she pulled a shawl over her shoulders. Everyone, including her former psychiatrist, insisted her problems wouldn't disappear because she chose to be alone. Nick often told her to find a man, but she laughed it off. More than anyone she knew her needs, and a man never made it on the list.

"Loneliness helps you gather strength." The small voice defied its owner, her dead ancestor, Yanni.

"This isn't going to be easy."

"Did you think it would be little one?"

"I'm not sure. The feds are involved."

"No," Yanni answered. "Just one for the time being."

"You know more than you're telling, Yanni." Allison hugged the shawl tighter.

"No, child. I only see small pieces of the puzzle. But I do know this is a path."

"A path?" God, she'd heard that more times than she could count, and still Allison had no idea what it meant.

"Yes. One that is yours. It has been here waiting for you to arrive."

Allison turned slightly to glare at her great-grandmother.

Yanni shrugged. "It is the way of things."

"And where does this path go?"

"I cannot see it," Yanni said. "'Tis cloudy and uncertain."

"Of course it is," Allison replied dryly.

"The force beyond what I see is dark and ominous."

Allison shuddered. She'd felt that presence, and he knew she had.

CHAPTER TEN

At the station, a young reporter waited anxiously. "Detective." The reporter ran up to Jake and Lancaster. "Rory White, *Gloucester Daily Times*. I'd like to ask you some questions about the murder."

"Where's Satch, the Times' regular guy?" Lancaster eyed the wet-behind-the-ears kid. Wire-framed glasses slipped down his thin nose, and his khaki trousers had a freshly ironed crease.

"He's on vacation. I hear the FBI is in on this." White glanced at Jake. "That means this is something more than a simple homicide. Can you tell me about that?"

"Look, White. Either you're not from around here or someone didn't explain the procedures to you. The chief will address the media. You will be given a press release when the chief is ready. Until then, the only thing I have to say is no comment." Lancaster's finality was hard to miss. "Now step aside, please, so I can go do my job."

Jake followed Lancaster into the office, leaving the reporter in the lobby. "You handled that well."

"Damn pests," Lancaster muttered. "Can't turn around without bumping into them when something like this happens. Why don't we take out an ad and give the killer all the information we have, which isn't much, and tell him what our next move will be?"

Jake nodded. "I know what you mean. They expect you to

catch the guy, but they hamper your progress by giving a blow by blow account of your actions. It's a vicious circle. I generally steer clear of the media."

"Yeah, it's the chief's job," Lancaster grumbled. "But it still doesn't deter them." He scratched his chin. "So let's go over the facts."

"The first vic was five-five, brownish red hair and slender in build. Patricia Gardner is five-three, brownish red hair, and slender in build. He kills them late at night when he's sure no one will hear and leaves messages on the wall in their blood. The first scene had a message leading me to Gloucester."

Lancaster frowned. "They look alike."

"Yes, more or less."

"So do you think he's killing the same person over and over?"

"It's certainly a possibility," Jake replied, even though deep in his gut he knew the answer was yes.

"Sister, girlfriend, someone he feels wronged him."

Jake's phone rang. "Austin."

"Jake, I've compiled a list of possible cases from all the gathered data. There were thirty seven, but based on locations and timelines, I've dwindled it down to two. The first lived in Baltimore and the second in Philadelphia."

"Two?"

"Yes. And, I've found nothing in your previous cases."

"Okay, Margo. Send me the information about the two possibles and I'll take a look."

"Oh, and Zack got called to do a consult on another case so he will be delayed in getting to you."

"Thanks."

Lancaster stared at him over his cup of coffee.

"There are two possible cases that might be linked to this guy. I'm having the information forwarded so I can check it out. I should be able to put together a more updated profile in the next day or two."

"What do we know about the first vic?"

"Good New England family, honor student, well-liked, full ride to college on academics. Living with her boyfriend and working part-time while getting her Masters. She was pretty and outgoing, had lots of friends."

"Except one," Lancaster offered.

"Except one."

"All the background checks were done."

"All."

"It's not chance that he's finding the women who meet the criteria by accident."

"No."

"Which means planning."

"Which Allison Brody corroborated, if you believe her story. Planning and patience. He waits for the right moment."

"That won't be good for us."

"No." An old memory from college popped into Jake's head. A pretty girl found dead two days after he'd found her waiting naked in his bed. She was five-four, slender in build and had brownish red hair.

Jake didn't like the direction this investigation was headed.

Jake scrolled through pages that Margo had sent him regarding the two previous murders. He stared at photographs memorizing each detail, reviewed autopsies and crime scenes, committing everything to memory. Lancaster spoke to the officers who were conducting the interviews of

Patricia Gardner's employer, neighbors, and the people at the restaurant where she'd last been seen alive.

Jake's concentration wavered because of strange noises coming from outside. "What's all that racket?"

"They're getting ready for the parade to kick off the annual Waterfront Festival. The local merchants have booths and provide refreshments. It's a big deal that draws in tourists. There's even live music at the end of Stacy Boulevard by the food setups."

Jake shot Lancaster a dry glare. Lancaster shrugged. "Hey, it's a big 'to do' for us small town folk."

Jake snickered at Lancaster's comment, knowing that he wasn't really small town folk. Then a thought occurred to him. "Lots of unfamiliar faces round and about?"

"Yep."

"Perfect place for our friend to be mingling."

"Let's get out there."

Detective Lancaster sent word for some uniforms to follow him. He stopped at the door. "What are we looking for?"

"Tell your men to keep their eyes open for anything." Jake had been sensing something since he got to Gloucester. He couldn't describe it, but he would know if The Surgeon was close. "What has the chief said about the press conference?"

"He's waiting until after the festival. He doesn't want to cause panic and keep people from coming to town."

Maybe he should, Jake thought, but he didn't say it.

Wandering through the crowds, Jake and several policemen kept watch for anything unusual, which wasn't an easy task since out-of-towners were everywhere and The Surgeon could blend in. Every once in a while he could make out a light blue shirt, part of the police detail assigned to the fest.

Jake paid little attention to the booths where the locals smiled and peddled their nautical wares. He kept his focus on the hordes of people who strolled around the area.

Closer to the end of the street, something he heard or felt gave him pause. He couldn't place it at first. Slowly, he pivoted. A familiar steely gaze peered through the crowd. Jake focused on a pair of gray-blue eyes. The other man saluted, turned, and got lost in the milieu of people. Jake sprinted to the spot where the suspect had been standing. His head whipped to the left and then to the right. His body did a complete three-sixty hoping to catch a flash of the man. He ran a rough hand through his hair, cursing silently.

Lost him.

While staring after the ghostly figure, something out of the corner of his eye caught Jake's attention. His nerves were humming. He changed position to better watch the activities.

A bubbly little blond laughed while she wrapped a small picture frame in tissue paper. People responded to her openness and enthusiasm. It was a pleasant sight, even for his hardened resolve. She turned and said something to her partner in the booth. When she shifted again, he saw Allison Brody.

Allison's movements were fluid and graceful, but she consciously avoided direct contact with anyone. Timid, she stayed in the shadows, continually conversing with the other woman who didn't seem to notice. Or, more likely, she'd grown accustomed to Ms. Brody's behavior.

A flash of The Surgeon winking at the giddy blond singed his brain. Had he bought something in their booth? Did Allison Brody smile sweetly and brush fingers as she took his money? He slowed his thoughts and reined in a surge of unexpected feelings.

Jake pushed his way through the growing crowd. A boiling energy coursed through his body the closer he got to Allison Brody. He didn't know what to make of it, but it left an uneasy feeling.

"Ms. Brody." He spoke loud enough to get Allison's attention at the rear of the booth. He hadn't taken time to really notice her when she'd appeared at the police station. Her dark hair bounced. Her glossy lips were full and lush. Shivers exploded across his skin, landing with heaviness in his groin.

Now speechless as she sauntered toward him with cool indifference, Jake prayed no drool escaped his gaping mouth. She wore white shorts that hugged curvaceous hips, sending thoughts to places they shouldn't go and making his pants tighter. The sunny yellow-striped shirt blended with softly tanned skin. She looked like a goddess.

"Hello, Agent Austin. Would you like something?"

Her greeting was cool and reserved. Obviously, he hadn't made a good impression at their first meeting, and she certainly wasn't going to let him off easy.

It took a moment for words to form. "Did you sell anything to a man, about my height, bleached white hair, a few minutes ago?"

"I haven't really been dealing directly with the customers, but no one by that description stopped here. Why?"

He scowled, not sure if it was because she hadn't noticed the suspect or because of the hard-on making his shorts so damn restrictive.

He cocked a brow. "Didn't you sense something or have a flash that the killer might be near?" he said sarcastically.

"I've actually managed to go for several hours without connecting to the monster in question, agent. Besides, I thought you weren't interested in my flashes."

She crossed her arms in a defensive pose, scrunching those nice breasts together. He'd struck a nerve. Maybe that's why he'd said it. But, he wouldn't be deceived by her innocent look or the loaded comment. "That's right, Ms. Brody. I'd just as soon have you stay out of police business." Jake hissed the remark, turned and stalked away.

****

The earlier tingle in her spine now made perfect since. Allison pretended the heaviness in her chest and the air didn't signal a brush with evil. She stared into the crowd hoping to pick out the killer. As if.

She shifted, uncomfortable with the notion an unseen force had again thrown her into the path of Agent Austin, even though he mocked her abilities at every opportunity. She clutched her arms with a cold sensation, quickly chased away by a warm, wicked smile. Her body hummed with energy.

"Wow!"

Allison spun around at her friend's exclamation.

"Who was that?" Kat said.

"Agent Jake Austin."

"Oooh, the Fed."

"Yeah, the Fed," Allison muttered. "Close your mouth."

"He's an awesome specimen of the male gender."

Allison grimaced. "If you like the tall, dark, and brooding type. He's not someone I'd want to spend time with. He's unpleasant." At this moment, she wished she hadn't let Kat talk her into working the booth today. A weakness she agreed to occasionally, despite her predisposition to stay as far away from people as possible.

"Oh, momma. Give me unpleasant."

Her best friend since high school, Kathleen Rubin had the uncanny ability to succinctly state things. Allison said, "Come on let's get back to the customers."

She stared in the direction Austin had disappeared and frowned. For some reason, she heard a child's rhyme in her head. *One little, two little, three little dead ones.*

Allison had helped Kat close up the booth then got in the car to drive home. For some reason she couldn't explain, the car steered toward St. Joseph's Chapel, another location she'd recognized in the vision. It bothered her that he could infiltrate her mind so easily and she couldn't prevent it. Her brilliant idea… to see if she could sense him. She felt stupid as she parked and got out, casually walking around the side of the church, then back toward the car. Against sane judgment, Allison lowered the barrier sending out invisible feelers. If she could sense something, find anything to lead the police in the right direction, it would be worth the risk. Not to mention putting Agent Jake Austin in his place with smug satisfaction.

CHAPTER ELEVEN

Lancaster paced the small conference room. "Christ, I can't believe we have nothing to go on. Not even a witness who thinks they saw someone and can give us a description."

Jake hadn't told anyone of the suspect he'd seen. "If he changes his appearance all the time, he will fit in. It would keep him anonymous."

"Hmmph," Lancaster grunted and sat down in a chair. "You were here at the crack of dawn. Don't you sleep?"

"Not often."

"How do you function?"

"Years of practice."

Lancaster yawned. "Well, I can't do it. I'm heading home. You gonna call it a night?"

"In a while."

Lancaster pushed himself up using the table for leverage. "Can I ask you something?"

"Sure," Jake said without looking up.

"Are you any closer to figuring out why this guy is interested in you?"

"No. Good night, detective." The lie had tumbled easily from his lips. He knew every word of each report by heart from reading them so much.

Thoughts that should have been on the case drifted to Allison

Brody. To be truthful, that beautiful subject had diverted the direction of his thoughts a lot lately. It was irritating. Even his libido had a mind of its own around her. The last thing he had time for was a distraction and that's what she was, a monumental distraction.

Jake stood and stretched until the muscles in his back screamed in agony. Nothing more could be done tonight. He'd go back to the Stern Trawler and rest. If he was lucky.

****

"How can you eat so much and not gain a pound?" Kat said, as Allison sat down at the table with a loaded plate of spaghetti, egg rolls, garlic bread, and salad.

"Superior metabolism."

"I hate you."

This was their monthly ritual when Kat came over to have dinner and girls' night at Allison's house. They had been doing it for years, a very small pleasure Allison allowed herself.

Over a mouthful of spaghetti Kat mentioned her new beau.

"Sean? Who's Sean?"

"Oh, haven't I told you about Sean? Well..." She took a deep breath before barging through the story. "I was driving up the coast the other day and my car happened to break down at almost the very spot where Sean had stopped. Can you believe it? What luck."

Her excitement made Allison smile. "Uh, huh. Luck."

"Truly, I wouldn't lie about something like that. Anyway, he was taking photographs for a travel magazine. We started talking while he looked at my car and I found out he's staying in the area so I invited him to dinner, as appreciation for helping me with the car."

"Are you nuts? You don't pick up strange men and have dinner with them. Haven't you heard about the murder of that woman?" Allison's incredulous tone started Kat on a tirade about their friendship.

Kat got a goofy look on her face and rolled her eyes. "You spend too much time alone, you know. You need to get out more."

"So you keep saying," Allison replied dryly. The fear for her friend was warranted. A killer had come to town and was targeting young women.

"Well, you do. Staying locked up in this house isn't normal or healthy."

"So I've been told. Would you believe me if I said I think you're right?"

Kat stopped her chewing and stared at Allison. "What?"

"Oh, nothing. I just—well—I went to see Paul Kincaid the other day. Professionally. Then, he took me to dinner."

Stunned, Kat said, "Dinner? You and Kincaid? In, like, an actual restaurant with people and everything?"

"Yeah."

"So spill with the deets, honey."

"There's not much to tell. I haven't been sleeping lately."

Kat frowned.

"Nightmares. So I called to talk. I went to the office, and after our session, Paul confessed the old feelings were still there and he suggested I seek another psychiatrist. He called later to ask me to dinner."

"And you said yes?"

"And I said yes."

Kat shook her head. "I don't believe it."

"I couldn't believe it myself. But, we were friends and dated in college even before he became my shrink. That was his ace in the hole."

"Bastard."

"Stop. It was a nice evening. He even brought me that rose." She pointed to the small vase that held the flower.

"Wow! This sounds like something major. I generally don't get flowers until the third date."

"Stop, would you?"

"And after dinner?"

"He brought me home, kissed my cheek and left."

Kat's bright smile deflated. "Oh, how boring. That's certainly not a good ending to a great evening. You didn't ask him in for coffee?"

"Nope."

Sighing she said, "I'm definitely going to have to go over the finer tips of dating with you. It's been too long since you've been out in the real world. You're rusty."

"No, actually, it was very civil. I'm not sure I want any more from Paul. I've not wanted anything more for years." She looked at her hands, avoiding her friend's stare.

Kat's lack of response signaled an understanding that only best friends shared.

"While I'm thinking about it. Do you remember the last time I wore my locket?"

"The one your dad gave you?"

"Yes."

"No, why?"

"I planned on wearing it for the date, but couldn't find it anywhere." She frowned in concentration trying to remember when she'd worn it last.

"It'll turn up, hon."

Allison hoped so. It was her most prized possession. "Anyway, you'll have to keep me posted on how things go with Sean."

"You know I will. Now, let's get these dishes cleaned up so we can watch our chick flick."

Allison said, "You rinse, and I'll load the dishwasher."

"Deal."

Allison struggled with yet another restless slumber.

Sinister laughter emanated from every direction in the vast darkness. She whirled wildly trying to find an exit while an eerie mist

clawed at her legs. It felt as though a ton of bricks had been piled on her chest. She couldn't catch a breath.

As quickly as the darkness and terror had fallen, it vanished.

An enormous field of tall grasses and bright flowers welcomed her. Allison threw her arms above her head and crooned a song of happiness. A male voice whispered words she couldn't understand, but there was no fear. The world turned a magnificent emerald color, soothing, calming, peaceful in a way.

With a thankful sigh Allison tumbled into deep sleep, dragged down into the realm of the sandman, not frightened of the plunge.

Palm trees swayed with ocean winds and the sun offered warmth, coaxing flowers to greet the day. Fish openly swam toward shore, unafraid of being snatched from the water. Dolphins jumped playfully in the distance as seagulls sang their warbled melody.

Only in this place was she who she wanted to be.

The breezes carried more than the fragrance of the local fauna. Waves of something more primal brushed her body, leaving yearning aches in sensitive places. A few feet away wearing cutoff jeans and no shirt stood Alex. His tanned skin gleamed with sweat and sun streaked hair danced around hypnotic eyes. They met in this secluded cove, two teenagers growing up together.

I'm dreaming, Allison reminded herself, though wishing she could go back in time. *"Alex?"*

"Yes."

He raised one open hand and then the other, waiting silently for her to comply. The mere contact of their palms sent desire through her. The hairs on his legs tickled her skin. Her nipples strained against the bikini top as they pressed against each other.

Alex bent his head and touched her lips with his. The contact so brief it startled her. She'd been expecting more. "What's happening?"

Alex stared hard at her mouth and then met her eyes. "I'm in love with you."

Surprised, she stepped back. This was new territory. They'd never spoken of love. "Are you sure?"

He laughed and his eyes sparkled. "Pretty sure." Alex cleared his throat. "Rennie?"

Only her father and Alex called her Rennie. Of course, Alex didn't know her real name or what she really looked like. In their dream world, she had light coloring, high cheekbones, green eyes and bigger breasts. These were attributes from her mother, the most beautiful woman she'd ever seen. Her beauty wasn't movie star flashy or sleek as a model. Her mother had quiet elegance and old-world charm. Allison's father once said that when he looked at her mother, he saw the beauty of the ages. That's what Allison wanted. Instead she inherited the coloring of her gypsy heritage, dark and mysterious.

Her hands shot out and pushed him back. "Hold on." She unceremoniously sank to the sand. She couldn't breathe.

Alex dropped down next to her. "Not the reaction I'd hoped for."

The scene disappeared. Allison curled into a fetal position. Tears silently ran down her cheeks and she opened her eyes. Could the killer be Alex? Is that why he easily invaded her mind, because he'd been welcome there many years ago? "Oh, my God, Alex. It can't be you. It just can't be."

****

Allison's alarm trilled at 9:30 a.m., breaking into the lovely two-hour sleep. Reluctantly, she smacked the clock and dragged her otherwise sleep-deprived body toward the bathroom and the shower she hoped would wake her up.

She sat down to breakfast a short time later. A long florist box lay on the table. "What's this?" she asked Martha. The housekeeper who had worked for her family for years, and even though she was officially retired, still came in to fuss about Allison's house.

"Don't know." Martha poured coffee into Allison's mug. "It was on the porch along with the paper. It has your name on it."

Inside the box lay a single black rose in a bed of red tissue paper. Dark beauty with a sense of evil surrounding it. Allison's blood froze and her fingers were like ice.

"Oh, my," Martha breathed. "I've never seen anything like it." She moved toward the box. "I'll get a vase to put it in."

"No," Allison blurted. "I mean, no thanks," she said more calmly. "I'll take care of it." Her appetite gone, she wiped her mouth and stepped outside.

"He's telling you."

Her eyes reluctantly drifted to the porch swing to see Yanni with a worried expression. "Telling me what?"

"That he knows who and where you are."

"I know him."

"You do?"

"It's been bothering me since he'd mentioned that we've connected. I figured it out last night."

"And what do you think you know?"

"Many years ago he and I connected… in dreams."

CHAPTER TWELVE

Jake finished a brisk morning run and headed back to the Stern Trawler for a shower. Passing by the small wooden table on the way to the bathroom, Jake stopped to pick up the picture of Allison Brody in the old newspaper article. Even at the age of nineteen, she was incredibly beautiful. Time had whittled away teenage immaturity, leaving a classic masterpiece of lithe build and mystical enchantment. Strength with caution and quiet intelligence rounded out the mystery. He couldn't get Allison off his mind. A feeling of déjà vu said he'd seen her somewhere before.

He picked up his cell. "Austin."

The sharp timbre of the caller's voice held his attention. "Enie, meanie, miney, moe, which direction will I go?" Laughter echoed through the phone. "What's the matter, Jake? Cat got your tongue?"

"Why are you doing this?"

"Our game has been fun, but it just got better."

Every muscle in Jake's body tensed. "What the fuck does that mean?"

"Temper, temper. I'm sure you'll find out soon enough."

There was a click and then a dial tone.

"Damn!"

Jake showered, dressed, and anxiously headed to the police station.

"So anything new on the case?" Jake asked Lancaster the minute he saw him.

"Good morning," Lancaster said.

Jake stuck hands in his pockets. "Morning."

"All the interviews are completed and every possible angle has been examined. We still have nothing. I expect the tox screenings any time now."

Jake stared out the window, unconsciously rubbing the back of his neck. The sky clouded up and a dreary rain tumbled from those clouds wetting the pavement. The phone rang but he paid no attention to the conversation. A few moments later the door opened and the room exploded with sensations. Each nerve synapses popped like a firecracker on the fourth of July. He glanced over his shoulder to see Allison Brody.

Jake could tell there was something on her mind. The weird vibes bouncing off her made him edgy.

"Ms. Brody, how nice to see you again." Lancaster reached out to shake her hand.

She gave him the briefest of smiles and moved away. "Thanks, detective."

He motioned her toward a chair. "Please have a seat." Sitting across the table from her, Lancaster asked, "What brings you here today?"

Austin stood several feet away. It had gotten hard to breathe again.

Allison kept her gaze on the detective, finding it easier to meet his understanding eyes than Austin's turbulent ones. She was surprised her voice sounded normal as she spoke. "I'm not sure how to interpret this, but I knew I should tell you about it. So here I am."

"Tell us what?"

He'd startled her. The heat from his body seeped into her skin. Allison hesitated, then tilted her head and studied his grim expression.

Tall and lean, broad-shouldered and slim-hipped, he wore black pants and a dress shirt buttoned at the cuffs but not at the neck. A day's growth of beard, black as night like his hair, surrounded full lips. His eyes were the oddest shade of green and burned her with one look.

Allison pressed her lips together to moisten them. "This

morning the housekeeper found a box on my doorstep and brought it inside."

Austin's brow creased, his eyes suspicious. "A box?"

"Yes, a florist box addressed to me."

"What's wrong with a pretty lady getting flowers?" Lancaster said, in an attempt to lighten the atmosphere.

"It's a single black rose in red tissue paper." She noted the questioning glance Lancaster shot Austin. "I think it's from him."

"By him, you mean the killer?"

"Yes," she answered softly.

Lancaster cleared his throat. "Why would you think the flower was from the killer?"

"Was there a note? Austin said in a low tone.

"No, just the box with the single rose."

Austin moved closer. "Your name, but no note. Why would you assume the killer sent it?"

She kneaded her forehead to keep the migraine at bay, but kept her voice level and her gaze cool. "I don't want you to think I'm up to my carnival tricks again."

Austin crossed his arms. "Please enlighten us."

Allison glanced at Lancaster who nodded. "When I opened the box I felt... scared, like something dark had risen and wanted to latch onto me."

Surprisingly, Austin didn't smirk or make a sarcastic comment.

"Where is the box now?" Austin demanded.

"In my car. I didn't know what to do with it and I wasn't going to leave it at home."

"We need to see it."

She led them to her car and opened the trunk. The stark white box lay on a background of gray.

"Who else touched the box?" Lancaster said.

"My housekeeper."

Lancaster picked up the thin box using his handkerchief. "No markings." A sergeant was walking by so Lancaster stopped him. "Take this to forensics. Tell them I need anything they can give me like yesterday."

The sergeant nodded and left.

"Black roses can't be everywhere. I've never seen one. I'll have an officer make some calls to find out where it came from."

Allison stood wrapping arms around her waist watching the men's discussion.

Austin said, "He could be making them himself."

Lancaster shrugged. "It's possible. Would he go to all the trouble?"

"Yes."

"Has he done it before?" Lancaster said.

Austin turned those compelling eyes on her. "Not that we know of."

An officer escorted her back to the conference room, and brought a bottle of water. She had no idea where Austin and Detective Lancaster were. Allison closed her eyes and reached out with heightened senses. Deception, lies, partial truths floated inside this place. Unfortunately, she did not sense Austin or Lancaster nearby. Something told her they were no closer to finding this maniac today than they were yesterday. Not comforting.

An invisible pulse pushed at her shields which intensified the headache. Immediately, she retracted her senses and prayed he wouldn't get inside. She recognized the attempts to break through. Later the migraine would ferociously zap her mental and physical strength. Grabbing her purse, Allison rose to leave. As she reached for the door handle it twisted. Detective Lancaster and Austin entered the room.

"Ms. Brody, thank you for bringing in the box. If it is from the killer, we may retrieve a fingerprint or other information to bring us closer to catching him." Lancaster offered in a polite tone.

Austin stalked the room, restless. If he clenched his teeth any tighter, she thought for sure his jaw would break. He stopped so close she wanted to step back, but didn't.

"I suggest you take a few days off work, Ms. Brody, and stay close to home. If this killer has cast his interest in your direction, it will be dangerous."

Allison raised her chin and stared directly into Austin's eyes.

"Time off would probably be a good idea," Lancaster chimed in.

Their advice was sound, but her new awareness of the killer went beyond their knowledge. "Thank you for your concern, gentlemen, but I can't take off right now. I have a new project at the store that I need to get up and running. My boss depends on me and I won't let him down."

Austin leaned against the wall and watched her while speaking to Detective Lancaster. "Perhaps it would be prudent to put Ms. Brody under police surveillance."

"Meaning what?" she said.

"A uniformed officer or two would accompany you everywhere, every minute of the day."

"I decline." She turned to Detective Lancaster. "I'll tell you this. Use it or not. Believe it or don't. He's already picked at least two more women. He's not finished. Good-bye, detective." She intentionally ignored Austin, and left the room.

The pounding in her head increased to an almost blinding level. She needed to get home. Rummaging through her purse, she scored a bottle of Ibuprofen and downed two, swallowing hard. Her fingers clutched the cell phone.

"Martha, its Allison."

"Hi, sweetie."

"Can you call a cab and have it pick me up at the police station?"

"Is something wrong?"

"A migraine, blurred vision. I don't want to drive."

"I'll call them right away. Are you going to be okay?"

"Yes. I need to get home to a warm bath and my medicine."

"I'll be waiting for you."

"Thanks."

Ten minutes passed before the cab got there. She was happy and grateful to the driver for opening the door. Any jarring movement sent shooting pains straight to her brain. She was woozy on the drive. Martha waited on the porch when the cab pulled up. Allison handed bills over the seat to the driver and opened the door as the housekeeper rushed to her aid.

CHAPTER THIRTEEN

Allison awoke to a shadowed room. Casting a glance toward the clock she noted several hours has passed without dreams, or nightmares. Cautiously, she sat up. So far, so good. No nausea, and the pain in her head had receded. Propping against the headboard, she wrapped arms around her knees.

At thirteen, when her abilities appeared along with puberty, acne and the development of breasts, she'd started having wonderful dreams. On a tropical island somewhere in the middle of an unknown ocean, she met a boy not much older than she. They were both shy in the beginning, but eventually formed a deep bond of friendship. Practically every night they met on the beach, swam, and played with the dolphins. Sometimes, Alex would climb a palm tree and drop coconuts for milk. He built a lean-to where they would lay and discuss their hopes and dreams for the future.

They talked about school, and what they wanted to be when they got older, all the things young people think about but only share with their best friend.

Alex had been her best friend.

Over time, deeper feelings emerged. No longer did he give her a quick peck on the cheek, but lingering kisses on her neck, her mouth. The natural progression of their relationship led to other intimacies. Together they learned about each other bodies. Every so often, they would skinny dip in the ocean. Alex developed as well. He went from a thin, quiet boy to a toned, confident young man. Allison fantasied of meeting him in the real world one day, kissing him, touching him.

The last night she met Alex on their beach, they made love for the very first time. The intensity of that coupling stayed with her even as she woke.

The next day her parents died.

She had begged Yanni to help bury her abilities, forever.

She'd left part of herself on that island in the dreams. A huge chunk of her heart still resided there, with him. That was ten years ago. She wondered what he'd done when she hadn't come back, afraid now she had the answer. Did her disappearance contribute to this outcome? These victims resembled her in color and appearance.

Allison never knew anything of his real life, but obviously, he knew her. Was it chance that he'd appeared in Gloucester? Or planned?

They had never talked about where they lived. "What am I going to do?" She posed the question to the empty room, but vowed to find Alex.

"Fate is a beech."

Allison jolted. Yanni stepped out of the shadows.

"Yanni, you do surprise me." A bitter laugh escaped. "Yes, fate is a bitch."

"You plan to find him."

"I see no other choice." Allison rubbed her arms, uneasiness clawing its way up her spine.

"You will need help."

"No, I should do this alone."

"What about the police?"

"I've offered my assistance, for all the good it's done. The fact that I may know the killer, I'll keep to myself."

"You can keep that part secret if you wish. What about the other?"

"Other?"

Yanni settled on the edge of the bed. "The federal agent."

"Oh. He's a minor irritation."

Yanni scoffed. "Do not be so foolish. You must understand all the players and their roles, or you will not succeed."

"Great. Now you're going philosophical. Did you know Plato or Socrates in another life?"

"Not another life, the afterlife. Too stuffy for my taste." She scrunched up her face. "They walk around in bed linen."

Allison couldn't hold back the laughter. It felt good to laugh.

Yanni disappeared in a sparkling vapor. Allison crawled out of bed and went downstairs for tea.

"And how are you feeling?" Martha asked when Allison walked into the kitchen.

"Better, thanks."

"Are you going to be okay or do you want me to stay?"

Allison smiled. "Go home to Albert. I'll be fine now."

Martha nodded.

"And, Martha. Thank you for being here."

"All you have to do is call."

"I know. Good night."

The grandfather clock chimed five and the phone rang.

"Hello?"

"Hi, Ali. Just calling to let you know I'm back."

"I'm glad you made it back safe."

"How did it go with the cops?"

"Suspicion, disbelief. You know the same, but I expected it."

"Are you okay?"

If she didn't sound positive, Nick would show up on her doorstep. "A few headaches, but nothing I can't handle. Don't worry."

"I worry, you know that."

She loved her brother. Being the eldest, it fell upon her to care for the younger siblings. As time passed, Nick filled in as caretaker for Lucy while Allison got her degree at the local college.

"Yes, I know and I love you for it."

His heavy sigh stretched through the phone. "I could stay with you."

"No, Nick. I wouldn't be able to concentrate with you here. Besides, Yanni is popping in—regularly."

"Okay. But if you start feeling bad, you better call."

"I will. I promise."

It hadn't been more than three or four minutes after she hung up that the phone rang again. "Hey, Kat." Caller ID came in handy.

"I am so psyched, Allison. I bought the most beautiful blue gown. Wait till you see it. I look hot." She rambled on without a breath. "Oh, by the way, I invited Sean to come too. He rented a tux. Talk about dreamboat."

Allison chuckled. "Kat, what are you going on about?"

"Allison." She choked and then, as if speaking to a petulant child said, "Charity ball, tonight eight o'clock."

"Oh, my God, I totally forgot. I've been so wrapped up in this—well, never mind. "Maybe I shouldn't go."

"You are not sending me to this to-do alone."

"What about Sean?"

"You know what I mean."

"I'll pull one of my old dresses out of the closet."

"You'll do no such thing. I'll swing by and pick you up in about twenty minutes. I saw an exquisite gown today that would be perfect."

****

"I've had a plain-clothes officer tailing Allison Brody since she left here," Lancaster told Jake.

"And?"

"She got to the end of the building and stopped. The officer said she seemed disoriented or something. He wasn't sure. She called someone and moved up the block a little more then sat down and waited. A cab came and the cabbie assisted her into the back seat."

Jake's brows drew together. "She needed help? Do we know why?"

"No. But when they got to her house, the housekeeper helped Ms. Brody into the house."

"The cab left and our guy found a place where he could keep an eye on the house. Oh, and after she left this morning one of the other officers said she saw Ms. Brody at a restaurant with Dr. Kincaid."

"Kincaid?"

"Paul Kincaid. He's a psychiatrist."

"A shrink? Do we have any information on this doctor?"

"He's being looked into."

"And tell your guy to lay low. It's better for now that she not know she's being followed."

Lancaster nodded. "Yeah," he said into the phone. Lancaster sighed. "All right. Keep an eye on them, but don't get too close."

"What's going on?"

"Allison Brody and the Rubin woman are shopping," he replied dryly.

"And?"

"It just seems—I don't know—strange, especially after she had to be helped into the house earlier today."

"I guess she's feeling better."

"Obviously."

Jake's jaw tensed and his sharp gaze focused on the bulletin board where pictures of the victims hung.

CHAPTER FOURTEEN

This had to be one of the most idiotic things he'd ever done. Surveillance meant observing, not interacting. He should have stayed away, but the chance to get up close and personal with Allison Brody forced him to ask Lancaster about the best place to rent a tux.

To the right he saw Rory White, the reporter, talking to people with camera in hand.

His cell phone vibrated and he pulled it out to check the caller. Quincy. Jake ignored the call as he'd done with several from Margo and Peter. He couldn't talk to them right now, or wouldn't, until he figured out what the hell was going on.

It wasn't hard to pick out the most beautiful woman in the room. A slinky red off-the-shoulder gown allowed a tantalizing view of perfect breasts. Her mahogany locks were fashioned off to one side and his gaze followed the delicious line of her neck. Gold flecks danced in exotic eyes like fire, beckoning poor souls who dared to look deeply.

Jake straightened as Allison stopped a few inches from him. "Good evening."

"Good evening." He bowed in gentlemanly fashion, keeping careful distance.

"What are you doing here?"

"Surveillance."

Her bottom lip stuck out in a small pout. He wanted to pull her close and tease it with his tongue. "You're following me?"

"Not exactly."

"Then what are you doing here, exactly?" She stepped back.

The orchestra began to play a waltz. Holding his right hand out, he asked, "Would you care to dance, Ms. Brody?"

She froze for several seconds. Jake knew she kept distance. Something about touching.

"Certainly." Allison set her goblet on the tray of a passing waiter.

With Allison in his arms, Jake glided across the floor in perfect time with the music. His eyes stayed glued to hers, oblivious to those around them.

The music ended and Allison pushed away and headed toward the terrace doors. He grabbed two flutes of champagne and followed.

Moonlight spilled over the tended garden which was the perfect backdrop. Allison drew the crisp misty air in. Her hands held onto the stone banister almost as if she needed the support.

"You feel it, don't you?" Jake whispered close to her ear.

She didn't respond or face him.

"You skin tingles, your heart races." He moved closer still. "It's chemistry."

"It's more," she breathed, but still wouldn't look at him.

"Body chemistry, pheromones." His arm reached around to hand over the champagne. "We're two consenting adults."

She took the drink. "How do you know I haven't put a hex on you with a magical potion brewed in my cauldron?"

"Not likely since I don't believe in that stuff."

"Do you have an explanation for everything?"

"Yes. Actually, I do. There's always a logical answer. You just have to find and accept it."

Spinning around Allison slapped her free hand against his chest. "Very clinical, Agent Austin," she snipped. "It sounds as though you explain away everything you can't understand." She curled her fingers in his shirt, her mouth a fraction of an inch from his. "Can you do that? Explain me away?"

Sweet Jesus. Jake knew he should walk away. His control slipped a notch. He yanked Allison flush against him. If he could be rough enough, scary enough, maybe she'd stay away from this case and him. Maybe he'd be able to fight the attraction.

Too late.

He kissed her. How could he not? With one hand, he gathered her thick mane and crushed a frantic, hungry mouth on those soft lips. His tongue swept through tasting sweet wine. Before Allison noticed his blatant hard-on, he broke away.

At that precise moment, Paul Kincaid barged through the doors. "Oh there you are, Allison." He eyed Jake. "I thought you might like to dance."

She stuffed the empty glass into Jake's hand. "I'd love to Paul." She placed her hand on Kincaid's arm. "I was ready to come back in anyway." She dismissed him without a glance, and Jake felt the sting.

Noninvolvement had been a necessary condition in his line of work, a matter of survival. He cursed Allison for getting under his skin and clouding his focus, for filling his head with fantasies. "What the fuck was I thinking?" he mumbled. Stuffing hands into his pockets, Jake stomped down the stairs. For certain the undeniable attraction between them added another wrinkle to this already fucked up case.

Allison's pulse raced and her heart drummed ferociously around Jake Austin.

The ribbed shirt he'd worn had crisp lines and gold cufflinks winked in the light. The color of his hair stood out in contrast to the white collar it curled around. Tailored trousers hugged his muscular thighs. Her eye followed the satin stripe down the side which showcased a well-built physique and her mouth watered.

Instincts screamed to walk the other way, but she hadn't listened. Something deeper called.

The dance had been incredible. Touching him drained much needed strength and her shields wavered. And that kiss set off warning bells. Her breasts tingled. She was breathless, and stunned. If Paul hadn't come, who knows what she would have allowed Jake to do next.

Extra protection, shields, layers, barriers of any kind were a definite must if she saw Jake again. With that decided Allison grabbed her wrap and waved goodbye to Kat and Sean.

Her meditation and determination shored her defenses. The dreams were not occurring as often. The migraines, however, had tripled. Medicine, cool cloths, and dark rooms did little to ease the effects. She looked a fright. Heavy dark shadows circled her eyes, deep lines around her mouth. Thank God for the wonders of makeup. Paul had suggested time in the hospital so tests could be run. She'd adamantly refused.

Once or twice she'd lower the shields hoping to sense Alex without his awareness. Those experiments failed. Immediately, a dark force latched on and pulled her. Frantic, she'd fought the way back and erected the walls again.

In those brief encounters, Allison felt nothing of the boy she'd once known and loved. She unlocked the car door and started to slide in when she noticed a white florist box on the back seat. Her stomach sank. She carefully lifted the lid. The black rose inside looked like it had been splattered with blood.

CHAPTER FIFTEEN

Jake studied the massive bulletin board that reduced two women's lives to lab results and morbid photographs. One of the officers dropped off a brown envelope with his name written on the front.

"Detective Lancaster, there are some people here to see you," Officer Logan said over the intercom.

"Okay, I'll be right there."

Jake opened the envelope and spilled the contents onto the table. Lancaster whistled. Spread out before them were photographs of him and Allison talking, dancing, and on the terrace face-to-face. One picture showed Allison and Kincaid embracing. Jake stared at it for several minutes longer than the others.

Lancaster passed him a look. "Something you want to say?"

Jake shrugged. "I went to the ball to check things out."

"Check things out or check her out?"

"One and the same." His sharp response betrayed more than he liked.

"If you say so. I got the list of attendees from surveillance. The reporter was there. Do you think he sent these?"

"It's possible."

"But you don't think so." Lancaster opened the door. "I've gotta go see who these people are."

Jake nodded and returned his attention to the bulletin board, but not before putting on a glove and pushing the photographs back in the envelope to give to forensics. He wanted to burn the one of Allison and Kincaid. Several times he'd imagined his fingers around the good doctor's neck.

Lancaster returned a few minutes later frowning. He didn't comment on the meeting, so Jake didn't ask. Lancaster snapped on a glove and pulled out the photographs to thumb through them. "So what do you think the message is with these?"

"I think it's the killer taunting me. Letting me know he can get Allison if he wants to."

"Can he?"

"Yes."

"Is she the next victim?"

"She's too old."

"If he's changed other things, as you suspect because you can't find the supposed clue, how do we know he won't alter the type of victim?"

"He won't."

"You seem certain."

"Reasonably certain, detective. As the case progresses I intuit more about the UNSUB. That's how I create the profiles we use to catch them."

"The chief has called me twice already, wanting to know if we're any closer to catching this guy. He's preparing to give an official statement to the media this afternoon. Although he's not pleased that you and I have been working together, I've explained that you have classified information that could help our case."

Jake raked fingers through his too long hair. Did he?

His mind should be analyzing data and comparing similarities, but instead he pictured a pliant body, brunette hair spread over his pillow, a soft moan. He swore her scent still lingered on him. Cursing, Jake rubbed his forehead to dispel the image.

The door flung open.

"Oh, by the way." Lancaster cleared his throat. "Some other feds showed up."

"Thanks," Jake said dryly. "Hi, Peter, Margo."

Peter Carmichael glared at Lancaster. "Would you please excuse us, detective?"

"Sure. Lancaster saluted Jake with his coffee cup and hastily retreated. The minute the door closed, Peter swung an angry scowl his direction.

"The agreement as I recall was you scout things out and report regularly. What the hell is going on? This isn't like you, Jake."

"Hi, Jake." Margo waved. "You look like shit by the way. How's the investigation going?"

"Just peachy, Margo. Thanks for asking. Don't blow a gasket, Pete. There's not been much to report." *Things got complicated.*

He and Peter had worked together for years. Peter was one of the best field agents in the bureau and his friend. Peter knew him well. He'd have to tread lightly.

"I call the shots on the investigations and you know it. I can't make decisions unless I have information, which you stopped providing."

"The Surgeon is here, Peter. I'm starting to learn how he thinks, trying to develop a reliable profile. You know how I work and you've never worried about looking over my shoulder." Jake leveled a look at his friend. "I need some fresh air." With a half wave, Jake exited the room and found the nearest door to the outside. His mind exploded with a barrage of what-ifs and how screwed up life had gotten.

On the street, the young reporter ran up to him. "So, Agent Austin, can you comment on how the investigation is going?" He stood with pencil in hand.

"No comment." Jake started walking.

"Really? Okay," White snickered. "How about explaining what the FBI was doing at a social affair at the Carmody Hotel."

Jake stopped. "No comment!"

His icy glare must have jolted the young man because he retreated. "Yeah, well. Thanks."

Three hours later Jake sat at the table in his hotel room staring into space. His computer screen had several windows open with images reminding him how deadly this game had become.

In Jake's head the past and present collided.

Coming back from the library he noticed several police cars. He squeezed through the crowd to get a better look.

"What's happened, Blake?" Jake called out to a young officer he knew.

"Someone skinned a cat and then nailed it to a wooden cross over by that tree." The officer nodded in the direction of the

campus security and other policemen.

"It's probably a college prank."

"Not the general hell week stunt. And, it's not hell week."

"True. Well, I better get back. Take it easy, Jake."

"You too."

The resonate sound of the phone jogged Jake out of his memories.

"Austin."

"I saw her first, Jake." The voice was brutally cold.

"Who?"

"You fucking know who. The beautiful brunette you waltzed around the floor last night."

"What do you want?" Jake asked calmly, even though his stomach churned.

"How smart are you?" The phone went dead.

****

Allison had a meeting at GTT with Gil, the man who ran the family business. She and her siblings owned equal shares in the company and the dividends had put her, Nick and now Lucy through college. As the oldest, Allison sat on the board and attended the quarterly meetings.

She dressed in a burgundy suit she'd designed and made herself. She wore enough jewelry to still look professional, slipped into black three-inch heels and headed for the car. As she stepped out the front door she tripped on the white florist box that lay on the porch. Allison didn't want to touch the box. Leaving it on the porch was not an option either, so she went back inside and grabbed a towel.

The second she touched it, a small pulse started at the base of her skull. The box acted as a conduit, linking them. She dropped it in the back seat and slammed the door. Climbing into the driver's side, Allison headed for GTT. The more miles that passed the harder it was to concentrate on the simple action of driving to a place she'd been a million times. Her eyesight blurred so she pulled into a small park area.

Blindly fumbling, she found Detective Lancaster's card.

"Gloucester Police Department."

"I need to speak with Detective Lancaster," Allison said as she got out of the car.

"I'll try his line."

The phone rang twice. "Lancaster."

"Detective, it's Allison Brody. I need—" She stopped speaking. The detective said something but she couldn't hear for the buzzing in her head. Allison fell to her knees, dizzy. The cell phone slipped through her fingers.

The vision began at a quaint little house with a pastel-colored bedroom, paisley wallpaper and a white comforter that had been thrown to the floor. Gloved hands circled a young woman's neck.

Allison grabbed her head and closed her eyes to make the vision go away.

The young woman grabbed at the killer's arms and scratched at his face. His grip tightened and closed her airway. The woman slumped on the bed, her head lolling to one side.

The images moved forward.

Blood seeped into the colorful bed sheets and pieces of words written in the victim's blood crawled down the wall to a coagulated stop. *Three to get ready.*

Allison wilted to the ground unconscious.

****

Allison woke up in Addison Gilbert Hospital, disoriented. An IV dripped clear liquid in the tube. The pain in her head had dulled to an ache and her vision had cleared. She tried to scoot up on the bed but was too weak.

Paul entered the room, followed by Detective Lancaster, Jake, and other people she didn't recognize. Paul placed a hand on her forehead and cheek then used a pin light to see how her pupils reacted. He glanced at the monitors.

Slowly, the images and the scene that precipitated the blackout returned. She grabbed for the container on the table and vomited.

A nurse came in, took the container, and wiped her face with a cool rag.

Paul held her hand. "How are you feeling?"

"Not good." Her scratchy throat ached. "Why does my throat hurt?"

Detective Lancaster came forward. "Witnesses at the park said you were screaming hysterically before you passed out."

Allison didn't remember screaming.

"What happened?" Lancaster said.

Paul handed her a cup and she took a couple of sips. "I left my house for a meeting and found another one of those boxes on the porch." She stopped to take another drink of water.

Paul frowned. "What boxes?"

Lancaster waved his hand. "Let her finish. Go on, Allison."

"I put it in the car and left. My head started hurting. The farther I drove, the worse the headache got. I pulled over to call you and the pain got so bad I guess I blacked out."

"I told you those headaches were trouble," Paul said. "We need to run tests to find out what's causing them."

Her gaze went past Paul and Detective Lancaster to land on Jake. He leaned against the wall with his arms crossed, but he in no way looked relaxed. His intense glare focused on Paul. If looks could kill, Paul would have had invisible daggers imbedded in his body. She didn't know what to make of Jake's body language.

Lancaster broke into her thoughts. "We found the box and sent it to forensics. Good thing using the towel."

"I hope it helps."

"We'll see."

The fair-haired guy who stood by the door cleared his throat to get the detective's attention.

"Excuse me." Lancaster smiled and moved to stand with the others and converse in whispers. The group exited the room.

"I'm going to find the ER doctor who admitted you. I'd like to keep you overnight for observation."

"I don't want to stay here, Paul."

"We really should do a CAT scan at least, Allison. I'd feel better if we had some idea why this is happening."

"And you don't think I would too?" Although she knew exactly what was causing her headaches.

"Then let us run tests."

"I'll think about it."

Paul grimaced, but said nothing more before leaving.

Allison raised the bed to sit up and took another sip of water. "You don't need to hide in the shadows. I know you're there."

Yanni appeared beside her bed. "Tis dangerous for you to keep suppressing your abilities. The evil is too strong, and if you do not gain full strength, you will not beat him."

"I'm very tired. Can we talk about this later?"

"Austin watches you with a hunger. Do not take him lightly

for he is a powerful force to be reckoned with."

"You don't need to tell me that. I've felt that force close up." That night on the terrace when his flippant, totally male attitude ticked her off. But, he'd been right. Body chemistry was definitely at work here.

Her controlled, somewhat peaceful life had been disrupted and not one, but two dangerous men fought for her attention. She sighed and closed her eyes. "I need to sleep."

Yanni placed a hand on her cheek. "Gather strength and shore your mind. You will need those weapons when the time comes to fight."

CHAPTER SIXTEEN

In the hallway, Peter turned on Jake. "So who is she and what does she have to do with this case?"

Jake looked at his friend. "She came to us a couple of days ago claiming to see through The Surgeon's eyes. She offered to help."

"A psychic?" Margo said.

Jake clenched his jaw. "She never said the word psychic, but yeah, I'd say that's it."

Peter glared at him. "So you did what? Let her assist in the investigation?"

Jake balled his hands into fists. "No, Peter. I told her I didn't believe it, and we'd stick to regular police procedures." He glanced at Allison's door.

"There's got to be more to it. Why did we find her passed out in the park?"

"The black rose is the third she's received. She believes it's from The Surgeon."

"Why?"

Jake shoved the hair out of his eyes. "She's a pawn in his game. I just don't know where she fits."

"It's a game? Why do you say that?"

Jake moved as a stretcher passed. "Because it is. He's toying with me. He mentions me by name, draws me in, and leads me on a merry chase. A game."

Lancaster had gotten on the phone the minute they'd stepped

out of the room. "There's been another murder."

Jake looked one more time at Allison's door.

Lancaster said, "I've assigned an officer to stay by the door until she's released."

A ring of tape had been strung around the crime scene. As they proceeded up the front walk Lancaster pulled an officer aside. "Keep everyone out for a few minutes."

"Yes sir."

Lancaster logged them in and followed Jake as they went through the front room. The first thing Jake noted was how undisturbed the house seemed until he reached the bedroom. An overwhelming coppery smell

hung in the air and a heaviness, a deep sense of loss. Displayed for all to see was the body of a pretty, young woman, who should have had a long life. Instead, she'd become another piece in the killer's game. "Do we know who she is?"

"Sylvia Miller," Lancaster offered.

Jake quietly nodded. He methodically surveyed the scene from the doorway, memorizing every detail. He entered the room and moved toward the bed and the body. The same configuration carved in the skin, the same gory mutilation of the female anatomy, the words written in the victim's blood.

Three to get ready.

Jake touched nothing and pivoted in the spot where he stood, examining the entire room.

He grunted before following the same line back to the door and brushed past Lancaster on his way outside.

"You didn't find what you were looking for, did you?" Lancaster asked.

"No. I'll wait for forensics. Maybe I'll canvass the area with your officers and talk to the neighbors."

Almost on cue, two other vehicles pulled up. One was the forensic team. The door on the van next to them opened and Genevieve Tobias jumped out. She grabbed a camera and put the long strap around her neck. It swayed below her belt, but didn't interfere with her purposeful stride.

Peter said, "We've been officially asked in by the chief and the mayor."

Jake looked at Lancaster who shrugged. "Logical."

"Hey, Tobias, how's it hanging?" Margo said nodding toward the camera.

"Thirty-five and by the fly, Margo." Her gaze slid to Jake and he acknowledged her.

Peter stepped away to answer a call. Jake watched the forensic team suit up and haul in their equipment.

When Peter and Lancaster rejoined them Jake said, "Detective Lancaster, I'd like you to meet Genevieve Tobias. She's the forensic photographer who works with our team."

She smiled. "Nice to meet you, detective."

"Ma'am."

Jake went on. "The guy lurking behind her in the dark shades is our forensic pathologist, Dr. Zach Quincy."

"Doctor." Lancaster nodded and did a quick shake of hands before Quincy retreated.

"You'll have to excuse him. He'd just finished two extensive cases and was looking forward to a break," Tobias offered.

"Completely understandable."

Margo jumped in. "Peter, I'm going back to the station to get my computer set up."

"Go ahead, Margo. I'll catch a ride back with someone." He looked directly at Tobias.

Lancaster spoke to the officers who were going door to door. Jake visualized the previous night. He picked out the site where the killer would have hidden, waiting for his opportunity.

In the conference room at the police station, Jake, Lancaster, Tobias and Zach gathered to discuss the initial autopsy results of the newest victim.

Jake said, "Okay, Zach. You're on."

"Not much you don't already know, Jake. She died between two and four a.m. this morning. Looks like the same type of weapon used in the New York killing. From the cuts in the skin, I'd say probably a knife with a serrated edge. She died of strangulation and was disemboweled postmortem. No external signs of rape or other sexual abuse. No marks on wrists or ankles to show that she was restrained in any way. No defensive injuries, but there was stuff under the fingernails. It looks like she might have scratched him. The words on the wall were written in the victim's blood."

Lancaster said, "Have they found any traces of anyone else in that house?"

"No, detective."

Tobias opened the file in front of her and passed over photographs of the scene and the body. Jake held the picture of the message. Three to get ready. He repeated them lyrically, silently, with a rhythm only one other knew.

"So we're not much further than we were yesterday."

"Not much," Zach confirmed.

Margo hunched over her computer. She rarely spoke when she worked, except to provide necessary information.

The door opened and Peter strolled in. He briefly looked at Tobias then sat down at the end of the table. "They released the Brody woman from the hospital."

All Jake's senses went on alert. "When?"

"About an hour ago. Kincaid took her home."

"Surveillance?" Jake asked.

Lancaster nodded. "Just like before, low profile. We don't want to tip The Surgeon, if he's watching her."

"He's watching," Jake snarled.

****

Paul leaving was a huge relief. Allison couldn't take another minute of his fawning. To her mind, the terrible headaches and blackout were minor compared to what was at stake. Who knew how long the killer would wait to strike again?

Allison changed into a nightgown, pulled on a robe and went downstairs to the study. How sturdy were the barricades she'd developed in her mind? Would they keep Alex out long enough for her to form a plan?

Anger erupted.

Throwing her head back, Allison roared. The room shook, books flew from the shelves of the hand-carved bookcase her grandfather had built; the lighthouse painting hanging on the west wall fell.

"Your powers are growing."

"What?" Allison whipped around to see Yanni sitting on the windowsill.

"Intense emotions, anger, fear, have strengthened your resolve and in doing so, have allowed your abilities to evolve."

"What are you talking about? I've never done anything like

this." Allison flung her arms out in a wide circle encompassing the disheveled room.

"I tried to tell you, Allison," Yanni said as she hopped to the floor. "Visions are only one part of your gifts. We are special you and I. Not only do we house all the secrets of our line, but we were born on the equinox and that phenomenon enhances all the abilities the human mind and body possess."

"What are you saying?" Allison laid her head between her hands and massaged her skull.

"With time and determination, you too could be a powerful force."

"You make me sound like another one of Mother Nature's disasters."

A soft, gentle hand touched Allison's forehead. "Not disaster, little one. Treasure."

"This is crazy. I'm crazy." Allison shot out of the chair, putting as much distance between herself and Yanni as possible. "I'm a freak, a mistake." Twisting the ends of the belt on her robe and with anguished sincerity she said, "People condemn what they don't understand. And they

don't understand me. Please go," Allison whispered as she closed her eyes and withered to the sofa, suddenly drained of energy.

Alone, Allison worried. Worried what he would do to her mind if she couldn't repel him. Worried what it would do to her sanity if she kept on this course.

She opened the French doors and wandered onto the patio. Her flimsy nightgown billowed in the breeze, the robe left inside. Her feet dragged as though they were cemented in concrete. The journey to the sandy cove took a while. Water lapped the shore and limbs on the trees rustled with the wind. Allison didn't notice. She sought one thing.

Luna.

In her family tree, the women were strongest at night. She raised her arms above her head causing the sleeves of her gown to fall to her shoulders. They formed a vee with fingertips outstretched toward the full moon, drawing a life force from its rays. "Be still and silent in the night, when creeping down to find your light. The secret of a woman's power, a full moon on the bewitching hour."

Allison sank to her knees. "Luna, oh beautiful moon, whose guiding light gives me strength. Help me understand what is happening. What cosmic tumblers have fallen into place to cause this drastic change in my world?" She hung her head and cried, too caught up in anguish to notice the dark form by the trees.

CHAPTER SEVENTEEN

Peter and Lancaster sauntered into Cameron's and sat down at Jake's table. "Another murder, no evidence, no leads. I'm glad the chief asked your team to come on board."

Jake leveled his gaze. "We need to keep our eyes open and senses sharp. Stress that to your men. Make sure they stay close to Allison Brody. I don't care if she sees them or not."

"I thought she was too old to be a target."

"Based on the previous murders and his M.O., she is too old," Peter said.

Jake nodded. "Still, there's some reason she's involved. Until I figure it out, I want her watched."

"Won't seeing her surrounded by police spook him?"

"Not likely. He's arrogant, confident, and loves rubbing my face in it when he one ups me. We need someone close to her."

"What about you?"

"Me?" Jake took a bite of his sandwich. "How do you mean?"

"I thought—uh, thought you might want to stay closer to her."

Peter reached for the sugar to put in his coffee. "The Surgeon has started this game and somehow Ms. Brody is tangled up in it. It would be best for you to stay away from her, Jake."

Jake clenched his jaw, threw money on the table to cover the bill and left.

****

Allison switched on her computer. She decided to toy with some new promotional ideas, a pleasant respite. It provided a way to step back from the situation and calm down.

She also got online to see if any of her chat friends were available.

Her fingers froze. The most recent message was from TheSurgeon@....Going against better judgment, Allison opened the message. The screen danced and changed, exploding with color. Red lettering in a bold elegant font appeared.

You're so delectable. My mouth waters for your taste.

Allison's sweaty palm clamped onto the mouse. Heart pounding, she clicked on the attachment and waited. Pictures appeared on the monitor. One of her getting into her car at the house the day she found the last florist box. The zoom had captured her shocked expression. The next

showed her in the display window at R&N's working. The final pictures unnerved her more than the first two. They had been taken last night in the cove. He'd been there, close enough to take the pictures. She had not sensed him.

Allison's concentration faltered and her shield slipped. The darkness crept inside with the cold hatred and fury of the killer. His intimidation tactics frightened her, as he'd wanted. Unwilling to give in to the notion that someone she had once loved could be so completely evil, Allison focused the energy and pushed back the darkness with light. "Damn you. What is your game?"

Ignoring the evil would not make it go away. Her cell phone was in her purse along with Detective Lancaster' s card. She wandered to the kitchen and put on water for tea.

As she stood in the room absently stirring honey into a mug, the doorbell rang. Very unusual for her to have guests in the afternoon—or ever. Caution, surprise, and a chill thrill ripped a hole in her protective fabric as she swung open the door to find Jake Austin on the porch.

The light green shirt made his eyes that much deeper in color. His chest was more remarkable when not hidden by a suit coat. He slid hands into the back pockets which made the jeans tighter. "Hello."

"Hi," she said and leaned against the door frame. "What brings you out this way, Agent Austin?"

Even though he acted casual, intensity rumbled around him. "Can we talk?"

"Come in." She moved aside to allow him access to the house. "Would you like some tea or a bite to eat?"

"No, thanks."

Allison closed the door, all too aware of Jake's closeness. "I'm in the kitchen, right through here."

She led the way.

Gripping the counter edge with one hand, she stirred her tea with the other. "What can I do for you?"

Without so much as a by-your-leave, Jake toured her kitchen, looking in cupboards and lifting lids on containers. "If you're looking for drugs, I only do the prescription kind and they are sitting in the windowsill. I keep my Ouija Board and crystal ball hidden in the pantry," she said dryly.

Jake stopped perusing. "You've got a smart mouth."

She leaned against the counter. "My apologies if I've offended you, but you were searching my kitchen without a warrant."

He coughed and shoved his hands into the front pockets this time. "I wanted to know more about what you do."

"What I do?"

"Yes, you're psychic powers or whatever."

Allison studied him for a few minutes. "Why?"

He brushed a hand through his hair, long fingers separated thick strands. It amused her to think he was at a loss for words.

"I'm sure you already have a file on me."

Jake ducked his head and gave her a sideways glance. "Not much in the file, really."

Stunned and a little ticked he'd actually checked her out, she gritted her teeth. He cocked an eyebrow, waiting. How could she tell him that she wasn't at all sure of her so-called powers? She'd chosen to leave that life long ago. "I'm of gypsy heritage on my father's side. Gypsies have a long history of psychic powers, palm reading, tarot cards, and fortune tellers."

"I've seen the movies." His eyes twinkled.

"Very funny." Allison took the mug and sat down at the table. She motioned for him to sit also. "The powers, abilities, gifts— whatever you want to call them—are passed down to only the females of the line, not to every female, and they differ from generation to generation."

"So the males get nothing?"

She scowled at him. "Not exactly. Some get heightened senses. They know when they're being watched or feel when something bad will happen. It never develops more than that. And, again, it doesn't happen to every male and it skips generations sometimes. We are very good with animals too," she added. "Anyway, on rare occasions, if a female is born on the equinox she inherits all the powers in some form or other and they are enhanced tremendously. Or that's the theory."

"Theory?"

Allison shrugged. "In eight generations, it's only happened twice. My great-grandmother and me."

Jake studied her. "I ask the question again. Theory?"

Uncomfortable, Allison toyed with a napkin. "Look, agent. This is speculation and mumbo jumbo by your standards. You being here certainly isn't because you're interested in my abilities." Allison ran her index finger around the rim of the mug, waiting.

"I'm grasping at straws, Ms. Brody." Jake stood to pace. "You claim you can see things through his eyes. I'm intrigued."

A raw, sensual power emanated from him. "I don't have an answer for you, Agent Austin."

He stopped in front of her chair. "Would you please stop calling me that?"

"What?"

"Agent. My name is Jake. Can you call me Jake?"

"If it pleases you."

That threw him, she could tell. He frowned. "I can't say that I understand it. I won't even say that I necessarily believe it, but..." He sighed. "Will you help me?"

"That couldn't have been easy for you."

"Nothing's been easy." He thrust his right hand out urging her to shake. "So what do you say?"

Part of her warned it would be unwise to collaborate with this man. She'd made it a point to avoid touching people for years, but found herself closing her hand over his. A surge of energy shot through her arm, straight to her stomach, and lower. She got lost in his eyes then roused herself.

"In the spirit of our newly formed—collaboration, I should tell you about an email I received from The Surgeon today." She eased from his grip, which tightened the minute she mentioned the email.

"I need to see it." The urgency was back in his voice and his body tensed.

For an instant, Allison noticed a red aura surrounding Jake. "The computer is in the other room." She signed on. "I've only received the one."

Jake sat down and looked at the email. Silence stretched as seconds passed. He cleared his throat. "Do you have an empty disk?"

"Right here." Allison leaned over his left shoulder behind the monitor to retrieve one. She stayed close as he copied the email. He smelled of fresh soap and shampoo. It wasn't overly strong, but pleasant. She stopped just short of sniffing his hair. How stupidly teenage was that?

"Okay." Jake stood, sending Allison stumbling back. "Well." He paused holding the disk. "I'll be going then." As he brushed past her, he stopped. "Oh, here." He handed her a cherry lollipop.

Puzzled by the gesture, she said, "What's this for?"

Jake shrugged. "A peace offering."

Sexual sparks pierced her heart. "Unusual and..." Her left brow arched, tugging the corner of her mouth with it. "Unexpected." Maybe under all that machismo there actually hid a sensitive soul. Allison pulled the wrapper off and stuck the lollipop in her mouth. "Ummm, I love cherry."

She twirled the candy around a few times. Wickedly pushing the stick in and out between her lips, never breaking eye contact.

Jake shifted positions. "I'll see you later."

"You certainly will," she whispered.

Allison studied the black car as it drove away.

"Interesting," a cheerful voice said.

She closed the door and found Yanni lounging on the settee. Dangling from her ears were red, sparkly earrings, matching the color of her blouse.

"What's interesting?"

"Him."

"If you like the type." Allison plopped down in the over-stuffed chair and hung legs across the arm.

"Do you?"

"Yanni. Why do you keep turning up like this?" She set the lollipop on the table.

"I am meant to help you."

"Really?"

"Do not be annoying. You know it is my purpose."

"Do I?"

Yanni rolled to her stomach. "Tell me what you have learned."

Allison sighed. "Very well. I believe the killer is Alex."

Yanni's eyes grew wide. "The boy? The one in your dreams?"

"Yes. It's the only explanation as to why we connect. Even he intimated that we'd linked before. It took me a while to put it together." She drew her knees up. "it's been a long time since I've thought of Alex—a very long time."

A tingle skittered across Allison's skin. Her eyesight blurred. "He's here—outside, looking at the house. He stays in the woods."

Yanni crossed her legs, Indian style, put her palms together and raised her hands above her head. She separated them and brought them down slowly, taking deep breaths. With eyes closed, she said, "I see him. He is cautious. He knows about your shadows."

"Shadows?"

"The policemen who have been tailing you since you went to the police station."

"He's been watching me."

"And others."

"He killed that poor woman. I couldn't stop it."

"You did not know which one he would choose."

"But I should have tried. I shouldn't have let Jake push me out the door."

"Try harder next time."

Allison's eyes closed. "I feel anger in him. Anger with me and—Jake."

"We must work on your control and shielding. There are other techniques I can teach you."

"I—"

Yanni raised her hand and the bracelets fell back clanging. "You will need protection."

"What are you talking about?"

Yanni swung her legs to the floor and crawled to where Allison sat. She grabbed Allison's hands. "The time will come when you and he meet face-to-face. Do not be fooled into thinking he will do you no harm. Time changes people. If this is your Alex, you cannot know what the years have done to him. Life is sometimes cruel."

She hadn't gotten past the fact that this killer might be the boy she'd fallen in love with a lifetime ago. "Okay. Where do we start?"

For the rest of the day, Yanni coached Allison, tiring and relentless in the instruction.

Allison thought about a ball of fire and stretched out her right hand. The heat moved from her chest to shoulder then down the arm. When she peeked, she thought she'd see a small flame sitting in the palm, but there was nothing. Disappointed, she dropped one hand and with the fingers of the other, rubbed at the headache.

Allison fell backward to the floor, her arms thrown out as if to make a snow angel. "I can't do anymore. It's been six hours. My brain is about to explode."

Yanni clapped her hands. "Pay attention. You have a decade of learning to do in a very short time. Your life may depend on it."

Allison opened one eye and stared at her petite task master. "Is there something you're not telling me?"

"Of course not," Yanni blustered. "But the future is uncertain. You cannot know when you will need to focus all your powers."

Allison sighed. "I understand, but I also know if I don't get some sleep, I won't be good to anyone."

"Once more, then we will be done for the day."

"Very well," Allison agreed then lifted herself back up to the lotus position.

"Hands around, up together. Yes, that's it. Now exhale as you slowly lower them. Concentrate on centering your energy."

Allison focused on the soft tone of Yanni's voice. She felt the heat vibrate in her chest like a wild fire that fought to be contained.

"Harness the power so you can direct it," Yanni said.

"This is impossible."

Yanni stood. "To achieve, you must first believe." She held out her hand, palm facing upward. A ball of orange fire hovered in her palm. She focused her gaze on the dancing heat and it grew larger, turning blue, bright red and orange again.

Astounded, Allison said, "Amazing. I didn't imagine it possible."

"That is why you failed." Yanni closed her hand extinguishing the flames. "We will try again tomorrow." She disappeared into green smoke.

"That is so cool," Allison whispered.

The sun hung lazy in the sky as Allison walked to clear her mind. Not knowing why, she walked to the guest house which sat on the cusp of the cove.

The porch had a small swing, and affixed to the chain with a satin ribbon was a red envelope. Allison sat on the swing and carefully opened it. A card tumbled into her lap.

Like the moon you glow, a beacon in the darkest night. Like the sea your blood flows steady, your spirit takes flight. Like a pendulum my anticipation swings to and fro, waiting for that moment when you let yourself go. You name is whispered in the evening breeze, wraps around the branches and trunks of trees, a moment will come not too far away when we'll be together forever and a day. When you're ready to hear what I'm longing to say, that will be your judgment day. Anxious, I'm waiting for you to see that your future and destiny lie with me.

She stared at the neatly written words on the page, caught up in the flow of the prose and the musical rhythm. Even though the verse was unsigned, she knew the identity of the author. The meaning of the message sank in and her hands trembled crumpling the paper.

CHAPTER EIGHTEEN

"Hey, Quincy, hold on," Peter said as Jake entered the room. Peter pressed the speaker button. "Go ahead."

"We finished the autopsy on this new one."

"And?"

"Findings are the same." Peter heard Dr. Hallowell mumbling in the background something about young pups getting in his way and he couldn't make out the rest. "Any trouble?" Peter asked cautiously.

Quincy snickered. "Nothing I couldn't handle. I'll have the report to you shortly."

"Okay." As Peter hung up he looked at Jake. "So?"

Jake walked over and handed a disk to Margo. "He's been watching her."

Margo slipped the disk into the laptop and opened the attachments. Tobias whistled at the picture of Allison on the beach with her arms outstretched toward the moon.

"She's a night creature." Tobias tilted her head. "Were you aware of that?"

"I'm learning."

Tobias lifted a quizzical brow. "Really?"

Peter said, "What do you think this tells us?"

"Either his focus has shifted or widened," Margo supplied.

"Surveillance?"

"Still there," Jake said. "For all the good it's doing. He still manages to get close enough to take these." He pointed to the monitor.

"He could have a zoom lens," Margo offered. "If she's psychic, how come she doesn't know he's there?"

"Maybe she does," Lancaster said as he walked into the room.

"What do you mean?"

"She says she sees through his eyes. If he's watching her, she might have known he was there."

Jake frowned. *Why didn't she tell me?*

Tobias glanced at Peter and then back at the monitor. "Could she be in on it?"

Jake shook his head. "He works alone."

"Have you checked her out?" Peter asked Lancaster.

"I ran a check after she came in the first time. The copy is in that stack somewhere." He pointed to one of the stacks of papers on the table. "Good family, comes from money, doesn't need to work but does anyway. Little sister, Lucy, is in a local college. She's been there the whole time. We have witnesses who will confirm it. The brother, Nick Brody, is a geologist. He just returned from a dig. His alibi is solid. Parents were killed in an auto accident ten years ago. The parents' housekeeper stops by to clean up. No motive."

Jake paced. "Except for being part of the carnival side show, she's clean."

Rolling her eyes at Jake, Margo said, "So what do we do now?"

"Keep our eyes open, follow up on any leads, and hope the killer makes a mistake."

"I'll get some officers out to the woods by Ms. Brody's house and see if they can find anything," Lancaster said.

Jake moved to the windows. Luck wasn't an option. He felt helpless in more ways than one. He wandered to the table and picked up the folder on top of one stack. There was little he could do at the moment except carefully study the photographs for the tenth time. There had to be something he was missing.

Lancaster advised them that Allison Brody had arrived saying she had another message from The Surgeon. "I'll get her settled in one of the other rooms."

Jake sat reading the words over and over. He heard harsh

whispers in the corner of the room where Peter and Tobias stood. Not sure he wanted to know what they were arguing about he directed his attention back to the note and Lancaster.

"He's going to kill her," Lancaster said. "It's plain as day right there on the page."

Jake didn't respond.

"Are you going to talk to her or should I?"

"Give me a minute." Jake's voice vibrated. He appeared calm on the surface, but underneath volcanoes erupted and his stomach churned. "FBI Conduct Rule Number One says no fraternizing with a witness in a federal investigation."

"Technically, she's not a witness."

Jake's jaw clenched as he stared at the card.

"What does the book say if you break the rules?"

"I don't break them." Okay, so maybe he had small infractions.

Lancaster shook his head. "There is something passing between you and Allison Brody. You can't deny that."

Slamming his hands on the table, Jake bounced up from the chair. This drew the attention of everyone in the room. "I fucking can deny it. I have to." Jake paced the room. He pushed fingers through tracks in his hair, pulling on the ends. "If he thinks I have any interest in Allison Brody, he'll take great pleasure in killing her. He might even take the time to torture her first."

Peter moved closer to Jake as Lancaster calmly asked. "Why would it make any difference that you care for her? The other women he's killed had someone who loved them. Why are you making this so personal?"

"Because he will, dammit!" The room grew definitely hotter, or was it just his rising temper? "I have to go." Jake didn't miss the worried glances passed between his colleagues, but they refocused on other duties. Stopped with a hand on the doorknob and his back to Lancaster, Jake said in a hushed voice, "Do you ever wonder what makes a man cross the line?"

"The line?"

"Between good and evil."

Lancaster's gaze lifted toward the ceiling or the heavens. Cocking one eyebrow, he shrugged and said, "It's different for each one, I'm sure."

Jake grunted and left the room.

He stormed into the place where she waited, barely able to

contain his anger. "Allison."

She stood at the window, hands clasping her sides at the waist, arms wrapped around her body in a fierce hug. She looked vulnerable. "Jake."

"Have you noticed anyone lurking around your house or work lately? The same face you may have seen more than once?"

"No."

Her response was sharp and crisp, her frame rigidly straight. *Shit.* Jake's lips clamped together. He glared at her back wanting, willing her to look at him.

"You might want to discontinue working alone at night for a while until we catch this guy, or he moves on."

"Why?"

"I can't explain why he's so fascinated with you, but working late by yourself is reckless now that we know he's watching."

"I will not cave to fear or threats."

"Work during the daytime hours."

Her legs threatened to buckle. Jake's emotions hit hard and that unrelenting gaze was on full blast. His eyes were unyielding and her breath caught. Thankfully the windowsill was there because her knees turned to gel. Light from the window danced over his stern but gorgeous features. Sexy stubble covered a tight jaw line and mussed hair hung to his collar. Jake looked nothing like a federal agent.

Of course, he had no idea that the reason she worked alone at night was because of her difficulty being around people. This information she would have divulged had he even asked, but he didn't. He ordered her to rearrange her life, a life that had already been disturbed by his presence. She'd managed to erect a thin barrier to block the gruesome visions, but she had no shield against Jake.

"I suppose you could arrest me, Agent Austin. Have one of the officers following me do it." Her gaze slipped away and she turned her back to him again.

In seconds he was there, imprisoning her between the window glass and his hard sinuous body. Arms on either side, he pressed against her. "Do you want to die?"

"No," Allison whispered.

"Then why do you make it so damned difficult to protect you?"

The current between them electrified the room, his hard erection impossible to ignore. Anger spilled out as she pushed him away. "I will not become a prisoner because of this murderer," she yelled. "And you can't stop me from working. I've broken no laws." Two light bulbs exploded.

"Woman," Jake growled.

"Woman? Look, agent," she offered an insolent sneer. "I'm a free citizen." She moved forward, pressing her index finger in Jake's solid chest. "You can't tell me what to do." Allison stormed out of the room.

Jake followed. "Sergeant," he called.

"Sir?"

"Detain that woman."

The shocked look on the sergeant's face fled quickly as he blocked her way.

"What?" Allison roared.

The commotion brought Lancaster and the others from their locations. Jake's team stepped into the cramped hallway.

"What the devil is going on here, Jake?" Lancaster shifted his gaze between the two of them.

Without taking his eyes off her, Jake said, "Ms. Brody and I were having a discussion that wasn't quite finished."

"The hell it wasn't." Allison glared at him. "I have nothing more to say to you."

Jake half dragged, half guided her back to the open door. "Then you can listen. Thank you, sergeant."

Lancaster stepped into the room. Allison wrenched free from Jake's grasp and moved as far away as the room would allow. Lancaster stayed by the door to serve as referee.

Tension filled the room, but both remained quiet. She stationed herself in one corner facing the wall, silently counting to a thousand in an attempt to calm down. That arrogant, annoying man sat on the edge of a table with his legs crossed at the ankles focusing on an unknown object in the distance.

"So, are either of you going to tell me what's going on?"

"He's being unreasonable," Allison said over her shoulder.

"She's being uncooperative." Jake offered in a weary agitated voice.

Neither of them moved.

"I don't take kindly to being ordered around."

Jake scowled. "I'm trying to protect you."

With a breathless laugh, Lancaster said, "Why don't I drive you home, Ms. Brody?"

"Thank you, detective, but I have my car."

"Then let me walk you out."

Jake curtly nodded, but didn't move and that upped her irritation. As if she needed his permission.

"I saw a board in that room with several pictures of women. The last picture on the right, who is she?"

"The Surgeon's latest victim," Lancaster replied.

"I saw it," she whispered.

Jake's head whipped toward her. "Saw what?"

Allison wrung her hands. "I saw him kill her. He was already in the bedroom so I had no way to determine the location. I couldn't be sure if it had occurred in the past, present or would in the future." She sank into a chair. "I watched him do it." Allison put the back of her hand to her lips trying not to scream.

Lancaster patted her shoulder. "It wasn't your fault. You had no way of knowing."

Jake moved closer. "Will you be okay to drive?"

"I'll be fine, Agent Austin."

He clenched his teeth. "Fine."

Allison left through the door Lancaster held open without a word or a glance in his direction.

"Make sure the surveillance team stays close," Jake told Lancaster.

Jake sat in his room staring blankly at the laptop open on the table. Again, when his concentration should be on catching The Surgeon, unwillingly his thoughts focused on a more beautiful opponent.

A loud knock dragged him from the small table. He opened the door and Peter stepped into the room. "Do you want to explain that commotion today?"

Jake didn't answer.

"You're a professional, and what I saw today was not professional. And I'm not even going to go into how you look."

Jake sat down in the chair he'd vacated.

Peter strolled from one end of the room to the other. "This is the first time I've seen you act irrationally, and with a woman?" He turned. "Are you going to fill me in?"

Jake sighed heavily and rubbed his hands across his face. "Hell, I can't explain it. From the moment I set eyes on Allison my head has been screwed up."

Peter grabbed hold of the back of the chair as Jake rose. "I don't believe it. You're in love with her. Shit!"

"That's absurd," Jake argued. "There's something strange going on, I'll admit, but love hasn't entered into it. I've only been here a few days."

The look Peter threw at him was one of frustration. "Please, Jake. Do I not work with Tobias, my ex, on a regular basis? I definitely know all about beating your head against a wall because of a woman."

Jake leaned against the small dresser, and growled low in his throat. He needed to hit something. Where was a punching bag when you needed it?

"I know this has been hell—the killer naming you in his messages and I understand how you feel, but—"

"Can you? Can you understand how it feels to see your name written in blood on the wall of a woman who was brutally murdered?

"Jake."

He glared at his friend. "Knowing that if you don't figure it out, more women are going to die?"

CHAPTER NINETEEN

Rage and fury blew through the killer. First the dance, now pressing against Allison and whispering intimately into her ear. How dare Jake touch her? Allison belonged to him and Jake would be shown the error of his ways. He'd make sure of it.

****

Allison threw her keys on the entry table and dropped the purse next to them. The bristling anger had simmered on the drive home. The man had a way of turning her inside out. Her emotions felt bruised and battered after spending a few minutes with Jake. It's funny how both men had come into her life unexpectedly and managed to wring her dry.

She started up the stairs, but the phone rang. She rushed to answer it. "Hello?"

"Allison, it's Paul."

"Hello, Paul." She was relieved to hear a friendly voice.

"I wanted to follow up on how you were doing before I leave town this weekend."

"I'm doing okay." *Except for the killer who has taken up residence in my head and the federal agent who threatens to break my heart.*

"Allison?"

"I'm fine, really. Where are you going?"

"I made reservations in Cape Cod for a change of atmosphere."

"Cape Cod?"

"Yeah. I try to go up there every couple of months to clear my head and relax. You wanna come? We could hang out, get drunk and act goofy, like old times. Oh, wait. That was just me, but you could join in. What do you say?"

"Paul—I"

"Don't worry, Allison. I'll get two rooms. No expectations. Two friends having a relaxing weekend."

Putting distance between herself and the problems might help to focus. Not to mention, if she could prove to Paul that she wasn't having a neurotic breakdown, he would quit circling. "All right, when do we leave?"

"I had planned on leaving around three today."

"Sounds good. I'll be ready."

"I'm not guaranteeing that I won't try to convince you to have tests done."

Allison chuckled. "Do your best." She hung up and ran upstairs to pack.

She hummed as she threw clothes into an overnight bag and scooped up facial cleanser and a toothbrush. Yanni's lessons about control had helped tremendously with the headaches. She'd have to talk to Nick about getting some Amber crystals. Unfortunately, crystals wouldn't solve her biggest problem…Jake.

****

"What?" Jake's voice rang through the halls of the department.

"She left town with Paul Kincaid."

"The shrink?"

"Yes, sir."

Frowning, Jake roamed the conference room with angry strides.

"The surveillance officer followed them until they left town. He went back to Ms. Brody's house and spoke to the housekeeper who said they went to Cape Cod for the weekend."

"That's just great. Damn woman. Can't stay put. Police surveillance doesn't do anything if she leaves Gloucester." Jake nodded. "Thanks, Logan. I appreciate everything you and the others have done. I know this hasn't been the most pleasant of duties."

"On the contrary." Logan grinned. "It's been interesting."

"You're too kind." Jake's statement dripped with sarcasm.

Lancaster entered as Logan left the room. "What's that all about?"

"Allison Brody and Paul Kincaid went to Cape Cod for the weekend."

"They did what?"

"Left? Why would he take her out of town?" Jake wanted to hit something, again, like Paul Kincaid's face. Or perhaps a concrete wall to bloody his hands and take his mind off the pain in his heart that he couldn't or wouldn't define.

Lancaster's lip raised in a tilted grin. "You're taking this rather calmly."

"You're being a smartass."

"I can put an APB out for Kincaid."

You have no idea. I'd like to chase them down, grab Allison by the hair, put her over my knee, and beat her ass. Jake paused a moment to picture that scene.

"Go ahead and put the APB out." Jake yanked his cell phone out of the holder and dialed amidst murmurs from the others. "Excuse me a minute."

"Jake." Peter warned from the other side of the room where he'd been quietly observing.

"Don't worry. I'll hold it together." For now. Jake stepped into the hall. On the second ring, Linc picked up.

"You have reached the phone of Linc Anderson. Please leave your message at the sound of the beep, and I'll call you back. Beep."

"Stop fooling around. I know that's you."

"Damn."

"I need you to check something for me."

In a flat voice, Linc said, "I live to serve."

"Find all the places people can stay in Cape Cod for the weekend. I'm looking for Paul Kincaid." That's hoping he used his real name.

"I'll call when I find something."

"Thanks, Linc." He strolled into the room. "Detective, can you run Paul Kincaid?"

"You think he's the killer?"

"Doesn't fit the profile, but I'd still like some background on the guy. Call me when you have the report."

"Where are you going?"

"Do you know any cops in Cape Cod?"

"One."

"Can you call and ask if they can keep an eye out for Kincaid's car?"

"Sure."

"I'm heading that way. Linc is checking all the places they might stay and he'll send a list." Jake slipped through the door.

Tobias stuck her head out and said, "You're going after them?"

"Yes."

Laughter rumbled through her. "Do you want me to tag along?"

"Not necessary."

"Peter wants to see you." Tobias yelled.

He stopped and watched her grin as she made the sawing motion across her neck. "Tell him I'd already left and you couldn't catch me."

Peter stepped into the hallway. "That would be a lie."

Jake sighed and retraced his steps to the room. Peter had returned to his laptop. The glare he gave Jake spoke volumes. "I won't throttle her, although it does hold some appeal."

Quincy walked in. "What did I miss?"

"Jake's going after the psychic," Tobias offered.

"Did we lose her?"

"No, she bolted." Jake said.

"Ah!" was all Quincy said then turned to talk to Peter.

Lancaster motioned for Jake. "I spoke with the guy in Cape Cod. He said his people will watch for the vehicle."

"Thanks."

"What are you going to do about Kincaid?"

The thought of them together, Kincaid's hands on Allison's flawless skin, her kissing him, under him. Jake's jaw tightened. "I'll restrain myself, unless Kincaid pushes it."

"Jake," Tobias called. "Do you think going after her is necessary for the case?"

"She's our link. The killer is treating her different than the others. Special. I'm uncertain what he'll do when he finds out

Allison left."

CHAPTER TWENTY

"Hi, Nick."

"Is everything all right?"

"I'm fine," Allison said.

"How are the headaches? I sent amethyst and rose quartz to the house. Did you get them?"

"You never cease to amaze me. I did get them and I have them in my pocket as we speak. It certainly doesn't hurt to have a brother who's a geologist."

"Well, you can't beat a good healing stone."

She smiled. "You still keep up with the old ways."

"Some. Of course, I'm nowhere near as knowledgeable as Yanni."

"Who is?"

"Have you had anymore visions?"

Allison glanced at the gas station door. "Yanni has been teaching me control and how to build shields to protect me from the intrusions. It's helped with the headaches and the visions."

"How's the investigation going?"

Allison saw Paul exit the building. "I can't talk about this right now, Nick."

"You sound anxious. Is there something wrong?"

"No."

"Let me be there with you."

"I'll feel better knowing you're close, but not so close that the killer notices you. Let me call you later."

Nick sighed. "Do what you think is best, but Ali, this is more than you're used to handling. It may be too much, too soon."

"I know. I'll be careful. Love you."

"Love you too."

Paul got into the car. "Is there a problem?"

"It was Nick checking on me."

"I haven't seen him in a long while. How's he doing?"

"Good. He's visiting Lucy."

Paul glanced at her as he pulled out of the lot. "Isn't she going to college somewhere?"

"She's at the community college."

The rest of the drive was serene. No talk just the car and the road which was conducive to the relaxation Paul had claimed.

They arrived at a quaint bed and breakfast where Paul had booked two suites. They checked in, changed, and went for a nice dinner at a small, cozy restaurant. The food was good and afterward they took a chilly coach ride around the village then walked along the beach. Paul slung his arm comfortably around her shoulders and pulled her close to block the breezes coming off the water. Allison enjoyed the salty spray and the sound of the waves splashing the shore, but she was grateful for the body heat.

Paul kept her entertained with humorous stories about college days before they headed back to the B&B.

This had been a good day. She removed make-up, brushed her teeth and hair. A soft glow hovered in the quiet suite from the small lamp on the table by the bed. The velvet pouch containing her amethyst, fluorite, agate, opal and sugilite stones sat within reach.

Allison opened the adjoining door after a soft knock. Paul stood there in pajama pants, freshly washed and smelling of toothpaste.

"I wanted to make sure you had everything before I went to bed."

"Yes, thanks. I'm good."

He lifted his hand as if to stroke her cheek, but let it fall. "Goodnight then."

As he turned away, she grabbed his hand. "Paul, I want to

thank you for bringing me here. You were right, I did need a break."

"I'm glad." He grasped her hand. "I really do care about you, Allison."

His words were sincere. She gave him what she hoped was a bright, assured smile. "I know." She leaned forward and kissed his cheek. "Goodnight."

Once upon a time, Paul's bare chest and damp hair would have had her heart all aflutter. Now, the only thing that shifted her breathing and made her heart do the two-step was a handsome, albeit surly FBI agent. Jake knew how to set her temper off, but she couldn't pretend there was no attraction.

Allison rested her forehead against the door for a moment. In the last few days, she'd dealt with too many emotions. Between the killer, Jake, Yanni, and Paul, she was slowly losing her mind. Allison climbed into bed and switched off the lamp.

In the middle of the night she woke in a cold sweat. The pounding in her head kept time with the beats of her racing heart. The killer banged on the locked steel door in her mind. Something had enraged him, and the psychic ability surged enough to punch holes in her blockers. She added another layer to the barrier as Yanni had taught. Unfortunately, the extra energy needed to do it deprived her of strength and the headache enflamed. On shaky legs Allison staggered to the closet to retrieve pills from the overnight bag. Downing two, she wet a washcloth to wipe her face, and crawled back into bed, praying for mercy.

Very faint in the background a song played. Allison listened hard trying to tune it in more clearly. Instead, roaring over the music, was another rhyme. *Hickory, Dickory, Dock.*

The sun beamed through the crack in the curtains. A knock on the adjoining door prompted Allison to pull on a robe. Standing there with a towel around his middle and still dripping from a shower, Paul said, "I ordered breakfast from room service. It should be here any minute."

About that time, someone knocked on her door. The young lady who served the food handed Allison a message.

Paul tipped the woman.

The script was on beautiful flowered stationary with writing she had seen before. Each letter evenly written, the penmanship almost perfect. Icy dots of sweat broke out on Allison's body. She squeezed her eyes shut, praying she was mistaken.

Hickory, dickory, dock, Allison ran up the clock, the clock struck one, nowhere to run, hickory, dickory, dock.

Her expression paled.

"Allison, what's wrong?"

Someone pounded on Paul's door. The sound echoed through the room which now felt claustrophobic. Paul marched over and yanked it open.

"Where is she?"

Allison stiffened. The note fell to the floor.

Jake pushed his way further into Paul's room.

She swallowed hard at the look on Jake's face while he took in Paul's state of undress and the fact that she wore only a thin robe.

"What are you doing here, Austin?"

Jake ignored Paul and zeroed in on her. She turned away, not able to cope with the condemnation.

"What the hell were you thinking? No, wait, you weren't thinking."

"Who the hell do you think you are barging in here?" Paul hollered.

Again Jake didn't answer him. "Surveillance does no good if you skip town, Ms. Brody."

"Stop!" Allison screamed.

Immediately, both men were at her side. She picked up the paper and handed it to Jake. "I've had enough." Allison shoved by them. "I'd like to go home. Please excuse me." She slammed the bathroom door.

****

"Austin, I want to know what you're going to do about this." Paul fumed. "He followed us to Cape Cod for Christ's sake. Why would he do that? Is she in danger? Is she?"

Jake answered in a frigid tone. "Dr. Kincaid, I've had Ms. Brody watched around the clock since I realized there might be a link to the unknown suspect. That is…" He leveled a stare on her. "Until the two of you left town. I won't even go into questioning what kind of psychiatrist takes his patient to Cape Cod for the weekend."

"First." Paul held up his index finger. "She is no longer my patient. And second, it's none of your damned business." He turned to Allison. "Were you aware he had you under surveillance?"

"Yes."

"For crying out loud." Paul stormed toward her. "Why didn't you say something? I wouldn't have taken you had I known how serious this matter had become, or that you were somehow involved with this investigation. That explains a lot about your recent behavior." He faced Jake and Detective Lancaster. "So what do we do now?"

"We are conducting our investigation and will increase the number of officers on Allison's surveillance."

"Is there anything I can do? I don't like the effect this has had on Allison. I'm afraid her blacking out is a precursor to other episodes."

Allison gripped the sides of the table while watching them discuss her as if she weren't in the room. Picking up a 'Don't Worry, Be Happy' coffee mug, she hurled it against the wall beside the huddle.

The flying pieces had the three men scurrying out of the way. Peter and a uniformed officer burst into the room. Lancaster's hand went immediately to his gun holster.

"I'm glad that got your attention." Allison stalked toward them. "I'll have you know I've been taking care of myself longer than you might think." She glowered at Jake. "And you." She rounded on Paul. "Cozying up to me and spewing nonsense about friendship, and then you go telling him I'm psychotic." She threw her arms in the air. "I don't think we'll be having dinner anytime soon."

"I said no such thing." Paul moved toward her and whispered. "Deny it if you want, but I know you've been popping more pills than you should because of these headaches and lack of sleep."

She wrenched her arm from Paul's grip. "I will continue conducting myself as I see fit. If I get a lead that will help your investigation, I will let you know." She stormed toward the door and Peter and the officer moved out of the way.

CHAPTER TWENTY-ONE

Still outraged when she arrived home, Allison grumbled while unpacking her things. "Imagine, talking about me as if I wasn't there. Men! They're all jerks."

"It has been so for centuries."

Allison hadn't stopped unpacking. Yanni materialized and Allison knew the exact moment it had happened. That skill was improving. "Oh, great. So you're saying not to look forward to change in the male behavior any time soon?"

Yanni inclined her head. "It is best to concentrate your efforts on things you can actually change."

"You can't fix stupid." Allison opened her closet and hung some things. "Paul jumped right on the bandwagon agreeing that I need to take time off, hide away. What can I do?" She mimicked Paul's voice. "And Austin takes the cake. Suddenly, he's worried about me? I don't think so. He needs me to help him catch the killer."

"Is that what you really think, little one?"

"Yes—I don't know." Allison all but threw her unused clothes in the drawer. "No one is going to stop me from doing what I feel is right. I make that choice."

Waves of anger stilled flowed as Allison picked up the landline before it rang. Another improved ability. "What?"

"You shouldn't slam doors so hard." His quiet voice was

smooth, almost soothing.

"Who is this?" she asked, even though she knew. Her skin tingled in a creepy sort of way.

"I think you know, Allison."

"You're using the phone now? How sweet." Being flippant wasn't the best move, but she'd already had a hell of a day.

"Another form of communication. Certainly not as intimate, but effective nonetheless."

"What do you want?"

"You. I thought that became obvious of late."

Fear gripped her throat. *Try to talk to him.* She was unable to speak.

"No words for me? Pity. They will come." Click.

Yanni paid careful attention as she returned the receiver to its cradle. "He surprised me, calling like that."

"That is what he intended." Yanni stepped in front of Allison. "You must not let him gain control. You will not recover." With a poof, Yanni vanished.

Allison examined her reflection in the mirror. *Okay, Allison, you got his attention.* Every instinct said to run far, run fast, but she wouldn't go.

She couldn't.

Allison descended the stairs, still shaky from the call. She headed for the kitchen hoping hot tea with honey and lemon would calm her nerves. Her eyes fixed on the house phone which rang. She hesitated before answering. "Hello?"

"Well, I guess that answers that question." The cheeriness in Kat's voice brought a brief reprieve to Allison's frightened, disturbed mood.

"What question?"

"Why you came home early."

"How did you know I'd left, and came home early for that matter?"

"As to your leaving, I stopped by Friday night to see if you wanted to catch a movie or something and Martha told me where you'd gone. Today, I was on my way to the store and saw you fly out of the police station with a trail of smoke behind you. If I had to guess, I'd say this has something to do with that hunk of a man who works for the government."

"He's infuriating, unrealistic, and keeps trying to give me

orders."

Kat chuckled.

"Grrr. I'd really rather not talk about it right now."

Undaunted, Kat said, "Okay, but we need to discuss the Penny Sale for Our Lady of Good Voyage. It's coming up soon."

"Ugh! Why do I let you talk me into these things?" She pinched the bridge of her nose and took calming breaths. "I promise we'll do lunch next week to go over it."

"Allison." Kat used her motherly tone.

"Yeah?"

"You know I'm here to listen and help."

"I know and I appreciate it. It's been a long time since I've dealt with my abilities and I need to get it straight in my head first. Figure out my next step."

"The three A's. Assess, analyze, act. Just like your brother."

Not usually. "Talk to you later."

A warm bath and hot tea did little to calm her nerves. Anger stayed closed to the surface. Anger at the killer for tuning her life into a

horror movie. Anger at herself for not being strong enough to block the connection. And disappointed with the inability to subdue increasing desires for Jake, who could rip her apart with one word. She'd better never meet destiny on a dark road because she'd kick its ass.

Restless. Jittery. Allison didn't like feeling that way. She needed to be ready in every way to deal with Alex. Pulling a ring of keys out of the kitchen drawer she headed for the study to unlock the gun cabinet. Her grandfather once said that both she and Nick should know how to handle and understand the workings of a weapon. Her hand went straight for the thirty-two caliber handgun and some ammunition.

Daylight would be fading soon, but with loaded weapon in hand, Allison ventured out back to the small secluded cove behind the house. She stopped long enough to snag a few aluminum cans from the recycle bin. Martha loved her diet soda.

Perched on a log down by the water, three cans glittered in the diminishing sunlight. Allison counted off twenty-five paces, turned and squared her shoulders. "Okay, now what was it grandpa used to tell me? Extend the right arm." She drew her arm up. The gun felt heavy in her hand, but she leveled it in front of her body.

"Keep elbow slightly bent, put left hand on butt of gun to securely hold the weapon, line the target in sight, gently squeeze the trigger."

The gun exploded. A piece of wood flew into the air. Allison frowned. It had been several years since she'd brandished a gun for target practice. Again, she followed the remembered procedures. This time when she fired, she heard a clink ricochet from one can, but it only wiggled. While preparing to take another shot, a booming voice interrupted her concentration.

"What the bloody hell are you doing?"

Allison twisted to see Jake storming toward her re-holstering his weapon.

"I'm practicing," she replied in a clipped tone, then faced the target again.

As she fired another round, she fell back against a wall of rock solid flesh. Muscular arms circled her and grabbed the gun. "Give me that before you hurt someone. It's illegal for you to fire a weapon within the city limits unless you're at a shooting range. I should take you in."

A call came from the house. "Austin?"

"It's under control, Logan." Jake yelled.

Jake expelled the magazine from the thirty-two. "Have you lost your mind?"

"No. It's a reasonable precaution."

"This is never a solution." Jake shoved the gun in his belt after locking the safety. The breeze turned chilly and she shivered. Jake took off his jacket and laid it around her shoulders.

The jacket carried his scent and warmth to chase off the chill. A tingle raced up her spine that wasn't from the cold. She stilled, lifted her head and stared at the tree line. Although she didn't see him, she knew the killer stood there, watching. Jake slowly moved to put himself between her and the tree line. Jake stared in the same direction.

"Jake, let's go inside."

He stayed in that position for a few seconds more, then nodded and followed her to the house. Logan was waiting when they returned. "You can go back to the station." Jake said. "Ask Lancaster to send a couple of people to check those woods that face this property."

"Did you see something?" Logan said.

"Maybe. I know they didn't find anything the last time, but I'd like them to check again."

"Okay."

"And, Logan." The officer looked at him. "Tell your guy outside to stay alert."

"Yes, sir."

Allison put on the kettle and started the coffee maker. She needed something to busy her hands. She fought against the foggy vision, a side effect of the constant bombardment of energy on her brain.

"Sit down," Jake growled. "You're shaking."

He led her to a chair. Jake opened cabinets until he found the coffee mugs. "Where are the tea bags?"

The killer was pushing. She sensed the anger.

"Allison."

She blinked.

"Where are the tea bags?"

"In the second drawer to the left."

Allison focused more now on Jake. The mere presence of him made the room smaller. He threw her off balance but made her feel safer.

She reached for the tea with trembling fingers and brushed across Jake's hand. A shock jolted her and she retreated. "You're close to him," she whispered.

"Who?"

"The killer."

Disbelief still reigned supreme in Jake, but Allison's voice had an unusual monotone quality and her eyes glazed over.

"Why do you say that?"

"He watches you… closely."

"Of course he does," Jake said cautiously. "We've been playing this cat and mouse game."

"No. It's more. It's not a game. It's personal."

Jake's heart raced. "Allison." He fanned his hand in front of her face. Slowly, her eyes returned to normal.

Allison blinked. "What happened?"

"You were in a trance or something."

"A trance? Did I speak? What did I say?"

"Nothing that made sense." He couldn't tell her how close to the truth she'd been.

"I'm tired." She rose. "I'm going to bed."

"Okay."

As she passed him she said, "Why did you come here?"

"You were a little irrational when you left the station. I wanted to make sure you were okay."

"I wasn't irrational, Jake. I was pissed. I think you know the difference."

He ducked his head. "Yeah. Okay. You were pissed."

"I don't like people thinking they can make decisions for my life, and I don't like being talked over like I'm invisible."

"Noted. Are you sure you're going to be okay?"

"I'll be fine," she replied absently as she ascended the staircase. "Goodnight."

"Goodnight."

If he examined it too closely, he'd admit that instinct drove him to follow Allison to the bedroom, strip her slowly, and spend the rest of the night making love.

He fought an inner battle between leaving her alone or staying to make sure nothing happened. Based on his interaction with Allison so far, common sense told him to go and let the surveillance team do their job.

Jake dialed Lancaster. "Let the surveillance team know that I'm staying the night." He signed off after Lancaster assured him the message would be delivered.

He'd crash on the couch and be gone early in the morning. She'd never know.

CHAPTER TWENTY-TWO

"What are you doing here?"

Jake opened one eye, testing the brightness before gradually opening the other to see Allison standing there in pajamas. He groaned. "What time is it?"

"Seven o'clock."

"Seven? Christ, I didn't mean to sleep this late." He never slept while on surveillance unless it was half hour increments. He'd checked on Allison several times throughout the night, but after the last time, he lay down and didn't get up again.

"You stayed?

You were out of it last night. I didn't think you should be alone."

"Afraid I'd hurt myself?"

"I did find you with a loaded weapon yesterday."

She shook her head. "Which I'd been taught to use."

He swung his feet to the floor, and rested his head back against the cushion. "Please can we not do this now? I haven't had coffee."

"Do you want some breakfast?"

"Breakfast?"

"Yeah, the first meal of the day, something you do every morning."

"Not everyone."

"So you don't want anything to eat?" she huffed, turned to leave.

"I didn't say that." He grasped her wrist. She tried to pull away, but he held on.

Without facing him she said, "I'm making waffles. Do you like waffles?"

"Haven't had them in a long time, but I could eat."

He released her. Jake checked the front door and saw the surveillance team a short distance away. A heavenly aroma wafted from the other room and he heard the television. She had the news on.

Adorable was the word to describe how Allison looked as she poured batter into the waffle iron. The pajama pants were too long and the shirt, if you could call it that, had skimpy straps and clung tightly, stopping midway down her stomach. He wondered if the soft material would crinkle if he touched it. "Can I help?"

"You can pour orange juice into glasses, and the coffee is brewing."

"You actually drink coffee? I've only ever seen you drink tea."

"I had coffee at the police station."

"But I didn't see you drink it."

"I've been known to take the caffeine plunge," she replied.

"Thank God."

He filled glasses and set them on the island, stretching before he sat on a barstool. Allison got the syrup out of the pantry, grabbed the butter from the refrigerator, and snatched a fork off the counter. "Dig in."

To his amazement, Jake finished four waffles. "I need to get to my room and shower. It wouldn't do for me to show up in the same clothes I left in."

"Certainly, this wouldn't be the first time that has happened."

"No, but Peter has been vocal about my appearance of late."

"I haven't been formally introduced yet. Which one is Peter?"

"The tall blond, who's kind of reserved."

Her brow lifted and peeked out from brown bangs.

"To the bureau appearance is part of the package."

"Package?"

"Yes. The Federal Bureau of Investigation represents a lot, just with its name. We're to wear suits, be clean-shaven, and have a trim haircut." He ran a hand along his stubbled chin. "Needless to say, I haven't fit the image lately."

Allison put her chin on her knuckles. "I like this image. It looks good on you."

Her comment surprised him, made him feel kind of warm inside. "I better go." Jake hesitated. It felt good having breakfast and spending time with Allison. Doing this normal activity seemed... familiar. "Thanks for breakfast."

She walked him to the door.

"Don't go anywhere alone," he said.

"It's not like I'm ever alone, Jake. My guard dogs are never far behind."

"Good. Keep it that way."

Allison grabbed the shawl out of the closet and went onto the porch. She loved fall. Birds were busy gathering pieces to enforce their nests against the coming winter. The trees swayed in the soft wind, their leaves whipped from the branches to play chase across the sky.

Jake stopped to talk to the officers in the police car. He smiled before getting into his car and driving away.

She watched as the sun danced from behind clouds which would help bring heat to the chilly morning. She hadn't felt this rested in a long time. There'd been no dreams at all, which was uncharacteristic. A few times her subconscious had sensed a presence, someone watching over her.

"Yanni," she called, but didn't get a response. "Humph. Just like her. Always around when you don't want her, and never around when you do."

Inside, she cleaned up the breakfast mess. In the den, she found the gun lying on top of her grandfather's desk. Smiling, she replaced the gun in the cabinet and locked it. The magazine was nowhere to be found.

****

The night sky rumbled with an approaching storm. Across the street from R&N's, cloaked by shadows, the killer's tall figure loomed in the darkness. The Surgeon studied Allison. Her flushed face and spiked hair begged for his touch.

He liked the hair pulled back, and imagined running his tongue over the small scar on her earlobe that he knew was there.

His fingers itched to caress the star-shaped birthmark on her right hip. A fierce urge to explore her secret places pulled at his tenuous control, but he resisted. *Not yet.*

He smiled. *She's special.*

Allison Brody made an interesting piece for the game.

Pulling the collar of his leather jacket around his neck, the Surgeon strolled down the sidewalk, humming.

****

This display was a companion to the back-to-school display in the north window. It showcased the fall styles. Allison massaged the pinch in her neck for the third time in the last hour. A sure sign it was time to go. A recognized tingle slithered up her spine, but she refused to be cowed by it. She gathered her tools, stashed them in the closet, and threw the switch on the junction box to light the window.

The cool night air provided relief from her overheated skin and Allison welcomed it. She locked the door to the store and quickly walked past the black and white police car with its red and blue topping that had become a familiar and comfortable sight. She waved to the officers.

As she unlocked her car a recognized tingle slithered across her spine and settled. Another storm stirred the clouds as she stared into the dark night, catching a glimpse of a lone figure turning the corner up the block.

At home, Allison dropped into bed and fell instantly asleep. Not long after, on that REM plane where dreams occur, she saw a solitary figure standing on a smooth, polished floor. *She didn't dare call out, too afraid of what would happen. A lonesome tune floated through the room and she became that figure. She sashayed, lost in the melody. One, two, three, one, two, three.*

Out of nowhere appeared a wall completely covered in mirrors. In the reflection, she wore a silky gown the color of jade. Her hair hung in long waves and tumbled down her back, a style she hadn't worn since her teens. The music changed and in the blink of an eye, a tall man with a strong arm about her waist waltzed her across the floor.

His tie and handkerchief matched the color of the dress and he wore a fine man's cologne. The man's shadowed face left him a mystery, but his smile held a certain virulent promise.

Panic set in.

Allison pushed against him trying to break away. "Let me go."

"You can't run away, Allison. Our game is getting interesting."
The killer's hand encircled her wrists and his lips roughly kissed
her neck. "We'll meet again, my beauty. Soon."

Alone with nothing but a black rose, Allison desperately
clawed her way back through the fogginess. Her movements
sluggish, she struggled to regain her senses.

Her eyes popped open.

Stumbling through the dark, Allison switched on the bathroom
light. Her pale reflection stared back. The circles under her eyes
were darker and her hair was a sweaty mass. She hung her head
low and splashed cold water on her face.

He'd gotten into her head again.

On the way back to the bedroom, an intense pain shot through
her skull. Her eyes rolled back and she plummeted to the floor.

CHAPTER TWENTY-THREE

Morning runs were a small pleasure for Jake. As he crested the hill, his cell phone vibrated.

"Allison Brody's housekeeper rushed out to the surveillance team this morning shortly after arriving at the house. She found Allison passed out on the floor." Lancaster said.

Jake tensed. "Is she okay? Did they call an ambulance? What happened?"

"No one knows, but they found a rose on the bed next to her pillow."

"What?" Jake all but roared into the phone. "How did it get there? What were you men doing? Sleeping?"

"No sign of forced entry. He got in and out the same way, leaving no evidence except the rose."

"Where is Allison?"

"At the house. Peter thought you'd want to accompany me when I go."

"I'll be at the Trawler in five minutes."

"I'll be waiting."

Outside Allison's house Jake barely glanced at the officers on scene. He made a beeline to Peter who was speaking with one of the paramedics. "How is she?"

"She'll be fine. She needs rest."

Jake paused in the doorway of the parlor. Allison was dressed in a royal blue gown and sheer white robe that flowed to the floor. Her hair fell over one shoulder and those exquisite eyes were glistened with tears. He moved on stiff limbs toward the divan to kneel in front of her. "Are you all right?"

"No," she whispered, keeping her eyes averted.

"Look at me, Allison. Look at me." The soft tone of the command did not make it less forceful.

Strands of hair hid her eyes. He touched the mass of silk, letting it sift through his fingers before tucking it behind her ear. His fingertips brushed her cheek.

Clamping his jaw, he sat back distancing himself. Every instinct screamed to hold her, but he ignored them. "Did he hurt you?"

"No, Agent Austin."

He frowned. "Don't do that."

"Do what?"

"Put the title between us. What's going on?"

"I'm losing my mind."

"No, you're not."

"I thought I could help. I thought I could..."

Fear gripped him. "He is a cold-blooded killer, who wouldn't think twice about finishing you which is why I wanted you out of it."

Allison flinched at the truth. The look on her face turned icy. "Thank you for relating the brutal facts which I've already seen." She rose and walked toward one of the officers.

Inwardly, Jake berated the careless, insensitive outburst. He fought the temptation to apologize, because it would do no good.

Peter moved to his side. "Did she remember anything?"

"I really didn't get a chance to ask."

Peter watched Allison talking to Detective Lancaster. "Any theories on what's going on?"

"Not all formed yet." He cast another glance at Allison then said, "I'm going up to the bedroom."

Heavy curtains covered the windows so no light got in, which made sense. The covers on the bed were in a knotted pile. Jake closed his eyes and in his mind walked the same path with the killer. Allison rolled to her side, but she looked different. Her hair was lighter, she appeared younger. She smiled. The scene changed and Allison looked as she had tonight, head thrashing on the pillow, hands gripping the covers. A gloved hand hovering, but not touching her. A black rose placed on the pillow.

Jakes opened his eyes. "Damn." The game had become more dangerous. He shouldn't have underestimated the opponent.

The only light in his room came from the laptop screen. This day had gotten him no closer to a solution. Jake sat on the bed, knees bent, and fingers steepled in front of his face. His Glock lay beside him, but provided little comfort for his furied mind.

At 12:05 a.m. he received a call.

"Up late again, agent? Thinking of me, no doubt."

Jake closed his eyes and leaned against the wall.

"What? No greeting for me? I'm hurt."

Jake picked up the Glock. His finger set and released the safety.

"I visited Allison last night. You should really say something to the officers. I did it quite easily. The room smelled of roses. I hoped I'd see the ones I'd been sending by her bed. Beauty at rest, that rich, thick hair splayed across the white pillow."

The tone in the Surgeon's voice softened as if he were reliving the scene while he related it. "It took restraint not to put my hands around her neck. My cock throbbed with anticipation, but I want more from Allison."

Jake's eyes were open now. One hand clenched the phone while the other gripped the gun. The thought of the killer's hands touching Allison almost propelled Jake through the phone to end this once and for all.

"I've never been sexually aroused by the women I've killed—except once, and you know which one I'm talking about, don't you, Jake?"

"Let's talk face-to-face," Jake said.

The killer laughed. "That would spoil the fun." He sighed. "Allison is more special than you realize, and that's what makes this so rich. She's a thirst I can't quench, a hunger I can't sate."

Jake's mind screamed with agony. He jumped off the bed and paced to the window to stare into the night.

"I'm going to have all of her, and you can't do anything about it. I'll like the idea of you helpless when I take her."

Jake slammed his forehead softly into the wall.

"Picture her spread eagle, tied to the bed—naked. I'll cut each piece of clothing off her body. I'll rub warm scented oils on my hands and massage until she squirms." The Surgeon paused in his description. "I'll feel her tight around me as I ram my cock inside. Mmmm." He breathed heavily. "Do you want to kill me, Jake?"

"No," Jake replied in as calm a voice as he could manage through clenched teeth.

The killer's tone turned cold once again. "We're more alike than you think."

Jake slammed the phone shut. The thought of killing him had crossed Jake's mind.

CHAPTER TWENTY-FOUR

"So that settles it. Mission accomplished and all that," Kat said.

"I'll be glad when this is over."

"Which thing are we talking about now?"

"The Penny Sale." Allison got up and took her plate to the sink.

Kat followed. "You seem different lately."

"How do you mean different?"

"I don't know, distracted."

Allison looked at her friend. "I'm having the headaches less."

"Uh, huh."

Allison knew that tone. "To tell you the truth, I'm relieved. It scared me when I passed out at the park."

"I'm sure it did. It scared a lot of people."

"Oh, don't start." Kat's look of innocence had Allison shaking her head.

"I'm just saying a lot of people care about you."

"Right. I have loads of friends."

Serious now, Kat took Allison by the shoulders. "I know you're up to something even if you won't tell me what. Be careful."

"Don't worry." Allison patted Kat's forearm. "I'm a little wired. Having a madman break into your house will do that to a person. Want to take a walk down by the cove?"

"I have a better idea." The sparkle in Kat's eyes warned Allison she would probably regret asking.

"What?"

"Let's go dancing."

"Dancing?"

"Hell, yeah. Blackburn's should be open and they have a kick-ass band this week."

"You know I don't like crowds, or people. Besides, it's been a strange couple of days."

"You need it," Kat said as she prodded Allison toward the door, switching off lights as they went.

"Kat, I'm not sure I'm ready for this. I should stay home."

"Honey, staying home did no good if the guy got in."

She had a point.

"Those watchdogs are always hovering anyway."

Sighing, Allison said, "All right. I'll go for one hour, that's it." She barely managed to grab her purse and keys before her friend shoved her out the door.

****

Jake had been even more restless after his talk with the killer, a man he had known so well a long time ago. He jumped in the shower hoping to relax his muscles. The steam usually had a soothing effect.

Not this time.

He shut off the water and flung the shower curtain open, frustration getting the better of him. Grabbing a towel, he buffed his hair and then wrapped it around his waist. He dashed to the bedroom when he heard the faint buzzing. "Austin."

"Jake, it's Lancaster."

"Hi, detective. What's up?"

"Your pigeon has flown the coup again."

"What?" He rubbed water out of his eye.

"Allison Brody and her friend left the house a few minutes ago."

"It's midnight for Christ's sake." He threw the towel on the bed. "Shit! That woman loves playing with fire."

"It seems so," Lancaster commented dryly.

"Have her tailed and let me know where she ends up. I'll take it from there."

"Sure thing."

Jake hastily dressed, grabbed his keys and flew through the door. His cell phone vibrated as he slid into the driver's seat.

"They're at Blackburn's."

"I've seen it. I'm on my way."

"Do you want backup?"

"No. I think I can handle the two women." Jake flicked off the phone; sure another confrontation with Allison was on the horizon and wondering how this one would end.

Pulling into the pub's parking lot, Jake saw the surveillance team and stopped to talk to them.

"That's the car they came in," Bennett said, and pointed to the vehicle.

At least they parked under a light.

"Okay, I'm going in to talk to them. I'd appreciate it if you guys would hang around though."

"No problem," Stephens said.

Inside it took a moment for his eyes to adjust to the dim lighting. Even after midnight, the hazy interior hummed with commotion and had more patrons than Jake would have expected. The band played an old tune Jake recognized. He scanned the booths, tables and bar area but saw no sight of either woman. The pungent smell of beer and cigarette smoke wafted in the warm air being pushed around by ceiling fans.

He cautiously maneuvered through a small crowd to reach the edge of the hardwood dance floor. Allison and Kat Rubin were dancing. A wave of relief washed through him. She was safe and unharmed, and damned sexy. Her lips moved with the words to the song the band beat out.

Allison laughed at something her friend said and Jake realized it was the first time he'd actually seen her laugh. The sweet sound overshadowed the song in his ears. A young guy moved in behind Allison and Jake went on alert. His hands immediately fisted, so he crossed his arms to keep anyone from noticing. The stranger touched Allison's shoulder. She stopped dancing and her smile faded.

Jake headed their direction. Allison was shaking her head and saying no thanks when he got closer.

"Come on, baby. Let's dance. We'll make beautiful music together." The guy's sloppy grin and slightly slurred speech said he'd had a little too much to drink.

"No, thanks. Why don't you go ask someone else? I'm really not interested." She stepped away and the guy dropped his arm.

"I'm a good dancer. I won't step on your toes."

In a steely tone, Jake said, "The lady said no, man. Why don't you go ask that redhead whose giving you the eye?"

The drunk looked at the redhead in question, smiled and took off.

Allison rubbed her arm where the man had touched her.

"Are you okay?"

"Sure. It's not the first time I've had an overzealous guy ask me to dance."

His eyebrows shot up to his hairline. He knew it wasn't true. She didn't get around people that often.

"I don't really see you as the bar and dancing type, so what are you doing here, Jake?"

"I should be asking you that question."

"Kat thought I could use a night out. You know, have some fun."

The music slowed and she began to sway.

"Kincaid thought you needed a weekend away, and we know how that turned out."

Allison moved closer. Her hands slowly felt their way up his sides, pausing when they reached the gun holster under his jacket. She wrapped

hands around his waist and rested them on his low back. Her body moved with the rhythm of the music brushing intimately with his.

Allison raised her eyes. She had amazing eyes—smoky. He released his arms to encircle hers, resting his hands on her ass. Shifting his position, he squeezed their bodies tightly together, front to front. They swayed across the dance floor. One of Jake's legs positioned between Allison's and her inner thighs and woman's center rubbed sensually against it. She took her turn exploring his ass through the jeans and it seriously turned him on.

Attraction tangled with desire, common sense, and duty. The air was thick with need and hunger. Jake's hand clutched Allison's hair. With his lips teasing her ear he said, "When you play with fire, you can get burned." His teeth nipped her lobe.

Allison pushed out of his arms and stalked back to the table to grab her purse and jacket. "Kat, we need to go."

"Oh, but I'm just getting to know Jimmy." Her friend pouted.

"I'll take you home," Jake offered. "Your friend can stay and have fun."

Allison glared at him and headed for the door. He fell in step with her. Jake waved at the surveillance team and opened the car door so Allison could get inside.

"You didn't have to bother yourself," she said when he slid in.

"It's no bother. This way I'll make sure you get home and stay there."

She crossed her arms. "I was ready to go home anyway. I don't like crowds."

"I saw the look on your face when that kid touched you." Jake said, as he pulled out of the lot.

"He wasn't a kid."

Jake snickered. "He was a kid, Allison."

"I was enjoying myself and I let my shield slip. When he touched my arm, I got flashes."

"Of what?"

She shrugged. "Not sure, really. Him, some young girl. It could have been an old girlfriend or someone new."

"So you don't know if what you see is from the past?"

"Not always."

"Then how do you know what you are seeing with The Surgeon is current?"

She shifted to look at him. "Because with him I am connected. I watch him do those things. I'm inside his head."

"Why are you connected to him?"

"You think I know? You think I want to see that?" Her voice rose.

"I'm sorry."

She stared out the window. "For what?"

"Everything." He drove to the house and parked. When he went around to her side, she'd already opened the door, so he offered his hand.

She surprised him by taking it.

He kept hold of her hand while they walked to the door. "So, do you get flashes when you touch me?"

Allison unlocked the door, stepped inside and faced him. "Right now my shields are at maximum." She smiled. "I can touch you all I want. Goodnight, Jake," she said and closed the door.

Stunned and brimming with sexual energy, he said, "Damn, I need a cold shower."

CHAPTER TWENTY-FIVE

Jake stalked into the police station. The damned cold shower last night made his lips turn blue and his fucking teeth chatter, but his erection remained. Sleeping had been out of the question when all he could think about was Allison's last words. That set off a barrage of imaginative scenarios involving her hands and mouth. Tossing his jacket on the chair, he removed the lid to drink his grande coffee.

Lancaster sat in front of the board nursing his cup for the morning. Bloodshot eyes were evidence that he'd had sleepless nights too. Jake had sympathy for the man and nodded a greeting on his way to where Peter and Margo were talking.

"No new cases have been reported," Margo advised. "It's like he disappeared."

"I'm sure he's out there waiting," Peter replied.

"Pete, can I talk to you for a second?" Jake said.

"Sure."

Jake motioned to the table where Lancaster sat.

"What's up?"

"I want Allison Brody put in protective custody."

Lancaster's cup stopped midway to his mouth. "What brought this on?"

At first the intensity of Jake's voice was low. "The Surgeon wants Allison with a need he's finding hard to control. First though, for lack of a better analogy..." He ran fingers through his hair and closed his eyes. "He wants to mate with her." Jake clenched his jaw.

"You mean rape her?" Lancaster said.

"Not exactly. It's different. He thinks Allison is a special gift just for him. He'll use the union to sanctify her as his own."

Peter sat back in the chair. "And how do you know this?"

Jake paused for a moment. "Because he told me."

Immediately conversation in the entire room ceased. Lancaster spoke first. "You talked to him? When?"

"Last night." Jake stood and moved to the window. "He called me."

"Great." Lancaster bounced up from the chair. "We'll check the Stern Trawler's phone records, see if we can trace where the call came from." He rushed to the desk and picked up the phone. Jake placed a finger on the button.

"Wait. He didn't call me on the landline. He called my cell."

The other man replaced the handset. "Your cell?"

Jake nodded.

Lancaster looked at Peter. "You can still try to trace it."

"Get the phone records from Jake's cell, Margo," Peter said.

"On it." Margo's fingers tapped the computer keys.

The flash in his eyes told Jake that Peter held anger in check only by the barest string of will. "Has the killer contacted you before?"

"Only one other time. After the ball."

"When he sent the pictures?"

"Yes."

"You didn't think it necessary to clue us in that the murderer contacted you?"

Jake felt as though the whole world rested on his shoulders at that moment. He dropped into a chair and hung his head. Raising gritty eyes, he focused on Lancaster. "I told you, he makes it personal. He taunts me, tries to break me, and this time he might succeed."

"You're in deep shit, Jake." Peter informed him. "You'll be lucky if you're not sent to jail as an accessory."

"I know."

"What were you thinking?" Tobias said.

Jake turned weary eyes on his colleagues and Lancaster. "He's gotten close enough to Allison to kill her. Our meager attempts at surveillance have provided no safety. Please, Peter."

"Detective," Peter said. "Can you ask Ms. Brody to come in? I'd like to speak with her about protective custody."

"Do you really think she'll agree to that?"

Jake shrugged. "I'll be her shadow if necessary. Hell, maybe I'll just kidnap her."

Lancaster's body rumbled with laughter which helped break the tension filling the room. "Warn me ahead of time. I've been in the room with the two of you during a… disagreement. I'll want to be far away from that altercation."

"Maybe you should go away." Peter paced the small room. "I agree she needs protection, but I also think you need to distance yourself from this case, immediately."

Jake started to protest, but thought better of it.

****

A uniformed officer walked Allison down the hall and opened the door to the conference room where people waited. She was nervous. Too many people, such a small place.

Her abilities had been expanding with Yanni's help, but crowds still made her nervous. Jake sat at the end of the table. She sensed conflicted emotions raging through him and wondered what this was about. The intensity of his gaze almost knocked her flat. Her last encounter with Jake had been embarrassing. She'd acted shamelessly. She blamed it on the stress of the last few days.

"Hello, Ms. Brody. We haven't been formally introduced. I'm Special Agent Peter Carmichael. I head this team."

"Hello." She shook his hand and instantly knew he and Jake were friends and this situation burdened that friendship.

The tall blond man was charismatic and dressed in bureau attire. The jacket had been discarded and his striped shirtsleeves were rolled to the elbows. While the look came off casual with the loosened tie that hung a little askew, Agent Carmichael wasn't relaxed.

Guiding her, Carmichael introduced her to the rest of the team. "This is Agent Sullivan, our computer guru. That debonair guy with the shades is the pathologist, Dr. Zach Quincy, and this is our forensic photographer, Genevieve Tobias."

Tobias wrinkled her nose. "Just call me Tobias. I hate the

name Genevieve."

Allison nodded. "Hello to you all. It's nice to see Agent Austin is supported by such a diverse group of friends."

"I wouldn't go so far as to say friends, exactly," Quincy said with a devilish grin.

Allison grinned also. "No, I'm sure with that temper, people don't hang around him unless they have to."

Quincy blinked and laughed. "How true you are."

Agent Carmichael walked up, shoved Quincy out of the way, and pulled out a chair for her to sit. "I've been told you might have information that could aid us in this case."

"Possibly."

He seated himself in the chair across from her. "I'm sure you can understand my skepticism."

"All too well."

"So what can you tell us, Ms. Brody?"

She clasped her hands in her lap. "I've only psychically connected with him a couple of times, but I sense a lot of rage and hatred. It's revenge he seeks."

"Revenge?"

"Yes."

"How can you be so sure?"

"I can't explain it other than to say I feel a sadness that drives his rage and that in turn fuels his actions. He's very meticulous in the preparations."

"His preparation? How so?"

"A certain type." She worried her bottom lip. "The victims all look alike, don't they?"

He looked at Jake.

"It's her he kills. The one who hurt him, but..."

Anticipation lingered in the room as they waited for the rest of the statement. She concentrated on something unseen by anyone else, then said, "He wants you there every step of the way, Jake."

Carmichael assessed. "Why does he want Jake along?"

Allison shook her head. "I don't know. At this point, I'd be guessing but most of what he does is directed and orchestrated to include him."

Jake stared at her with steely eyes, revealing nothing of his thoughts or feelings. It wasn't necessary. His aura had changed and the waves of emotion were shaking her.

"He uses a straight razor on the women after they're dead. He cleans it when he's done, and sharpens it for the next time."

Carmichael glanced at the pathologist who nodded. "Ms. Brody, we have discussed the changes in this case and the now unpredictability of The Surgeon's actions. Your name keeps popping up."

"I assume that's why you called me down here, Agent Carmichael." She sensed there was more to this visit. "Why don't you just get to it?"

"Based on the recent developments, we believe your life is in danger. We would like to place you in protective custody."

"No, thank you."

Jake glared at her and stood. At first, he spoke quietly. "He broke into your house, Allison. Anything could have happened."

"I sort of knew he was there, on a subconscious level. I dreamed we were dancing. It's what he wanted."

"He has taken this to a dangerous level."

"But he won't kill me, at least not yet." She rose from the chair.

"You don't know that for sure.

She gently prodded Jake with her mind, but found it closed tight. "I know more than you can imagine, Jake."

"How?" Agent Carmichael said.

"He's talked to me."

"When?"

"A couple of times it's been in my head, literally. But he did call me on the phone the other day when I left the police station after Cape Cod."

Carmichael turned to the woman with the computer. "Margo, check her phone records and see if we get anything we can trace."

The woman nodded and started typing.

Jake put his hands in his pockets. "Why didn't you tell me?"

"There is nothing you can do."

Unconsciously they moved closer to each other. Jake stared at her, and she at him. Carmichael coughed politely reminding them they had an audience.

She turned. "While I understand you're suggesting what you think is best, I do not wish the protective custody."

"Allison."

"I'm sorry, Jake. I am an officer in my father's company and have to attend meetings regularly. I'm not finished with the window designs at R&N's and Mr. Rubin depends on me because that helps his sales, especially with the back-to-school season. Not to mention my brother would scour the countryside until he found me if I disappeared."

"We'd take precautions and you could notify your family," computer girl offered.

Allison managed a small smile. "I'm sure you would." Her smile faded. "For some reason, I am connected to this killer. He's said things that lead me to believe we've met before."

"Met?" Carmichael's demeanor changed. "You've seen his face?"

Her hands moved up and down her arms as she walked around the table in the center of the room. "I'm not sure. I've blocked my abilities for a long time. Sometime in the past, I feel our paths have crossed."

With a scowl on his face, Jake said, "I don't believe you're linked to him."

"Your mind is closed to the possibility."

"Wait," Carmichael said. "What do you mean you've been blocking your abilities?"

Allison faced Carmichael. "I've attempted to ignore this link, block it but in doing so, I have to take too many doses of migraine meds and I almost died." Her voice softened. "I won't turn from this anymore. That's all I can give you. I'm sorry. I need to leave." No one tried to stop her. Hesitating when she opened the door she said, "You know where to find me."

CHAPTER TWENTY-SIX

Allison descended the darkened stairway when someone grabbed her from behind. He covered her mouth before a scream escaped. "Don't scream. I'm not going to hurt you. Do you understand?"

Chills danced across her neck where his warm breath caressed the skin. The killer had managed to get in again. The caliber of his voice and tone, although familiar, made her quiver. Strangely, it felt good in his arms and she fought to keep from leaning back.

He's a killer.

Why did she react this way? An attempt to penetrate his mind crashed into a cement wall and gave the onset of a headache. The intruder removed his hand. "You are a stubborn, willful woman."

He spun her around holding her arms. The breath whooshed out of her lungs and she shoved him with both hands. "Jake? Are you crazy? You almost gave me a heart attack."

"You should be scared as hell. Let us put you in protective custody. I got in and we already know he can get in."

She started for the front door. "Where are those officers?" she threw over her shoulder. "I'm going to have you arrested for trespassing."

He was on her in a flash. "Allison," he whispered. "We need to talk."

This time she leaned against his chest. Practice exercises on control with Yanni and these encounters with Jake had zapped her strength. Her body pulsed at the thought of the way Jake held her even in anger. She turned and hugged his waist. He rested his forehead against hers. "What do you want from me, Jake?"

"I want you to allow the protective custody so we can make sure he doesn't get to you again."

"Where would I go? What would I do?"

He pulled back. "You'd go to a safe house. You could do whatever you wanted as long as you didn't contact anyone."

"But I'd be able to tell my brother what is going on, right?"

"You could tell him what, but not where."

Allison pressed her head against his chest hearing the steady heartbeat. "For how long?"

His hands got lost in her hair. "Uncertain."

"All right. I'll do it," she breathed.

Their mouths met. Surprised that such a hard man would have soft lips, Allison enjoyed the sensations his tongue provoked. He increased the pressure of the kiss and massaged her scalp. She sighed and that tongue went on an exploration.

Allison felt weak after only seconds. She slid her hands up his back and squeezed tightly against him.

Jake pulled back and stepped away. Pushing the hair out of his face, he cursed. "What am I doing? This is wrong on so many levels, Allison."

She was bewildered. "Kissing?"

"Us, dammit. This." He pointed to himself and then her.

"Jake—"

He moved another step farther away. "I will make all the arrangements for the safe house and let you know when to be ready. Pack clothes for several days at least. I've got to go."

He was gone.

****

Allison lingered in the hot shower, willing her muscles, one by one, to release the tension. After what seemed like hours, she shut off the jets and stepped out to dry.

In bed she begged Luna, the moon goddess, to rejuvenate the magical powers. Drifting to sleep, she dreamed. Unfamiliar sensations danced on the edge of her consciousness and a beautiful melody played.

She strolled through a misty maze. At the crossroads she was unsure of which path to choose. She picked the one on the right and cautiously moved forward. Inside and all around she heard laughter. Twinkle, twinkle, little star, how I wonder where you are.

"Who's there?"

"Hello, Allison."

Allison continued on the trail. It wound right, then left, then right again, but still no way out. "Jake?"

"Come find me." A whisper caressed her ear sending wicked chills across her skin. "Roses are red, violets are blue, if I win the game, my prize is you."

Not Jake. "You won't get me this way." Her voice raised but she didn't scream. It wouldn't do for her to reveal how much he scared her.

****

Jake ran back to the car and headed for town. "Peter, Allison agreed to the protective custody. I told her I would arrange it."

"Okay, I'll contact the local office to get the location of a safe house and ask for a couple of their agents to take her."

"I'll take her to a safe place."

"Do you think that's wise, Jake? You're already too close to this case and in serious trouble the way it is."

"You told me to take time off. I won't let anything happen to her, Pete. I'd like to leave tonight. Moving in darkness will be better. I figure he's gotta sleep."

He hoped.

"I want regular updates. What about her brother and the others that need to be told she will be out of contact for a little while?"

"I'll buy a pay as you go phone and let her call them after we get where we're going."

"Do it," Peter said.

"I'm going back to my room and try to sleep for a couple of hours." Thanks, Pete."

In the dark room, Jake's mind couldn't escape Allison's pull. "Damn. What are you doing to me? This won't be good for either of us."

Her strength and conviction were commendable and he respected that, but he longed to see those eyes simmer with passion. His lips itched to taste her until she cried out in pleasure. Matter of fact, he could think of numerous positions he'd like to have her in, beneath him, straddling him.

Jake shifted to his side. His mind reeled, conjuring every reason why Allison Brody was a bad idea. All sensible, sane thinking was lost. But he had to protect her. *Control is the key.* But he had no control. The killer was the host of this deadly game.

CHAPTER TWENTY-SEVEN

The sun had not yet crested the horizon when Jake silently entered Allison's house. He crept up the stairwell to the second floor and Allison's bedroom. As quietly as possible, Jake pushed the door open and snuck inside, almost tripping over the packed suitcase. She glowed in the moonlight. *Sleeping Beauty*.

"Allison," he whispered.

Her eyes flew open, her arms thrashed. "Quit doing that," she said after realizing it was him.

"Doing what?"

"Scaring the shit out of me."

"We need to leave."

"I thought you were going to call and let me know when you were coming."

"No time. Come on. We have a car waiting." He grabbed her hand and pulled her out of the bed.

"I need to get some clothes on."

"You have five minutes."

"But—"

He grabbed the blankets. "At six minutes, I'll bundle you in these blankets and carry you."

Allison glared at him, spun and walked away. If he wasn't mistaken she cursed him as well. He was impressed when she returned four minutes later.

Jake hurried from the room, snatching the suitcase on the way out. With a few grunts, tripping once, and nearly toppling off a hill, he made it to the four-wheel drive vehicle parked on the gravel road about a mile or so away with Allison at his side heaving breaths from their mad dash.

"You made good time," Quincy said.

Jake opened the back door for Allison and then climbed in.

Quincy drove and Jake studied Allison's profile in the shadows. She was beautiful. The fiery eyes, however, warned of an unpleasant tongue thrashing. "Allison," he began, but she slapped him hard across the face.

"Ow, that had to hurt," Quincy commented, doing everything to keep the laughter from exploding.

Allison sneered. In a smart move, Quincy focused his attention on the road.

"Do you want to explain what the hell you're doing breaking into my house—again—and stealing me away in the dead of night?"

"I was trying to explain when you slapped me," Jake answered, rubbing his cheek.

"I agreed to go to the safe house. Of course, I thought the plan was to let me know you were coming so I could be ready."

"That was the original plan, but Peter and I talked it over and felt it would be better to move quick and under cover of darkness. We don't want The Surgeon to know you're gone for as long as possible."

"You could have let me know," she grumbled.

"I'm sorry for changing the plans without your knowledge."

Allison curled against the door, keeping as much distance between them as possible.

Dawn broke and Allison sat up to stare out the window. She hadn't spoken for more than an hour.

"Are you hungry?" Jake said, gently brushing a strand of hair.

"Starved," Allison answered roughly.

"The restaurant should be about two miles up the road," Jake told her. He looked at the driver. "We can get some food then you can shove off."

Quincy nodded.

A slight dimple he'd never noticed formed when the corner of Allison's mouth curved up. Those deep brown eyes looked at him, not with malice, but with awareness. Still early, there were no traffic sounds, only the steady murmur of the road. A nice change from the fast-paced, hectic life they'd both been living.

"Hey, is this going to be a sit-down meal?" Quincy asked.

"Uh…yeah, why not."

"Stellar. I'm starved too."

They arrived at a diner where Jake had parked another SUV the day before.

Allison fussed with her hair a little, slid on her shoes, and took a deep breath before jumping out the door.

Her heart hammered as she walked next to Jake toward the restaurant. Uncertainty and a bit of fear had her reaching for his hand and linking fingers. A gaze of green fire and raw hunger turned on her. He squeezed her fingers and brought them to his lips. The connection sizzled.

They were seated and Jake excused himself to call Peter. Allison leaned back watching Quincy. He kept busy positioning silverware, the menu, doing just about anything to keep from looking at her.

"I'm not going to bite your head off, Agent Quincy. Jake convinced me to come on this trip."

"He doesn't want to see you hurt. He can't let that happen."

"He wants to catch the killer. It has nothing to do with me."

"You're wrong." Quincy's eyes were earnest, but his tone soft. "It's much more." Quincy played with a napkin making it into an animal figure. "I never thought I'd see the day." He looked at her, sincerity plain on his features. "He's in love with you. He just doesn't know it yet."

She hadn't expected that.

"I can see it in his eyes every time he looks at you."

Jake returned scowling as he slid into the booth. She smiled at Quincy as she fingered the small napkin animal he'd made.

Quincy grabbed a menu. "So, what shall we have, something heavy and greasy or something light?"

"I think I'll have the western omelet with toast and juice." Allison replied.

A waitress appeared delivering water and took their orders.

"What did Peter say, Jake?"

"He was put off that I didn't advise him I'd be doing this tonight. I'm on his shit list." Jake shrugged.

"Again," Quincy mumbled.

Allison lifted her eyes and Quincy winked. She could have sworn she heard Jake growl as he gulped the coffee.

"So what now?"

"We go as planned. I'll take Allison to the safe house and you head back to Gloucester."

"He won't do what you want, Jake. He never does." Allison touched his arm. "I shouldn't have done this. Take me back."

"He can't hurt you if he can't find you. That's why I've gone to such lengths to get you away from there."

"I tried to help that last girl."

Jake turned in the booth to face her.

Quincy stopped fiddling with the origami figure. "What girl?"

"I thought I could find something—anything—that would reveal the next victim. I started visiting the places I'd recognized in the visions. I'd even had a small hope that I could warn her somehow."

Quincy's mouth dropped open.

Jake grabbed her arm and squeezed it a little tight. "Did he see you?"

"I'm not sure. A couple of times I got the feeling I was being watched."

"Do you realize he could have taken you?"

"He knows I'm there when we connect. I can feel him too, but I can't connect with him all the time. There are powerful shields in place."

Jake sighed. "Most people run and hide when they know a killer is stalking them. You seek him out."

"At least if he focuses on me I have some control."

"No, you don't. He's in control, Allison. That's what drives him."

She pulled her arm free. "He'll hurt someone else."

"When he does, it won't be because of you. It will be because of me."

The food arrived and Quincy gobbled his breakfast in record time, even ordering more pancakes. Jake wasn't as enthusiastic, but managed to get some eggs down. Allison pushed the food around on the plate, but barely ate. Her appetite had disappeared.

Wiping her mouth, she said, "If you'll excuse me, gentlemen, I'd like to freshen up."

Quincy nodded, but Jake didn't move. She glared at him. "Jake."

Reluctantly, he scooted out of the way. She felt his eyes on her the entire walk to the restrooms.

After washing her hands she assessed her appearance. Dreadful. She needed a comb and the extra toothbrush she'd packed.

The parking lot bristled with the breakfast crowd traffic, but she managed to maneuver her way to the SUV. A few minutes later, she heard someone sliding and gravel flew through the air.

She peeked around the door. "Hi."

"What the hell are you doing?" Jake groused.

"I wanted my comb and toothbrush," she said cheerily. "What did you think I was doing?"

Jake averted his eyes, and forced his hands into his pockets. He looked like a kid being scolded. She liked this cute side as much as she liked the sexy side of Jake Austin.

"You thought I was running, didn't you?"

He didn't answer.

"Where did you figure I'd go?"

"I'm sorry, okay? I'm sorry. I knew you weren't in the building."

This statement caused her to pause. She tilted her head. "How did you know?"

He seemed a bit shaken. "I had a feeling, something changed. I don't know, dammit. I just did."

Interesting.

"How'd you get in the truck?"

Allison held up her fingers jangling the keys. "They were lying on the table and I grabbed them when I got up."

She swirled, opened the door and rummaged around in the bag. Clutching her toothbrush and toothpaste tightly, she handed Jake the keys and followed him back inside.

"I think you should take me back."

"No."

She sighed dramatically. "What do you think he'll do?"

Jake's thoughts were on the past. "He'll look for you. Then he'll call me, rather pissed that I took you right from under his nose."

"It's more personal than you let on. Why is that?"

"It's complicated," he responded. His eyes turned frigid. "I can't offer you more than that right now."

They said farewell to Quincy and climbed in the SUV.

Allison battled with the decision to run. Breaking all connection with her abilities so long ago could have played a factor in Alex's dark path. She had to know.

The sun lazed and fluffy clouds offered it a cozy bed to rest as they drove up the secluded drive. Nestled on a hill beneath a tall, shady tree, the house waited. Two gables gleamed in the last rays of the sun. Allison pushed into the front door with her bag and wandered around the first floor. "This is a safe house?"

"The bedroom is upstairs," Jake offered.

He grabbed the bag and her hand, gently guiding her to the sweeping staircase. At the top, Jake opened a set of double doors then moved aside allowing her to enter first.

Wide-eyed, Allison couldn't speak. The view of the room had stolen her breath.

Jake chuckled softly. "It's great in the morning. All the windows help brighten the room."

The room spread from one end of the house to the other. The entire back wall had floor to ceiling windows and French doors which opened onto a huge balcony.

"You'll love it at dusk. The shadows come alive."

Still amazed that a safe house would have such spacious and beautiful surroundings she said, "You've been here before?"

"Yeah." He smiled. "I own the place."

Her heart stuttered. Her stomach dropped. *Oh, no.*

"You can put your things in here." Against the front wall sat a beautiful wood dresser with an elaborate mirror. "There are a few empty drawers. Allison? Are you all right?"

She jumped in response to hearing her name having zoned out for a minute. "Yes."

He stepped close. "Are you sure?"

"Thoughts—I have a lot of things running through my head."

Jake bent toward her, his breath warm on her neck. "What things?"

"You and me, alone in this house."

Jake straightened and moved slightly away. "Uh, you probably want to get settled in, so I'll go down and make dinner."

Allison wandered around the enormous room. A person couldn't get claustrophobic in here, she mused. A huge bed was positioned cattycorner at the south end, and a chest to match the dresser stood against the wall. The wood floor felt cool, but most likely warm with the morning sun. A huge, colorful rug adorned the middle of the room. The plushness made her want to lay down and roll around. The sheers on the windows were a shimmery blue, almost transparent, giving no sign of privacy. Deep in color almost royal, the loveseat to the left invited her to sit and gave a perfect view out the windows or to the big screen television that sat against the opposite wall with the entertainment center.

She'd done her best to ignore the massive bed which dominated the room. No one could doubt the male influence in the rich colors. *What am I doing here?* Allison drifted again to the windows.

"All will reveal itself in time," Yanni whispered.

Allison continued to stare outside. "But will it be in time?" She sighed with a heavy heart. "Someone else is going to die."

"I know, child."

"I need to get out of here."

"Follow the path." Yanni's voice crooned.

Allison knew things would happen even as she knew that she and Jake were an explosive combination—dangerous to her very soul.

Picking out the few things she needed, Allison ran water in the tub. Steam circled as she sank into its depth. Inch by inch the warmth seeped into each pore, every muscle. Heavy eyes closed letting her mind drift on waves of peaceful beauty.

A blinding flash and pain had Allison struggling to open her eyes.

Trapped.

The darkness grabbed on with incredible force, drawing her deeper and deeper into the killer's realm. *Roses are red, violets are blue, you may think you're hiding, but I can see you.* The cold voice chanted her name. *Come to me, Allison.*

Desperate, Allison flung her body forward and her eyes snapped open. Barely managing to stand she scrambled out of the tub and lowered to the floor clasping a towel, shivering.

Phone. She needed a phone.

Classical music floated through the house, subtly drawing her downstairs along with a delicious aroma.

Allison watched the efficient way Jake moved around the kitchen. He'd changed into a navy blue shirt, open at the neck. The khaki pants did much to define what he'd been blessed with. His feet were bare and he looked ready to take on the world. A woman could easily surrender to a man such as this.

He stopped when he saw her. "Hungry?"

She nodded. "Can I do something to help?"

"You can make the salad."

"Okay, point me to it."

They retired to the dining room where candles and wine waited. Yep, a girl could get used to this.

After finishing about half the food on her plate, Allison looked up to find Jake watching her. A little embarrassed, she wiped her mouth. He saluted with his wine goblet. She picked up her goblet and returned the salute. "So, I'm supposed to sit here and do nothing?"

"We wait, Allison. It won't be easy, but we wait."

"Um, in our haste to leave, I didn't pick up my cell phone. I need to call my brother." She held her hand up before he could argue. "He will be frantic. He knows I've been helping you and if he can't get a hold of me, he will think something awful has happened."

He nodded. "I have a cell you can use to call your brother, your company, and your boss at the store. Can it wait until tomorrow?

"Okay."

He focused those incredible eyes on her. "But, make them brief calls."

"Thanks."

Jake started clearing the dishes. "Why don't you take the wine in by the fireplace? I made a fire.

Allison walked into the next room. There were oversized pillows tossed on the floor next to a huge comfortable couch. A large, fluffy maroon rug lay in front of the hearth.

"My mother picked out the pillows," he said.

She set the glasses on what looked to be a handcrafted table, and plopped down on the floor, crossing her legs and snuggling against one of the pillows. Jake stoked the fire and added another log.

"It gets chilly here at night." He sank lazily to the floor, positioning his shoulders against the other pillow. "You might want to grab an extra blanket out of the closet."

"If it gets too cold, I will. Thanks."

A stilled silence, lasting only seconds, spaced itself between them.

"So tell me about your brother," Jake said.

"Nick?"

"Yeah. Are you close?"

"Very." Her mood brightened. "We were typical siblings, aggravating each other constantly."

"I know what you mean. I have brothers and sisters myself." A brief, sincere look graced Jake's face with a genuine smile.

"That's nice. You should do it more often."

"Do what?" He picked up the wineglasses and handed one to her.

"Smile."

They stared at each other until Jake looked away. "So, you were telling me about Nick."

"I'm the oldest, but you wouldn't think that if you spoke to Nick. He took care of me more than I ever took care of him." She sipped her wine.

Jake's forearms lay atop his bent knees. His aura had changed again. She still couldn't get used to being able to see auras. This was a new development in her abilities, but the strange thing was she could only see his.

"At thirteen, I began having strange dreams, events that would come true, and I sensed when things were going to happen. As if puberty wasn't bad enough." She took a deep breath. "Besides my dad, Nick was my champion."

"It must've been hard. You were so young."

"I never really felt young."

"And the dreams? Were they always horrible visions?"

Allison shook her head. "Not all of them. I had the same dream every night for years where I went to a beautiful tropical beach."

Jake's head slowly came up. "Tropical beach?"

"It was stupid girly teen stuff." She glanced at the fire. "I didn't know it, but the wealth of generations lay dormant inside me."

Intrigued, he said, "Wealth of generations?"

Allison stared at the burgundy liquid in her glass. "That's the term my great-grandmother uses."

"And what is she like? Is she still living?"

She thought about Yanni. "Not exactly. Yanni is full Romanian gypsy. With dark coloring and bangle bracelets. She's a character."

"And your parents were killed in a car accident."

Her breath caught in her throat. "When I was nineteen."

"Allison." He made a move toward her but she shook her head.

"It's okay. I've lived with it a long time."

"Did you have a vision?" Jake shifted position and put his glass down on the table.

Allison inhaled deeply. "I stayed at Kat's house that night because she had a party. I called. They were on their way out for an awards dinner. I asked my mother not to go because I had a bad feeling. She didn't stop to listen, or she didn't want to hear it." Allison shuddered.

"Why wouldn't she want to hear it?"

"My mother didn't believe in mumbo jumbo."

Jake watched her.

"My gifts come from my father's gypsy blood. She never believed it. After a while, I quit talking to her about my visions. My father and Nick were my pillars of strength. Even Kat tried to understand, but I knew it would be better if I said nothing."

Silence surrounded them again.

"It's late." Jake helped Allison to her feet. "You can go up to bed. I'll sleep down here."

Allison stared at his face. She wanted to kiss him, touch him. His jaw tightened. He held back his emotions with stiff reins.

"Goodnight, Jake," she said and climbed the stairs.

The room was pitch-black even with all the windows. Allison crawled into the bed, but didn't close her eyes, afraid she'd feel the evil again. She lay motionless for a while, watching the trees bend in the wind. Eventually, she drifted off.

Something niggled at her brain. It told her to get up.

Allison opened her eyes and looked around the room. Nothing out of place. She swung her feet to the floor, went to the door and listened, opened the door and went downstairs.

She stopped in the great room where Jake slept, covered in sweat. His head jerked back and forth, his features gripped in pain. He mumbled

and screamed out once. Allison reached down and touched his face, unable to watch the torment any longer. "Jake."

His long fingers closed around her wrist in a vice grip. "Jake!"

Jake's eyes opened. He seemed disoriented at first. Then as he focused and realized what he was doing, he loosened his grip. "What happened? Are you okay?"

"Yes. Are you?"

He sat up, his torso bare. "I'm fine."

Allison sat down next to him, lightly touching his shoulder and tracing a small scar. "What demons haunt you, Jake?"

"None more than anyone else."

"That's not true. I've felt your demon."

Jake brushed her hand aside. "There's still plenty of night left. Go back to bed?"

He wouldn't look at her and it hurt more than it should.

CHAPTER TWENTY-EIGHT

The next morning, Allison came down to the smell of brewed coffee. On the counter sat a plate of waffles. "Hi."

"Hi, yourself. Did you sleep well?"

"Sure." She wrapped her fingers around the coffee cup he scooted toward her. "What's this?"

He grinned. "Oh, I never thought to ask what you wanted for breakfast. I knew you liked waffles, so I went with that."

"I don't usually eat this big of a breakfast, but since you went to all the trouble."

"Tell me what you need, and I'll make sure we get it. Since I'm not here very often, there isn't much in the house."

"Well." Allison tapped the tip of her finger on her teeth. "Generally through the week, I eat light. Like an egg and toast or an omelet. When Martha shows up some weekends, she'll prepare some heavenly, uh—extremely filling meal and I end up not eating the rest of the day."

"Ah. Okay, I guess we'll talk later about lunch and dinner." He winked as he placed the syrup on the table. "Juice?"

"Sure." Allison dropped into the chair, eyeing the plate stacked high with waffles. "I'm going to gain weight if you keep serving me these." She groaned. "A lot of weight."

He sat down across from her and dug in.

Needing a breather when she'd finished off about half, Allison sat back and watched the sunlight stream across the room, highlighting the color of Jake's hair as he finished off his eggs.

With no pending crisis, no tension, he looked young and full of possibilities. There were laugh lines at the corners of his eyes and mouth, so she knew he was capable of such an act, and had done so at some time in the past. His voice sounded rich in tone and tenor. All the tightness that normally accompanied his frowns fell away.

She glimpsed the man Jake had once been and could be again, she supposed, were he to ever get beyond this ordeal with The Surgeon. For some reason, she felt that the *battle* between the two had changed Jake probably more than any other event in his life, as it had changed her. "So what are your plans for the day?"

He went to get another cup of coffee and she couldn't be oblivious to the way his jeans rode low on his hips and seemed, oh so comfortable.

"I have a few things to do around this place. I haven't been here much in the last two years."

"That's a shame. It really is quite beautiful."

"I've been working on it little by little. I come as often as I can, and I have a woman who comes in once a month to dust and check on the place."

He sat a small box down in front of her.

"What's this?"

"A throw away phone."

She looked at him.

"Use it to call your brother and your boss, and the company. After you're done, remove the battery."

"Why?"

"Precaution." He started to clear the table.

"Let me do that." Allison said. "I'll go crazy with nothing to do."

"Okay. Thanks. I'll be out in the garage for a while." His intense gaze leveled. "Don't forget to remove the battery after you make the calls."

"Yes, sir." She saluted.

Jake left.

After cleaning the breakfast dishes, Allison strolled around the house, taking more time to appreciate the furnishings and how the style of each room unmasked another small insight into the character of its owner.

The great room where they had talked last night could be described no other way. Spacious, but with a warm feeling, the room brought to mind cozy nights and hot memories. That rug held numerous possibilities. Allison picked up the blanket Jake had used and held it close. His scent coaxed fantasies of seeing him bare, on the rug. "Oh good Lord," she said and set the cover on the sofa.

Through the entry hall there lay another good-sized room. She assumed it to be the music room because it housed a fine stereo system, built-in racks containing numerous CDs, and a well-preserved piano. If she dared touch it, she'd surely find it in perfect tune. She sat on the piano bench, closed her eyes and tried to imagine Jake sitting in the same spot, performing a classical selection with all the skill of a concert pianist. The notes would flow through his fingers to the keys, creating a melody that brought a tear to the eye of anyone listening.

Jake Austin, the master of his own destiny, even if he didn't believe it—she did. *He's still infuriating.*

Allison went upstairs to finish her brief unpacking. In one of the dresser drawers, she found a huge pad of drawing paper, colored pencils, and charcoal pencils. She often used these to sketch out designs to someday create for the clothing industry. That was a dream—her dream. *How did he know?*

Retrieving the phone from her pocket, Allison dialed Nick.

"Where the hell are you? I've left messages. I was about ready to go to the police station and demand answers."

"Calm down. I'm okay. Let me explain."

"What's going on?"

"Yanni's been teaching me how to control my abilities. I've built shields in my mind. It's been invaluable. Still, if I relax for even a moment..." She remembered last night in the bathtub. "He sneaks into my head."

"I'm glad you have some sort of barrier, but I don't like that he can invade your mind. Who knows what this nut-job will do."

A little excited she said, "Nick, it's the first time I've actually felt like I can handle my abilities. Jake and his team listen to me when I tell them things. Of course, Jake is still skeptical, but at least they are listening."

"Who's Jake?"

She hesitated. "The federal agent I've been working with."

"By the catch in your voice, I sense there is more to that story."

"Not anything I can go into right now. I called to let you know I'm out of touch for a little while."

"How long is a little while? And why would you be out of touch?"

"The agent in charge felt it would be good for me to disappear because the killer has been able to reach me so easily. So, Jake brought me to a, um, safe house."

"You're at a safe house with this Jake?"

"I'll explain everything in more detail later. Would you call Mr. Rubin and GTT and tell them I've gone out of town for a few days. Make something up."

"I'll handle it."

"Thanks."

"You be careful and keep me posted."

"I will. Bye."

She curled up on the loveseat by the windows to draw designs she'd been kicking around in her head. Three designs: one elegant, one business and one casual seen from different angles. Alifare is what she wanted her line to be called.

Page after page filled with the sketches. Planning an off-the-shoulder number with a wrap, Allison turned to a fresh page and using short, quick strokes began the outline. It surprised her to see a face taking form instead. Deep eyes nicely spaced, a strong jaw, and features she recognized. A stern look she knew all too well, lips in a thin tight line. Her fingers brushed areas she darkened lines, and added shading.

Allison stared at the picture transfixed by the eyes. They were compelling, intense, with a touch of madness in their depths. Fingers played over the colored pencils and settled on blue. Rage and pain were scored in the dark lines. *Jake.*

"Hey."

She jumped, startled by his presence. "I—I didn't hear you come in."

Jake leaned comfortably against the doorjamb. "Obviously."

"I get lost when I'm sketching." Allison quickly flipped the page.

"I'm finished for the day. Would you like an early dinner?"

"What time is it?"

"Around four."

"We missed lunch." She smiled. "Good thing I ate those waffles for breakfast."

Jake smiled back. "I'm hungry too, but I could use a shower."

Allison rose and stretched her muscles. "I can cook, a little. I'll see what I can scare up for dinner." She scooted by him.

Jake watched Allison scamper off. Her essence lingered even after she left. She stunned him at every turn. He never knew what to expect. It was discomforting.

Frankly, it scared the shit out of him.

Those bedroom eyes and sensual voice turned him inside out. Last night when she'd touched his scar, he almost embarrassed himself and blew a load right then. Luckily, she'd left and saved his dignity, but he had an erection that would rival the gods. "Damn." *Another cold fucking shower.*

He'd often thought of this house as being large. Now, he wasn't sure it was big enough.

Freshly showered, Jake trotted down the stairs and stopped. Allison danced around his kitchen. She looked fresh and loveable in a pink fluffy sweater that stopped at her belly button. Her jeans were tight, hugging long legs and pink slouch socks peeked out. She looked like cotton candy and good enough to eat. Those thoughts made him stiff again.

She had found a pop station and pranced back and forth between the dining room and the kitchen putting stuff on the table. "Hi," she said.

"Hi." He followed her into the dining room.

"Sit." She switched off the radio and brought the drinks.

"You weren't lying when you said you didn't have much in the way of food, but I found boxed pasta salad and some cans of pink salmon. It's not much."

"It looks great," he said and pulled out a chair for her. "Tomorrow, we can make a list and go the store."

"I want to thank you for the sketch pad," Allison said.

"I knew you'd need something to do while you were here."

"That was thoughtful, but how did you know that I draw?"

"I saw sketches taped to your wall the day I came to your

house, and Margo said something to me after she checked your hard drive. You had notes for designs and there were sketches there as well."

"Oh."

"Look, Allison. Despite what you think, I would much rather have you at home sleeping in your own bed. But until we catch him…"

"I know. I know. We're stuck here."

"Precisely."

Allison concentrated on her plate, inhaling the rest of the meager meal like she'd not eaten in days instead of a few hours. Thankfully, he kept a small but stocked wine collection. He calmly drank his glass of wine, savoring the rich taste and watching Allison.

She looked up and their eyes met. "What?"

Jake set his glass down. "You cooked so I should clean up."

"Nonsense." She wiped her mouth. "If we work together we will be done in half the time."

She brought him the dishes and he loaded the dishwasher.

"I saw books in the other room. May I borrow one?" she asked.

"Help yourself."

"I'm going up to read. I don't want to deprive you of alone time. You're stuck here with me, after all." A vulnerability shone in her eyes.

Jake stared at her back as she left the room and sighed. "Dammit."

CHAPTER TWENTY-NINE

Allison screamed.

Jake ran up the stairs and burst into the room. The book lay open across Allison's lap and her head slapped back and forth. Her hands clutched the cover.

"No. No," she cried. "Look out. Run."

"Allison." He grabbed her shoulders and gently shook. "Allison, wake up."

Her eyes sprang open and her fists started flying. Jake had to deflect to keep from getting punched in the head. "Allison."

The fists fell and her hands covered her face.

Jake pulled her into his arms. "You're shaking. Just a bad dream. It's over now."

"It wasn't a dream," she mumbled. "He killed her."

"Killed who?"

Tears ran down her cheeks. "She's a teacher."

"Allison." He wiped the tears from her eyes with his thumbs. "Calm down. It will be all right."

She shook her head. "Not for her, Jake." Allison rolled away from him and stared at the wall.

"I'll be right back."

Jake went downstairs. He poured a small glass of whiskey, grabbed an extra blanket out of the closet, and returned to the bedroom. Allison lay in the same position.

"Here. Drink this."

"What is it?"

"Whiskey."

"Are you trying to get me drunk?"

He chuckled. "No. It will help calm you down."

Allison sat up and pushed the pillow behind her. He handed her the glass and opened the blanket. She downed the whiskey in one swallow then coughed before snuggling on her side to watch him.

Jake clenched his jaw. "Feel better?"

Allison nodded, but continued to stare at him.

"You'll be okay now." He turned off the bedside lamp.

"Leave it on. Please."

He left the door open.

Lying on the couch in front of the fireplace, he wondered if she had seen another kill? A vise had seized his lungs when she'd screamed. The sheer terror in that sound sent him into a panic. He laid one arm next to his head and stared at the flames. *I have no time for this, whatever it is.* Jake knew he had to stop this train dead on the track. He couldn't let Allison believe he was someone worth having. There was nothing he could give to her or any other woman. That stopped after—he shut his eyes—after the incident that started this murderer's game.

****

Jake answered the cell on the first ring. "Pete." He sat up, shading his eyes with a hand to keep the intruding sunlight from blinding him.

"We have another victim."

"When?"

"Early this morning. We got a tip."

"A tip?"

"Yeah, from him."

"Are you sure it was the killer?"

"He answered questions with specificity. It could only have been him."

"Why?"

Peter ground his teeth. "He said you would know why."

"Shit. He's figured out I took Allison."

"That's what we thought too. But, Jake, he released some sort of rage on this victim. In the other instances he'd been meticulous. This one looked like an animal had been let loose."

Jake ran his fingers through his matted hair. "I thought he'd call me, torment me, and berate me for taking her. Make it part of the game. I didn't expect this."

"The scene is being processed. I'll have Tobias email you the photographs."

"Are you sure you want me to stay out of it?"

"We'll deal with that later. Right now I need to concentrate on this. We need to catch this son of a bitch."

"Send me everything. I'll work from here."

"How's Ms. Brody?"

"So far so good." He didn't tell Peter about Allison's claim to have seen the murder. He still wasn't certain.

Jake got up, pulled on a shirt, and went to start the coffee.

Allison appeared a short time later. "Morning."

"Morning," he mumbled. He tried not to frown or clue her in that something had happened. "Were you able to get any sleep?"

"Yes. You were right. The whiskey did help." She spoke softly and her eyes were troubled.

"I'm glad." He placed a plate with toast on it in front of her and a glass of juice. "When you are ready, we can go into town and get groceries."

"That would be nice. I'd really love some tea and fresh fruit. I'll get my purse."

Allison picked up food as they walked down the aisles. Jake deliberated on the case. None of the UNSUB's actions had been consistent since he'd come to Gloucester. Why was Gloucester significant? And what did Allison have to do with it?

"Are you here?" Allison said.

"What? Oh, yeah." He paid and loaded the car for the drive back to the house. When they got there, he carried in a few bags. Allison unpacked and put stuff away. On the next trip to the car, his cell phone vibrated. "Austin."

"Again you have something that belongs to me."

Jake leaned against the car and said, "She doesn't belong to you, she never has."

"Bullshit. She became mine the minute we linked. I'd think you would understand that, Jake."

Not taking the bait Jake said, "Let me bring you in so I can help you." He could hear the madness in the killer's laugh.

"Help? I don't need help. I work on my own. Let's see." He paused. "You haven't caught me yet. You have a whole team of FBI agents and still I roam free."

"Stop—stop now."

"Give her back to me."

"No."

"I'll find her eventually."

****

Allison swore as she threw another piece of crumpled paper at the television across the room. She hadn't been able to complete one design today and she'd spent hours trying. Her thoughts strayed to last night's vision and that overshadowed everything else. She knew the murder had been committed. She believed Jake knew too, but he kept quiet. He'd been distracted most of the day and avoided her.

She was losing the natural light so she tossed the pad on the loveseat and opted for a snack. A computer would be a blessing. At least she could talk to her chat pals or search sites to get ideas for the windows. She liked keeping up on what the hot designers were doing with their lines. Still, another day had passed and she'd done nothing, watched nothing, heard nothing. She'd go crazy if this kept up. Luckily, she'd grabbed a couple of paperbacks at the store. Thriller. No. Romantic Suspense. No. Romance. Absolutely not.

Allison put the kettle of water on and decided to make omelets instead of sandwiches. She mixed the eggs, cut up ham, onions, cheese, red peppers, and put the skillet on the burner. Water was running, so she figured Jake was getting cleaned up. He'd been out cutting grass and doing yard work.

At the end of the hallway, a door stood ajar. She peeked in and saw him sitting in front of the computer, his hair still damp. He'd made this room a small office. "I'm making omelets. Do you—" She froze, stunned by the carnage that practically jumped off the screen.

Jake quickly switched off the monitor. "I'm sorry. I didn't mean for you to see those."

Allison blinked a few times. "I've already seen it. Last night."

Jake escorted her out of the room and back into the kitchen. The kettle was boiling so he pulled it off the burner, grabbed a cup, and made her tea. "Here. Be careful, it's hot."

"I'm all right, Jake." As all right as she could be after spending time in the mind of a killer.

"No you're not. No one should see those things."

"But I have." She picked up his hand from the table and pressed her lips to the palm.

He jerked back. "Don't." Jake skittered, almost falling. He straightened, and went over to the patio doors. She couldn't see his face, but knew something had changed, the distance between them had widened.

Allison stood, moved to the stove. "Are you hungry?"

"Not really."

She started to put the stuff away.

"Leave it," he said.

The steel-laced voice had given her another order. His kick-ass, take charge persona back in place.

Without saying a word, Allison left the room. How dare he bring her here with bull about it being for her safety, fill her with so many conflicted emotions, then brush her aside. He may be able to switch on and off like that, but she couldn't.

For a while Allison tried to read. She finally turned off the light and lay down. The daylight faded and the tree shadows danced with the wind. It was a magnificent show. In the stillness, she heard Jake playing the piano. Odd, the haunting tune sounded like the one she'd had stuck in her head for the last few days. In her mind's eye he sat on the bench, shirt open, eyes closed, envisioning the musical notes in his head.

She shivered. Something was coming.

With the melody floating around her, she reinforced her shields and tried to sleep. Tomorrow, things were going to change.

****

Allison woke suddenly. A faint glow from the hallway lit the room and a cool breeze rushed through. Several feet away, she saw Jake's silhouette against the blackness. In only his jeans, with one arm propped against the doorframe, he stared into the night. Layers of muscles rippled down his back. Sleek as a tiger, his moves were stealth and power. She had witnessed them often during their time together. Without turning he quietly said, "You should sleep."

No surprise that he knew she watched him. He had more

intuitions than he admitted. "What's wrong?"

"There's a storm coming."

Did he mean that figuratively? "And?"

Jake lowered his arm. "And you should sleep."

The brimming anger surged and she slapped her hands on the bed. "Dammit, Jake. I'm tired of you ordering me around. Quit trying to control me."

He turned, the small light glowing in his dark eyes. "What does control you, Allison? Your actions have been irresponsible."

"I control myself."

"Right." He crossed arms over his bare chest.

Tears formed that she tried to hold back. "What are we doing?"

"I don't have the answers."

"Who does?" One tear rolled down her cheek.

Jake's posture eased. "Maybe no one."

Allison gently wiped the tears away. "So what now?" For a moment, she thought she saw indecision or uncertainty cross his face, but it evaporated too quickly to be sure. He swirled back toward the doors. "You should sleep."

She squeezed her forehead, silently praying for strength. Quietly sliding from the bed in bare feet she padded across the room. One hand weaved around his stomach and the other up higher on his chest. He didn't move. Allison tried to read him, but again she found an impenetrable barrier. "Lay with me," she whispered.

"That's not a good idea."

A small protest which she ignored. She coaxed him to face her without much of a fight. "Why won't you let me close to you?"

Jake set her away and in a harsh tone said, "I have nothing to give you, Allison. I gave up my soul a long time ago." His eyes burned with the declaration.

"If you had nothing here," she pressed her palm to his heart. "You wouldn't care about this job, and I wouldn't be in this house."

The steady rhythm of his heart increased as she rained kisses across the smooth expanse of skin. "Stop." Jake begged in a husky voice.

"No," Allison said between kisses, unable or unwilling to end what had started.

Jake's hands turned into fists, his eyes shut tight. Practicing a technique she'd been working on with Yanni, Allison partially lowered her shield to him and the turmoil within. *Come to me.*

"Allison," Jake whispered.

Her mouth continued its journey.

"No more," he pleaded passionately. "What you'll unleash is not what you want."

Her head angled to one side. "You're wrong." In a softer tone she said, "I want to see every side of you." A finger stroked his jaw then she pivoted and walked toward the bed, swaying her hips. One of the straps fell off her shoulder and he sucked in a breath. Determined to rattle that arrogant demeanor, she lay across the bed giving him a full, clear view of the breasts spilling out the top. "Come to me," she whispered.

His eyes flamed with desire. Allison licked her lips and shifted. One nipple broke free of the gown and his nostrils flared. "Damn you," he swore and took long strides toward her. "Damn you," he uttered then grabbed her hair, pulling her head back to kiss her throat and nibble her earlobe.

At first, it was hard and unrelenting. She put up no fight. Let him ravish her and expel his anger—fear. The contained tension exploded shattering resolve and restraint.

The storm broke outside as he'd predicted, but a storm raged inside as well. Jake grabbed and kneaded her flesh. She cradled him between her thighs. As he kissed her jaw and collarbone, lightning and thunder blasted the skies. He nuzzled the soft hollow of her neck while fingers flicked and pinched her nipples. Rain pounded the house, echoing the urgency.

Mouths melded, tongues dueled. Fingers pulled on the hem of the gown lifting it off her body. Lips pressed softly on the skin above her belly button, between her breasts, and found her mouth. A growl vibrating his chest had the hairs tickling her nipples and she squirmed. Fingertips toyed with the waistband of the panties.

She arched. He shifted. The heat of him moved lower, lower. Tender lips kissed her core then the panties were ripped away. Slight, delicate brushes of fingertips across those lips, breath stalled in her lungs. Jake pressed her clit and her world erupted into sensual pleasure and sensations that ripped her apart at the seams.

One finger entered, pushed inside, and shamelessly she pressed against it riding it deeper. A groan preceded a second finger plunging to join the first. In and out with determined force. Allison opened her mouth to exhale and Jake's tongue invaded.

The kissing stopped, the hands ceased and Jake left the bed. Allison struggled to come down off the sensual high to watch him strip and crawl between her legs. No hesitation whatsoever before entering her. Although her body felt like putty, she wasn't prepared for the length and breadth of him. On powerful arms that bulged with the strain, Jake kept his entire body weight supported. In this moment his control was breathtaking. He sank deeper stretching the walls so tight she felt every pulsing inch of his erection.

Advance, retreat, demand, submit. Deeper, harder, quicker, faster. No mercy in the movement.

Everything stopped.

Jake rolled off. "I warned you."

Allison knew he waited for her fury and accusations. He wanted her to hate him. Gleaming in sweat, still primed for sex, his body was one of those created for fantasy. With her juices dripping from his arousal he attempted to push her away. Her breathing labored, her heart pounding, she said, "Again."

Jake's head whipped toward her. "What?"

"Again." Her eyes trained on him.

"Christ, woman." He jumped up, his nakedness not an issue. "I was fast—hard. No care for your feelings." His arms flew in the air as he preached. "I'm not what you want, what you need."

Allison knelt on the bed in front of him, face to face. No words, just hands, tracing the frown lines on his forehead. Gently touching eyes, nose, cheeks. Thumbs brushed across lips followed by her mouth. Desire flared in those dark eyes. She reached between their bodies to wrap a hand around his erection. "Again."

She pulled him back onto the bed. A brief reprieve from the battle, she mused. A mutual surrender.

This time she took control. Straddling him, she clasped hands and raised them above his head, holding them there while she kissed his mouth. He brought his arms down but she shook her head and pushed them up. "My turn."

Her lips moved over his jaw, his neck, and up to his ear. "Surrender to me, Jake," she said and bit his earlobe.

Jake's eyes glowed with emotion.

Allison kissed the spot on his chest over his heart. She flicked her tongue on a brown nipple and he lifted his hips causing the head of his cock to prod her ass. She scooted down so the thick flesh rested between her folds. Rocking caused sweet friction.

She continued the journey down his body hovering over his cock. It jerked and strained with anticipation. She moistened her lips and he slammed his head against the pillow. "It's my turn to order you around, mister. Don't move your hands. Understand?"

"Allison," Jake said in a choked voice. His hungry gaze watched her.

She licked from the base to the head in one long stroke, teasing the tip for a moment then closing her mouth around him.

His body tensed.

Oh so slowly, she moved down and up until he shoved his hips upward. Allison loved having him at her mercy. She wouldn't torture him—for too long.

"Ahhh," he howled then gritted his teeth.

She ceased with a loud pop and crawled up his body aligning her body right where it should be. Allison grabbed hold and lowered. Pleasure and sweet fullness.

She raised and lowered her body, hissing when the head touched just the right spot. The tempo increased and pressure built causing her muscles to clench tighter.

Jake glared at where their bodies joined and slammed his head against the pillow again. His hands clenched behind his head.

Her body wanted release. It was so close. "Now, Jake. Touch me now," she begged.

With a low growl, he released his arms and grabbed her waist. Her hands flattened on his chest to keep balance. The bulb in the bedside lamp burst and the climax tore through her with the force of a hurricane. He pumped two, three more times and roared.

Allison collapsed.

Some time passed before either of them moved.

She curled her body next to his and he wound an arm around her. "I'd have to disagree with the whole empty inside scenario, Jake."

He grunted and covered his eyes. "I can't talk just yet."

"Is it always like that?" she whispered, as she traced circles on his chest.

Jake lifted her hand, kissed her palm and shifted to prop against the headboard. "It's never like that."

Allison effortlessly nudged against him, her body trembling.

Her mouth touched heated skin and he hissed. She slid the sheet down and straddled his waist. Grabbing the headboard she leaned in and kissed him. "Let's see if we can make it happen again."

CHAPTER THIRTY

Allison felt Jake leave the bed. She pulled the covers around her shoulders and snuggled deeper, remembering bits and pieces of their night together. She'd never imagined sharing an intimacy like that with any man. *What have I done?*

"More than you know."

Allison cracked one eye to see Yanni sitting on the loveseat. "Tell me you haven't been here all night."

Yanni grinned mischievously. "He is very robust."

Allison groaned and hid her face.

"You cannot hide away forever."

"I'm not hiding."

Yanni let out an ungraceful snort. "You are. You cannot change your destiny."

"So you say. How do you know my destiny isn't supposed to be staying here until the killer is caught?"

Yanni frowned. "I have seen it differently."

Allison opened her mouth to argue, but Yanni disappeared. Maybe she's wrong. Allison hoped in vain.

I should have been stronger. He'll be gone soon and I'll be empty again. She closed her eyes tight, puffed out her cheeks and blew. "Yeah right. I should have done a lot of things different." Jake Austin would be another memory, an exciting memory, to lock in the treasure trove.

Being with Jake gave her a glimpse of what might have been. Even after lowering part of her shields, the only vibes within sensory range were the ones emanating from Jake. His power, his sex, overwhelming with such force that it blocked everything else out, at least for the time-being.

His hands braced against the marble shower wall and his head lowered, Jake let the hot water pelt the glorious tension from his neck and shoulders. All he could hear were Allison's low throaty sounds when he'd tasted every inch of her. Heavy-lidded eyes stared at him pleading for more. He'd stroked and caressed her body as if they'd been lovers for years. When he'd sworn he had no strength left, Allison lured him into another bout of incredible sex, dredging the last ounce of energy he possessed.

He wanted her, craved her physically beyond a doubt, but there lurked a deeper need. An emotional need he hardly knew how to deal with. It hadn't been a lie. He'd never experienced anything like that—ever. Only once did anything come close, but they were teenagers and it was young love.

All night in her arms. He sighed. "Damn."

The shower door opened and closed. Soft hands and lips inched up his spine. "Good morning."

Jake raised his head as Allison pressed her body so tightly against him the water barely got through. "Yeah." Indignation would wait.

He turned and took Allison's mouth, caressing the sweet cavern he lifted her against his length. She hooked a leg around his thigh and he pushed her against the wall. Exquisite breasts begged for attention and he obliged. Rosy nipples hardened in response.

"Hold on," he murmured as he grasped her thighs. She clung to his shoulders. He kicked the shower door open and walked into the bedroom, depositing her on the cushy chair outside the bathroom door. He dropped to his knees and gently gripped Allison's hips, pulling forward, until she teetered on the end of the cushion. With an arrogant smirk, Jake lowered his head, darting his tongue out, tasting various patches of her slick upper thighs. He moved closer and closer to the apex that housed her femininity. Allison squirmed and moaned, her hands clutching the arms of the chair.

At last, Jake's journey was rewarded when the tip of his tongue found the sensitive bundle of nerves to unlock Allison's passion. As he worked it mercilessly, holding tight to her hips so she couldn't pull away, Allison cried out, releasing her sweet nectar.

Without any time to recover, Jake draped her over the back of the chair, entering her from behind. Sliding his palms along her arms, he reveled in the feel of her body. Her sheath gripped tight with each thrust. He held her slim hips and pumped faster. Sensations clawed up his cock and heaved a vice on his balls as they slapped steadily against Allison. Gripping the back of the chair, she screamed his name as she climaxed.

He roared his completion and immediately dropped to the floor, pulling her down on top of him. His leg muscles quivered and his heart pounded. "We should never have started this."

She sighed. "It complicates things."

"I know."

"I didn't anticipate it."

He threw one arm over his eyes. "It certainly wasn't in my plans either. Yet, here we are."

"Yes. Here we are." She crawled up his chest until their lips met.

He kissed her deeply, enjoying the taste. Temptation to stay locked in this hideaway with Allison and play house was great, but it had to stop. Too many things needed to be done.

Reluctantly, he released her. "Let's get dressed."

Jake stood at the fireplace, his booted foot perched on the hearth when she descended the stairs. "I'm sorry."

"For?"

"Everything. I hope we can get past this complication without too much difficulty." *Very diplomatic, asshole.*

Her eyes flared and her chin lifted. "No problem. I'm sure I'll be able to put it behind me and move on."

His jaw tightened. "I think that's best for both of us. I have work to do."

"I understand. I'm sure your job keeps you very busy."

The room temperature dropped ten degrees in the last three minutes. "I have to go back."

"Fine. I'll pack my things."

"You're staying here."

Allison's eyes narrowed. "No, I'm not."

"I'm having another agent come to stay with you."

"Keeping me here will accomplish nothing, except to anger him."

"You don't know that."

"Yes, I do." She pointed a finger at him. "Don't expect me to sit here while others die. He wants me, Jake. I've felt the rage in him. It's escalating."

"That's exactly my point. It's better for you to be out of the way. He's obsessing and that obsession is focused on you."

"Yes. Me. He needs me. For whatever reason, we are linked.

"Stop saying that," he barked.

"I can touch his mind, and he can touch mine." She sat down on the hearth and put her head in her hands. "If he focuses on me, no one else will die. For once I can use these *gifts* to save lives."

The anguish in her voice punched a hole in his shell. "I won't use you as bait. That's not how we work."

She dropped her hands and sighed. "I don't have to ask your permission."

Jake glared at her. "You damn well do. If I have to arrest you for obstruction of justice and throw your ass in jail, I'll do it."

Allison jumped up. "Then arrest me because that's the only way you'll stop me from going home." She stomped toward the kitchen.

"Allison," he called, but was distracted by the vibrating phone on his belt. "Austin."

"You really are a bastard, you know that?"

"So I've been told by more people than I can count. What's your point?" Jake tried to feign a smile for Allison, who'd stopped and turned toward him.

"Bring her back."

"No."

Allison's eyes turned dark, almost black, focused blankly on nothing. Her skin paled.

"You think you're so fucking smart by taking her away. I'll show you who has the real power."

At that same moment, Allison pressed both palms against her temples. Her eyes rolled back in her head and she dropped to the floor.

"You better call 911, Jake." Click.

Jake ran to Allison's limp body. "Allison." His hands shook as he pressed fingers to her throat. The pulse was weak and her body was hot, feverish. He tapped her cheeks. "Come on, honey. Wake up." Jake pulled her across his lap and rocked. "Please. Please."

Desperate, he kissed her forehead. A bolt of energy zapped his brain snapping his head back. It felt as though he'd been punched by a world heavyweight. A strong pressure pushed on his temples and he pushed back with as much mental force as he could manage given the extreme headache pummeling him.

Jake crawled to the phone, dragging Allison with him, and dialed nine-one-one.

CHAPTER THIRTY-ONE

"What the hell happened?" Carmichael raged over the phone line.

"He did something to her, but I don't know how."

"We tried to track the calls, but got nothing. He's using throw away phones. Shit for all we know he's bouncing the signals all over creation."

He said he'd show me who had the power then Allison went down."

"Just like that?"

"Just like that." Jake rubbed his burning, scratchy eyes. "I've been at the hospital waiting. Did you find her brother?"

"Her friend Kat told us that he's visiting the younger sister at college. "We're trying to reach him by phone."

"They won't provide me with information on her condition until they talk to the family."

"Quincy's on the phone with the doctor right now. Shit, Kincaid just stormed into the room."

"Austin, you sonofabitch. This is your fault." Kincaid yelled in his ear.

Jake mentally battered himself. The other man had no idea how much truth that statement held. He heard someone murmuring on the line.

"They gave Quincy the same line, so he put Kincaid on the

phone. He figures being her doctor, more or less, might mean he's entitled to information. Hang on, here he comes."

There was more murmuring and Kincaid came back on. "This is bullshit."

"Kincaid give me her status, dammit."

The other man sighed. "They aren't sure exactly. Her body temperature has risen several degrees. She's hypoglycemic, the healthy color of her skin has been leeched away, and she's in a coma-like state. From the description you gave, Dr. Smith says it sounds like an epileptic seizure. He doesn't have any guess on how long she could be like this."

"So now what?"

"She's stable enough to be heliported to Gloucester."

"When?"

"Three o'clock today… as long as her condition doesn't change. We need Nick to give his approval for the transfer."

Jake massaged the tense muscles in his neck. "I'll meet you at the hospital then."

"You'll do no such thing, Austin. If I see you anywhere near her, I'll beat the living shit out of you."

"There's no way in hell you'll keep me from seeing her. Whether you like it or not."

There were some grunting and scuffling noises.

"Jake, this is Margo. Kincaid uh, left. Quincy escorted him to the door—sort of."

"Tell him thanks for me."

"When will you be here?"

"I'll leave as soon as I know they have everything ready to transport Allison."

"Okay, we'll see you then."

****

Jake watched from the hallway at Addison Gilbert Hospital as the nurses checked the monitors for Allison's vitals. She still had a fever with no cause that they could find. The thought of Allison never waking up made him sick. He reluctantly strode from the door, only a little assured with the police officer standing guard at her room.

"How's she doing?" Lancaster asked when he strolled in.

"Still the same." He walked to Margo. "How are things going

here?"

"Nothing new. Still waiting for the autopsy results and toxicology reports for the latest victim."

Jake ran both hands through his hair. He hadn't missed the censored glances Peter threw at him nor the way Tobias distracted Peter when she could. Their concern was warranted.

He stopped at the table and thumbed through files until he found the one on Allison. The newspaper article about her parents' death was on top. He stared at her young face. Laying the article aside he read information about her father's company and the charities her mother sponsored. He turned that paper over and froze. The woman in the photograph had blonde hair, full lips, and was absolutely stunning.

Someone's phone rang and it jolted him. He closed the file and aimed toward the door. "I'm going to check something. I'll be in touch."

"Do you need any help?" Lancaster yelled.

"Not for this." He definitely didn't want company on the trip to Salem, Massachusetts, where he hoped to find out more about psychic links.

****

Startled, Allison jerked and her eyes slowly opened. Her arms and legs were restrained with straps. It was cold, dark, damp. No light seeped through crevices, no warmth from any source. Where could she be and how did she get here?

"When I behold, upon the night's starr'd face, Huge cloudy symbols of high romance."

Allison shivered at the whispered words. The eerie voice came from every direction in the darkness. Hot breath singed her skin.

"And when I feel, fair creature of an hour! That I shall never look upon thee more, Never have relish in the faery power of unreflecting love."

"Where are you?" Allison said, a little breathless.

"I'm everywhere and nowhere."

"How can that be? You're not a god."

He chuckled. "Perhaps the devil?"

"Perhaps a man," Allison challenged.

"But what is a rose by any other name?"

"A learned man, no doubt. But I wonder—"

"Wonder away, fair maiden."

"What brings an intelligent man to this point in his life?" Allison tempted fate but the more she knew about her tormentor, the better her chances of escape.

"Brave words, Allison. Should you not be fearful of me?"

"I've had bad dreams before."

A full-bodied laugh filled the space around her, not an unpleasant sound. She sensed confusion, longing, a troubled soul. "Ahh, but this is not a bad dream, my sweet. For I have brought you to my domain. At this moment, the doctors are frantic to discover why you are comatose."

She felt him touch her hair and brush his fingers across her cheek.

"Even now, Jake Austin brims with the need to kill something. A caged tiger waiting to strike." As if it were a jest. "It is me he wishes to kill."

"I don't believe that. Jake would never—"

He grabbed her hair and wrenched. "Don't tell me what he would do. I've known him far longer."

Allison fought back tears as he released her. Show no weakness. It would be her downfall. "What do you want with me?"

With his mouth close to her ear he said, "Everything."

That one whispered word shoved fear into her chest. Her breathing began a rapid pace. "Why don't you just do it and get it over with?"

"Because my way is more fun. Haven't you guessed?"

"You like games."

"You'll find I like a lot of things." He ran his fingertip down the valley between her naked breasts, to her navel and beyond.

She instinctively tried to pull her knees up but the restraints prevented it.

"Don't worry, Allison. I'm not done yet. The journey is far from over."

He was gone.

Her mind worked frantically on how to get out of this place. Trapped in her unconscious with a deranged killer and no way to communicate with anyone else, she called out with her mind. *Jake.*

Jake sat next to Allison's bed. Her temperature had continued to rise. The doctors were baffled. They'd done every test and could find no reason why she did not awaken.

In Salem, he'd spoken to a psychic named Madonna. She explained as best she could the different kind of psychic connections and how they were possible.

"This particular incident you describe sounds like a type of vampiric aura."

"What is that?"

"It is the ability to siphon strength from living things. But he needs something personal to do it."

Although Madonna had been very kind in her explanations, Jake felt no closer to finding an answer on how to get Allison back.

The monitor beeped and he sprang to his feet. The small reflex of her system gave Jake hope. Allison was still with him, trapped in a place he couldn't reach.

Jake.

He rubbed hands over his face. Now he was hearing her voice. He needed caffeine.

Quincy strolled into the room with two cups of black coffee.

"Are you a mind reader?"

"Hell no. Shouldn't you be out chasing bad guys?"

The coffee tasted good, too good.

"So where's the persistent shrink today?" Quincy said.

"He does have a practice and other patients. I'd imagine that is keeping him a little tied up."

"Not for long, I'll wager."

Jake frowned. "Probably not." He paced the confines of the room. He lifted one hand to rub the nape of his neck, where tension had gathered in the form of knots. Quincy assessed his behavior with doctor's eyes.

"You going to keep stalking or tell me what the hell is really going on?"

Jake stared out the window. Darkness crept up the walls with the fading sunlight. Inevitable. He detested that word but it became more apparent that he needed to tell his team the truth. His job didn't matter any longer, only Allison mattered.

Jake.

CHAPTER THIRTY-TWO

At the police station, Lancaster huddled with Tobias, Peter, and Margo at the end of the table near the computer. When Jake walked in they all looked up.

"What's happened?" He stopped almost afraid to hear the answer.

"These arrived a little while ago," Tobias said.

Jake slowly walked toward her to take the photographs she offered. He scanned them, but remained calm.

"You're not surprised?"

"No, Peter. Not really. He took pictures of me and Allison at that charity ball. I should have guessed he'd go to the hospital to see her. It's another way to rub it in my face that he can get to her anytime he wants. Where was the officer on duty?"

"Some drunk was harassing a nurse and tried to get physical."

"You're telling me he paid some drunk?" Lancaster said.

"No," Jake said. "I'd say a timely happenstance gave him the opportunity he'd been looking for."

"The description I have is white male, between the ages of twenty five and thirty two. Introvert, doesn't help much. That could have been anyone of a number of people working at the hospital."

"He wasn't there when I sat with her."

Lancaster said, "How do you know?"

Jake shrugged. "I would have felt him."

"You're sure of that?" Peter said.

"Very sure."

"Explain."

"He is connected to Allison, but he is also connected to me."

Shocked, Lancaster said, "So now you believe in this psychic link?"

Jake nodded. "I've been doing research, getting more information."

"Why don't you and Detective Lancaster walk the last murder scene since you haven't been there yet? Margo, scan and email the pictures to Linc. See if he can assist you in turning up something at each of the murder sites where someone with our killer's vague description was seen in the vicinity with a camera. Maybe he's taken other pictures. I'll get agents back to the other locations to speak with neighbors again and the police officers."

"I'm already on it," Margo replied.

"Tobias and I will take the photographs back to the hospital and try to determine where he was standing when he took them. We can question people who might have seen him there with a camera."

Lancaster drove Jake to the most recent crime scene. The house hadn't been released yet, so crime tape still sealed off the perimeter.

With the standard gloves on, Jake turned the knob and entered the residence. Immediately the smell of blood hit. The disheveled room surprised him.

"It doesn't get any better," Lancaster offered.

The killer had vented his rage visibly. The cushions on the sofa were ripped to shreds; the pictures yanked off the walls and hurled across the room. To the right was the dining room and kitchen, to the left, the hallway and stairs to the second floor. He veered to the right slowly walking through the dining room, taking in everything. The china cabinet, shattered. Only one small sugar bowl remained intact. The kitchen had been torn apart as well. From the photographs taken Jake knew that under the spice rack a picture of Allison had been tacked to the wall by a serrated kitchen knife pushed in all the way to the handle. He ground his teeth. The message had been received.

Jake passed through a door on the opposite side of the kitchen and went down a small hallway. The laundry room sat off to the right. The stairwell leading to the bedrooms beckoned him. He'd put it off as long as he dared, so Jake slowly ascended the stairs with Lancaster close behind. He ran fingers along the banister, his skin itched with awareness that The Surgeon had crept up the same staircase. Silent and deadly, like the predator he mimicked. He went straight to the master bedroom at the end of the hallway.

Scenes of that night flashed through his head, a strobe effect. The woman slept alone in the bed, her husband out of town on business. The adrenaline and anger elevated for the kill. Across the room from the bed a television had been left on. He liked the soft light in the room. It gave him the ability to see her face when he took her last breath of life.

She must have sensed something because she opened her eyes and saw him standing there. A scream stifled in her throat as he clamped his hands around her slender neck and straddled her body to seal her fate. Her body bucked furiously to dislodge him, but his weight prevented it. Feverishly, she scraped fingernails across his face and jabbed his eyes. She'd obviously had some sort of training in personal protection, but she lost the battle when her windpipe crushed under the pressure.

Fury coiled tight in his gut because he didn't get the last gasp of life. She died too quickly. That alone fueled the rage already heightened because of Allison's disappearance.

Jake stumbled when he bumped into the side of the bed. Lancaster grabbed his arm to keep him from falling over. "You okay, Jake?"

Jake blinked a moment to orient himself. "Yeah." He stared at the bloodied wall where the message had been written. *Four to go.*

The room reeked of hatred so intense that it threatened to drag Jake under. "He unleashed his rage. This murder was punishment for me. He wanted something, I took it. This woman died to give me a warning."

"A warning?"

"That if he doesn't get Allison, more will die as savagely."

"Then why did he do that comatose thing to her?"

"Because I told him to fuck off."

"Do you want to venture a guess as to what will happen next?"

"I thought I did once. But now it's anyone's guess. Allison has changed everything."

Lancaster glanced at him several times on the drive back to the station. "So what the hell happened in there?"

"Theory is that a house can hold energy signatures. Murder has a violent energy and it's very strong. Sometimes a good profiler can pick up on that energy."

"Have you ever done it before?"

Jake stared out the window. "No, I've never tapped into it like that. I usually get weird vibes."

"Sounds like a kind of psychic thing."

Jake had almost laughed, but nothing about this was funny. He'd thought the same thing.

****

Cold. Dreary. "Mystical," Allison breathed.

"It is that and much more."

She jumped, startled at his presence. She hadn't sensed him. "Are you going to let me go?"

"Eventually, maybe."

"When it suits your purpose? When your game is stalled?"

He laid a warm hand over her right breast.

She gasped.

"You are more beautiful now than when you were young."

"You're Alex?" But it—he—didn't feel right.

"Anything's possible."

His vagueness confused her. "Why won't you tell me?"

"Because it amuses me to keep you wondering."

"What happened?" she whispered.

"Many things, not all of them pleasant. With you I had serenity, peace. One day you were there, the next you were gone." He pinched her nipple. She made a sound but didn't cry out.

"Things happened to me too."

"I suspected as much. Found you a new boyfriend, a lover?" he spat.

"No."

"That's irrelevant. We're here now."

"Here in the darkness."

"I like it dark. I thrive in the dark."

Then it was silent.

Allison shivered despite herself. She prayed for some light. *You have knowledge of the generations. Reach deep, the abilities are far greater than you can imagine.*

"Yanni, are you there?"

No answer.

"The knowledge of generations." *Concentrate.* She closed her eyes trying to call forth something that could get her out of this hell. The only thing she saw was Jake. The worry etched on his face as he watched her lay motionless in a hospital bed. He massaged his neck muscles and ran fingers through mussed up hair. *Jake.*

He was out of ideas. There had been no contact from the killer since the house and he didn't know how much longer he could stand watching Allison lie in the bed and not lose his mind. He ran fingers through his hair while rubbing his knotted neck. He grasped Allison's hand and let the lids fall over his tired eyes. *Allison? Come back to me.*

He felt so helpless.

Someone coughed. Jake opened his eyes. A travel rumpled man, tall with dark hair and eyes, stared at him, assessing him. "Who the hell are you?"

"I might ask you the same thing," Jake countered.

"I'm Nick Brody, Allison's brother."

He could see the resemblance now in the man who stood before him and the young boy from the newspaper article. "I'm sorry, Mr. Brody. My name is Jake Austin. I'm with the FBI here on this case."

Nick looked at him suspiciously. "Do federal agents make it a habit of keeping vigil at bedsides during investigations?"

Jake shifted uncomfortably and released Allison's hand. He met Nick's steady gaze with one of his own. "No, not generally."

"Then what are you doing here?"

How much should he tell Allison's brother? *I'm the reason your sister is in a coma.* He damned well wouldn't apologize for being here. "I dropped in to check on her. She's important to the case."

"I appreciate your kindness, Agent Austin." Jake shook the hand Nick Brody offered. "Her condition was unchanged when I spoke to the doctor at three this morning, but I'm just getting back and haven't spoken with the doctor to get an update."

"She's the same. There was a spike in her readings earlier today, but nothing since."

The look on Nick Brody's face was almost comical. He cocked his head slightly. "You're speaking to her doctor?"

Jake lifted his shoulders in a restless shrug and shifted again. He felt like a school boy in the principal's office. "I like to keep tabs on all parts of the investigation."

Nick nodded. "I see."

"Well, I'll let you be with your sister, Mr. Brody." Jake started out the door.

"She knows you're here. She senses it."

Somewhat surprised, Jake turned around. "Excuse me?"

Nick frowned. "Yeah, something happened. I could tell when I walked in. Have you felt her?"

Confusion warred with logic and the need to know more. "In my head she spoke to me. I think." He leaned against the door. "Maybe it was my imagination."

Nick whistled. "I can't even get that. When we were kids she used to try to reach out to me with her mind, but it was hit and miss. Amazing." Nick glanced at Allison and then back at Jake. "Exactly what kind of relationship do you have with my sister?"

"So… you think she could have really talked to me?"

Nick narrowed his eyes. "How much do you know about her abilities?"

"She claims to see through the killer's eyes. That she can reach his mind and he can reach hers. When she was young she would have visions and they would come true." He looked down at the floor. "That people treated her like a freak."

"People were uncomfortable around Allison when we were growing up. She would know things after touching people. That made

people nervous." Nick leveled his hard gaze on him. "You still didn't answer my question."

"We're… she's helping us with the investigation."

"I know. She told me that."

"We've been working closely together."

"You took her to the safe house."

Jake's lips formed a thin line. "Yes."

Nick sighed, staring down at his sister.

"You're close." It wasn't a question.

"Very."

"Can you talk to her and try to pull her back?"

Frustrated, Jake said, "Maybe…I don't know."

As Jake walked to the elevator, he wondered what it could mean. Allison called to him while unconscious. This left more unanswered questions.

CHAPTER THIRTY-THREE

Jake was getting groggy. He hadn't really slept since the night he'd spent in Allison's arms. It was catching up to him. His feet were heavy as he climbed the stairs. He managed to yank his jacket off then fell into bed.

He crashed hard.

Jake entered a misty place. His eyes couldn't focus in the darkness. His first impression was dungeon or torture chamber. His foot crashed into something hard. "Dammit."

"Who's there?" A soft voice called out.

"Allison?"

"Jake?"

The mist thickened. He grabbed hold of the object moving along the edge. After an inch or two, his fingertips grazed soft tendrils of hair. He clutched onto a handful and brought it to his nose.

"Ow."

Immediately he released it. "Sorry, honey. Are you okay?" Before she could answer, he kissed her. "Did he hurt you?" He kissed her again.

"Jake."

"What?"

"Can you stop kissing me so I can answer?"

"Sorry." He examined her strictly by touch. "You're strapped to this, whatever it is."

"I know." She hesitated. "He touched me a couple of times."

Jake stopped. "Touched you how?"

"It's not important."

A cold chill raced along his nerves. Cautious Jake said, "What did he say to you?"

"He tries to get me to talk to him." Allison shivered. "He doesn't always like what he hears."

It grew brighter and now Jake stood alone, Allison no longer close. He scoured the dimly lit place. A worn-looking wooden rack with strong, newly oiled chains sat in one corner. A stockade on a raised dais, a chain with metal cuffs hung from the ceiling and a leather whip snapped. Spotlighted in the distance was a large pendulum swinging back and forth, its blade growing ever closer to Allison.

She screamed.

Sinister laughter surrounded him. "Old horror movies. I hadn't thought of that. Ingenious. Thanks, Jake."

"Allison," Jake bellowed and fought to get to her. His leg was shackled to a stone wall.

The faces of The Surgeon's victims appeared, their voices mingled with Allison's cries begging him to help them. Jake kept his eyes on the pendulum while he tried to pull free. The blade swung inches from her mid-section. Then, total blackness and an ear-piercing scream.

Jake flew up in bed with a cry, reaching out. He scanned the familiar room. "A dream." He fell back hard against the pillow, closed his eyes, and worked to control the fear sending his heartbeat into overdrive. "A damn dream."

Knowing he wouldn't be able to go back to sleep, he climbed out of bed.

Jake steamed down the hall toward Allison's room. Everyone gave him a wide berth. That worked well for his foul mood.

On his drive to the hospital, he replayed the conversation with Madonna, the psychic.

Some say to use vampiric aura, you need to be within fifteen feet of the subject. Others believe that if you have an article belonging to the subject, like a lock of hair or piece of clothing, you can cast a spell on the item and place it nearby to prevent the subject from erecting shields or barriers.

Nick Brody stood off to the side speaking to Kat Rubin when Jake entered the room. Brody made eye contact, but continued his conversation.

There had to be something. The bastard had managed to get into Allison's house before and could have taken a lock of hair.

Jake began a gradual search of the area around the hospital bed. Under the bed, he felt between the slats of metal and the mattress. Nothing. He stood and slid hands down the left side, walking toward Allison's head. A vague awareness of the others in the room and their murmured conversation didn't cease his search.

His face hovered over Allison. Jake felt an odd sense of loss and absently rubbed the ball of ache in his chest. If Nick and Kat hadn't been in the room, he might have bestowed a kiss on Allison's still lips. That at least would have provided a small connection. He needed a connection to Allison.

Nick stepped beside him. "Anything I can do to help?"

Jake raised his eyes to meet Nick's bemused stare. "I'm not sure."

"What are you looking for?"

"I'm not sure of that either."

Nick lifted a brow. Jake sighed in defeat. "You'll think I'm crazy."

Nick nodded. "And watching you crawl all over the floor under my sister's hospital bed wouldn't have done that already?"

Jake straightened. "Good point."

"So?"

"I went to visit a psychic in Salem."

"Ah. And what did he or she say?"

"She told me about a type of power which can prevent a subject from putting up shields so that another can invade their consciousness, or something like that."

"And this information sent you here to skulk around and look for what exactly?"

Jake scanned the room. "A piece of clothing, lock of hair, keepsake. Something that would have to stay close for the killer to keep the hold on Allison."

"Hmmm." Nick snapped his fingers. "Ali did tell me that her locket was missing."

"Locket?"

"My father gave it to her when she turned sixteen. She's never without it. But she told me she had somehow lost or misplaced it."

Jake moved to the head of the bed and slipped his hand under the pillow. His fingers brushed something smooth and cool. He pulled them out to look at the small stones of different colors and sizes. His attention was particularly drawn to the dark blue stone.

"They are healing stones," Nick said.

"What are healing stones?"

Nick shrugged. "I have the same gypsy blood, learned the same stories, and I'm a geologist. While I don't have Allison's abilities, I do believe that certain gems and crystals have special powers."

Jake half smiled. "At this point, I'm the last person who would try to discount your beliefs. What is this blue one?"

"Moonstone."

Jake couldn't stop the perplexed look he threw Nick's way.

Nick shook his head and let out a slight laugh. "It's the woman's stone. It enhances everything female."

Like she needed anything to enhance her femininity. He replaced the stones under Allison's pillow. "What does the locket look like?"

"It's silver, hangs on an eighteen inch chain, and holds pictures of my parents."

Nick searched the windowsill and curtains. He checked the register, the bookcase and small closet. Jake continued his search around the bed. He removed his pocket knife and unscrewed the housing for the wires that were coming out of the wall. In a small plastic bag tucked up in the corner, Jake found the locket. "Got it."

Nick rushed to his side. "That's it. So he did take it."

"It looks that way. I wonder what else he took. Surely, he wouldn't have broken into her house and only taken one thing. He would have wanted a backup plan. I'll take the locket to the station and have it examined for prints."

"I'll check the rest of the room." Nick grabbed Jake's arm as he headed for the door. "What else did the psychic tell you? When should Allison wake up?"

"I can't be sure. But if I get this jewelry out of here and as far away from her as possible, maybe that will be enough for her to break free."

Jake walked to the bed and brushed fingers down Allison's cheek. He didn't look at Nick again. "I'll be in touch."

****

Allison's awareness of her surroundings had changed. Warmth filled her body and the black became gray. Opening her eyes to small slits let enormous bright light in so she shut them immediately.

"Ali? Can you hear me?"

She turned in the direction of the voice. It had to be a trick. Carefully, she opened her eyes again. "Nick?"

Nick squeezed her hand. "Welcome back."

Allison weakly clasped his hand. "Am I dreaming?" she managed through parched lips.

"No more than I."

"What happened?"

Nick explained the last couple of days.

"My throat hurts," she said.

"I'll let them know you're awake and get some water."

Within moments a doctor and nurse came in to perform an examination. "Damnedest thing," the doctor said. "Your body temperature is almost back to normal. Your vitals are strong and normal." He ordered food and recommended keeping her a day or two longer just in case the condition returned.

Allison stared out the window. It was dark. She shuddered. Her mind had been the site of the latest battle and she needed to prepare for the next round. She wanted to go home.

"Ali."

She'd almost forgotten about Nick. "Sorry."

"Where were you just now?"

"Wondering how this happened and if I can stop it from happening again."

"I can answer the how."

She slid him a sideways glance.

"I know, I know. That I could even begin to understand something about all this and you can't is unthinkable. But..." He ducked his head and stared at his shoes. "You're not going to believe where I got the information and how this whole matter was resolved."

"Try me."

Nick explained how he'd met Jake and everything that happened after.

"Jake?" She shook her head then stopped because it hurt. "He doesn't believe in anything paranormal."

Nick filled her cup with more water. "All I know is that I found him sitting beside your bed, looking like he hadn't slept in days. He was distraught. He blew in here yesterday with a story about going to Salem to find a psychic and she told him about this vampiric aura stuff."

Allison rested her head against the pillow. *So Jake talked to a psychic.*

The killer was still loose.

There were too many variables. She needed to get her strength back.

"You need to prepare." Yanni appeared by the window. "Learn the signs that he is coming. I had not prepared you enough. This should not have happened."

Yanni approached the bed. "He is strong and anger boosts his power. You have been coddling, trying to reason with him. You need to be fighting."

"Fighting what? An unknown, unseen enemy."

"Fighting evil. Do not be deceived by soft tones and sweet poetry. He must be destroyed."

"Do you know how ridiculous that sounds?"

"It is what must be done."

CHAPTER THIRTY-FOUR

She was awake. He could feel it, in his head, in his heart.

The warmth, the joy replaced by an uncomfortable throb in his back. The kind of persistent pain that spasms one vertebra at a time.

Jake scanned the area. Movement by a small alleyway drew him closer. *He* was there.

Jake took off like a shot, running full throttle. He leaped over a small white picket fence and through the alley. Without breaking speed, he bounced off a wall and tore through yards, yelling when a door flew open and almost whacked him in the face.

He'd lost sight of the prey after a couple of miles and stopped, bending his knees and bowing his head to catch his breath. His stomach ready to heave the bowl of chowder he'd eaten, he sat down on the road without a care of traffic and panted until his heart rate slowed and the nausea went away.

After a few more minutes, Jake stood, pulled his pants leg down, and brushed off his clothes. "Shit." He had a gash on his leg from hitting that trash can in the mad dash through the alley. He mumbled a few more expletives and pulled out the phone to call Peter. It rang before he could finish dialing. "Austin."

"Where are you?" Peter said.

"Taking an evening stroll," he replied in a dry tone.

"We got a call from Nick Brody."

Jake raised his eyes to the clear night sky. "What did he want?"

"He wanted you to know that Allison is awake."

He'd known. "I'm on my way."

At the hospital, Allison sat in bed laughing at something Nick had said. Kat held Allison's hand. Things got quiet when Jake and Quincy walked into the room.

"You got your color back," Quincy said. "How do you feel?"

"I want to go home, but other than that, I feel pretty good."

Jake stayed by the door and watched. There were no words to explain how he felt.

Nick kissed his sister's head and motioned for Kat. "Come on Dr. Quincy, let's step outside and discuss arrangements for Ali going home."

Jake moved to the windows while the others filed out of the room. He stuffed his hands in his pockets.

Allison sighed. "Are you going to talk to me?"

"I don't know what to say."

"How about you look better today, Allison, or glad to have you back with the living?"

He spun around at the last remark. "This is not a joke. He could have killed you."

She twisted her hand in the bed sheet. "I was careless and unprepared. That is going to change."

"I didn't protect you. Hell, I put you in harm's way."

"We didn't know he could do what he did."

Deflated, Jake sat down. "I couldn't go where he took you."

In a soft voice she said, "But you were there. I felt you in here." Her hand went to her chest.

"Do you have any place out of Massachusetts you can go?"

"I'm not leaving."

He grabbed her hand. "I want you out of this."

"He's proven he can get to me, Jake. I'm not hiding or becoming a prisoner to fear."

"I will end this. But I can't do it if I have to worry about you."

"You don't have to worry about me. I understand now. This was set in motion a long time ago."

"What do you mean?"

"It's complicated. Let's just say I know what I have to do."

"Allison, please. It's not your fight. Let me do my job."

She squeezed his hand. "I heard what you did in Salem. It must have been hard for you."

He shrugged. "I did some investigative work and came up with a possible solution to a problem."

"It was more. You know it and I know it."

He brushed his lips over hers. "I'll see you later."

Officer Logan was standing guard when Jake exited the room. "No male personnel gets in this room except for her doctor and Nick Brody."

"Don't worry, sir," Logan said.

Jake strolled up to where Nick and Quincy stood. "She's a stubborn woman." He and Nick shook hands.

"You have no idea," Nick said, and walked back to her room.

"I haven't brought it up until now, Jake, but do you think while we're here you might have your leg looked at? You may need stitches."

Jake pulled at his pants leg. The blood had dried and the material stuck to the wound. He'd forgotten about the injury. "Okay, let's stop off at the emergency room."

"Are you going to tell me what happened?" Quincy pressed the elevator button.

They stepped in and Jake said, "Evening strolls are more hazardous than I remember."

Two hours after leaving the hospital with a freshly cleaned, stitched, and bandaged leg, Jake walked into his room, slammed the door, and threw the bottle of antibiotics on the dresser. He maneuvered one arm and then the other around in circles, up and over behind his head to work out the soreness.

He plopped down on the bed after removing the torn pants, not bothering to take off his socks or shirt. His leg throbbed, his arm throbbed, his head ached, and his mood sucked.

The cell phone on the bedside table where he'd tossed it, vibrated. "Austin."

"Victory is mine sayeth…"

"What do you want? I'm in no mood for your bullshit tonight."

"My, my. Aren't we testy?"

Jake laid back. "It's late. Is there a point to this call?"

"Congratulations, Jake. You out maneuvered me this time.

Smart thinking, finding the locket. However did you manage to figure it out?"

"Connections," Jake replied.

"She's beautiful, our Allison, and very special. Her body is exquisite. Her round, firm breasts just enough. I love her voice when it comes in breathless whispers."

Exasperated and bone weary, Jake said, "Yeah, her eyes are the color of rich coffee and her hair as soft as silk, yada yada. What the hell do you want?"

"Don't pretend you don't care about her. We both know that's a lie. What do you want?"

"I want you to give yourself up and end this."

The killer laughed.

Jake threw his phone across the room where it bounced off the wall and landed on the cushion of a small wooden chair in the corner. "Bastard."

****

The sun rose over the horizon as dawn broke. A beautiful sight he supposed. Another day for him to fail.

Freshly shaved and clothed in a dark, blue suit which he'd finally had dry cleaned, Jake walked down the hallway of the police station to the room where pieces of this puzzle tumbled across tables and the floor.

He was studying a wall map of Gloucester when Margo came in juggling her purse, a cup of coffee, and two boxes of pastries. "Good morning."

Jake walked over and took the boxes from her. "Morning."

She dropped her purse on the floor, set her cup down, and pushed the button which started her computer humming. "Got new information late last night."

"Oh?" His interest piqued.

"The second interviews about the camera turned up a couple of witnesses saying they saw a guy on two different occasions."

Jake wondered at the carelessness. It was certainly not like the killer.

"Could be coincidence," Margo continued. "Both men had different hair color and we couldn't pin down a height other than between five ten and six feet." She sat down in front of her computer. "They are following up with a sketch artist."

"Good." He walked over and filled a cup with coffee already brewing.

The rest of the team and Lancaster strolled in a few minutes later.

"Pete, can I talk to you for a minute?" Jake called.

Peter moved to where he stood in front of the map.

"I have an idea."

Peter's full attention focused on Jake. "What kind of idea?"

"Margo is about the same height as Allison and same build, more or less."

"Yes."

"Suppose we do something to bring the killer out. Something that will make him come after her. Put a wig on Margo and Allison's clothes."

"If he's linked to her, won't he know it's not really Allison?"

The others came over to hear the plan.

"I'm hoping not if we bombard him with distractions."

"What would be tempting and distracting enough to bring him into the open?" Quincy said.

"Me."

Peter shook his head. "I don't like it."

"We have a connection. He's been taunting me. I think I can convince him." He glanced at Margo. "I can't speak for you though."

"Don't worry about me," she said. "I've been trained to handle myself. Just because I spend most of the time behind a computer doesn't mean I can't function in the field."

He shifted his focus to the map. "I've been studying this map of Gloucester. Here." He circled the dark line with his index finger. "You can get to most portions of Gloucester by 128. He could jut off here and come right into downtown to any number of streets. These other areas are too sparse for our guy. He likes to have a good population to choose from." Again with his finger Jake drew an imaginary circle around the middle, bottom portion of the map. "This is where he will concentrate his efforts."

"How can you be so sure?" Tobias said.

Jake looked at her. "Law of averages. He stands a much better chance of finding the woman to fit his criteria in a well-populated location."

"Logical." Lancaster offered.

Peter studied the map. "But he needs a home base, a place to plan and keep his stuff."

Jake glared at the map. His gut drove him toward a huge white area off Cherry Street. "What is this area?"

The others moved out of the way so Lancaster could get closer. "That's Dogtown Common. It's a large wooded area, several swamps." He frowned. "Numerous secluded places where someone could get lost for days if he didn't want to be found. I think I remember hearing about a murderer quite a while back who did just that. Sorry it hadn't occurred to me. I wasn't involved in that case." With the index finger of his coffee cup hand Lancaster pointed at Dogtown Common. "If our friend wanted to move about unseen that would be a good place for it."

Jake hoped they were on the right track. "Can we get uniforms to start a grid by grid search?"

"Why don't we widen our search for any kind of abandoned buildings, warehouses, things like that in areas off 128?" Peter said to Lancaster.

"I'll talk to the chief about adding more officers to help with the search. And, I'll contact law enforcement in those other areas." Lancaster left the room.

"You really think if we rattle his chain, get too close, we can smoke him out? Tobias said.

"It's a plan in progress."

Peter said, "Let's pass out the sketchy description details as well."

Margo nodded.

Peter turned to the others. "Okay, everyone. Let's see if we can shake this guy up."

****

"Good morning, Allison," the doctor said. "Things are looking good, but I would like to do another CT scan."

"I feel great, doc. Really." *I want to go home today. I'll be more comfortable.* She projected her thoughts at the doctor.

An eerie glaze settled over the doctor's eyes. "I think you should go home today. You'll be more comfortable," he repeated.

Amazed, Allison sent more. *Release me this afternoon. I need to go straight home.*

"I will get you released this afternoon. You should go straight home."

A quick pain made her break eye contact. The doctor shook his head as if to clear it and looked down at the clipboard where he'd written instructions for her release.

"Doc, you all right?" Allison rubbed her temples.

With a puzzled look he left the room, mumbling on the way out. "I'll get your paperwork started."

"That was weird."

"Not at all."

Allison looked over to see Yanni sprawled in the uncomfortable hospital chair.

"It is only a fraction of what can be done with practice and control. We will work on it more when you get home." Yanni vanished.

A nurse came into the room. "This was just delivered for you."

"Thank you."

A white florist box. She already knew what lay inside, but she opened it anyway. Her fingertip brushed across one of the soft petals.

The room dimensions wavered and Allison found herself moving swiftly with a stopwatch in one hand. He jumped over a row of shrubs and hid behind a tree, close enough to the house he could see inside.

Allison was breathing hard. Another vision.

He was planning his next move. The killer punched the stopwatch button and looked at the time. Elation washed through him as he strolled back to where he'd left the black Mercedes with tinted windows. He toyed with something in his hand. A quick click snapped the tool in place. In the glare of the streetlight, Allison saw the straight razor, sharp and deadly.

More waves and Allison was in the hospital room again. She grabbed the phone and called Nick to pick her up. After changing clothes, she pulled out the brush and started running it through her hair. She hung

her head forward and let the wealth of hair cover her face as she counted each stroke. At fifty, a male voice joined in the counting. She screamed and snapped her head back to see who had entered the room.

"Oh my god, you scared me." She threw the brush at him.

Jake jumped. "Hey." He caught the brush in midair.

"How long have you been standing there?"

Jake sauntered toward the bed wagging the brush. She grabbed at it, but he pulled it away. "They took out your I.V."

"I'm going home. Nick is on his way to get me."

Jake set the brush on the table. "You just woke yesterday."

"And I'm fine. I'll be more comfortable at home anyway."

"And more vulnerable. Here you are guarded and no one can get in to see you unless they are recognized."

"House arrest?"

"If I had my way," he murmured.

"You look good in a suit. Blue is a great color for you."

He glanced at her and grinned. "Distraction technique? Do you really think that works on a trained FBI agent?" Noticing the box, he tensed. "When did you get that?"

"It came this morning."

He flipped open his phone. "Pete, another black rose was delivered to Allison at the hospital."

"I'll send someone to pick it up, Jake."

"I have other information," she said.

He looked up. "Hold on, Pete. What is it?"

"He's already picked his next victim. He's in the final planning stages. I believe it will happen tonight."

"Did you hear that?"

"Yeah. This pushes up our timeline."

"He drives a black Mercedes with tinted windows. I didn't get a license plate number. His straight razor flips open like a switchblade."

"When did she find all this out," Peter said on the other end of the line.

"Hang on. How—"

"I saw it in a vision right before you came into the room."

"Get back here. We need to do this tonight."

"I'm on my way." Jake agreed. He hung up and stared at her.

"I know something else too."

"What?"

Whether you choose to embrace it or not, the three of us are on some sort of cycle. In the end, someone dies." She focused her gaze on his stormy one. "One of us dies."

CHAPTER THIRTY-FIVE

"You are not ready." Yanni said.

"I have no more time."

"It will take everything in you to deal with him."

Glancing out the window, Allison saw the last rays of the day swallowed by the darkness. She took deep breaths and lay down on the bed. Yanni raised her hands and lights went out. Candles all around the room sprang to life, their flames dancing to an unheard beat.

Yanni sang an old gypsy song, but Allison barely heard the words. She closed her eyes.

Yanni's song turned into a chant. A protection spell.

"Are you there?" Stillness. "Where are you?" Her voice echoed in the quiet room. "I feel him."

"Concentrate," Yanni said, then continued chanting.

The first sound or hiss sent chills across her entire body. Slithery, cool, a smooth tone laced with sarcasm. *"Well, look who's come to visit."*

The strong link between them shocked her even now.

"I've missed you. All of you."

She shivered remembering being tied down to that table.

"Trying to hide you from me wasn't Jake's best idea. I will repay him for that."

"He was doing his job."

"Tsk tsk, standing up for the noble FBI agent?" He snickered. *"Not surprising. He's always been able to invoke those feelings from others. I think there's more to it than him doing his job, Allison."* Impatience and irritation returned to his voice. *"Why have you summoned me?"*

"A barter."

"Barter?" A touch of amusement mocked his tone. *"You've piqued my interest. Go on."*

"I want you to stop killing people and…"

"And?"

"And leave Jake out of this."

His laughter was easy and real. She actually believed this amused him.

"Quit killing. Altogether. And what do I get in return?"

"Me."

"You put a high price on yourself, Allison."

"No. You did." Allison felt more certain of this decision now that she'd actually spoken it.

"Hmmmm. Very well." He purred in his answer. *"I'll agree to your terms, but you know Jake will have something to say about it."*

"I won't tell him. My deal is with you."

"Meet me at the old fish factories on Commercial Street, the fourth one."

"I know it."

"Eleven thirty tonight." The Surgeon chuckled. *"It will be memorable."*

Unsettled, she opened her eyes. "We need to pick out the right clothes. Come on," she said to Yanni.

Allison rummaged through the trunk at the foot of the bed. It took some scrounging, but she finally found the sculpted dagger and sheath. She'd paid a tidy sum to an antique dealer years ago to obtain the pieces—a part of her Romanian heritage. The carved handle felt cool as she gripped it. A wavy blade of tempered steel winked in the light. The leather sheath had soft velvet inside and a strap laced through it to fit around her thigh. "Perfect."

"What are you thinking?" Yanni asked while Allison threw open the closet door. "You need not get close enough to use a knife."

"My powers are uncertain. I need a backup plan and this is it."

"You need more training."

"No," Allison yelled out of the closet. "I need more time, but we've run out of that. I'll not let someone else die."

"This is not a wise decision."

Allison scoffed. "We know from past experience that I don't make the best decisions. But this time, I'm doing something right." She walked into the room. "I need to do this."

"Yes." Yanni sighed. "I believe you do."

"Now, the outfit has be able to hold his attention." Allison leaned against the wall and her stomach lurched. Jake's house looked better and better.

Before she changed her mind, Allison scanned all the clothes, settling on a long poppy print skirt with lacy overlay. The blouse dipped enough in the front to show ample bosom.

Allison took careful time in applying make-up, embellishing her features but not too ostentatiously. Shaky hands made it difficult to apply the eyeliner. She paused, inhaling deep in an effort to ease the rapid

rhythm of her heart. What she'd intended as smooth draws were more like gulps and she couldn't get enough air into her lungs.

Ignoring the fine tremors, Allison brushed her hair until it shone, leaving the curls loose. Mystery, allure, cunning. Those were the skills she needed.

At eleven p.m. Allison pulled out her cell phone and dialed Paul Kincaid.

Perplexed, Yanni said, "Why are you calling him?"

"You were right. I do need more training and in case my backup plan fails, I'll need help. I'll need him to get the Calvary."

"The what?" Yanni frowned.

"Hello?"

"Paul, it's Allison."

"I heard you were out of the hospital."

"Yes. They released me today."

"You're feeling well?"

"Very, but I—"

"I want to talk about your dreams."

Astonished. "My dreams?"

"I needed to understand what you were going through, how

you'd been living these last few years. Why you left school. Dr. Lomax took an interest in your case and you."

"He's a wonderful man."

"Don't I know it. It's been hard trying to fill his shoes."

"But you don't need to fill his shoes. You're a wonderful man too."

"It's no secret that I have had feelings for you since college. And, I thought you felt something too."

"Paul—"

"No, let me finish."

She quieted.

"I reviewed your file, focusing on the dreams, visions you had in the past. I found myself believing you. It doesn't make sense to me, but I believe you, Allison." He sighed. "That's it. That's what I wanted to say."

"Thank you," she whispered. "That means a lot." She sighed. "I'm going to ask you to do something for me."

"You know I'd do anything."

"For whatever reason, I have been drawn into an arena with this killer. I've got to stop him. Keep him from killing again."

"You can't possibly know what this killer will do. He's a psychopath, or at the very least, a sociopath. He could kill you, Allison."

"Or, I can draw him out, so Jake and the others can capture him. He wants me."

"And you're going to hand yourself over to him? It's too dangerous."

"Paul."

"Where do I fit into your plan?"

She advised him when and where the meeting would take place. "I need you to take this number and call Jake at exactly eleven twenty and tell him the details."

"I'm coming over there. I'm not going to let you do this."

"I'll be gone before you arrive."

"Allison—"

"Call Jake, Paul," she said and hung up.

"I have cast all the protective spells I know," Yanni told her. "You are in God's hands now."

Allison gazed into the mirror at her reflection. "A lamb to the slaughter," she mumbled and picked up her keys.

****

For a moment the room disappeared. The voices of those inside it turned to a soft hum. Jake blinked a couple of time. He saw a warehouse then a flash forward. Allison was talking to the killer, running fingers through his hair. The killer's mouth came down on hers.

Jake stepped forward.

Allison hadn't pushed away. She'd accepted the kiss willingly.

The Surgeon twisted, his mouth still locked on Allison's, but his gaze now locked on Jake. With triumph in those eyes the Surgeon lifted the razor.

A sharp pain splintered Jake's neck. He jerked when Peter placed a hand on his shoulder. "You okay?"

"Allison's in danger."

What she told him this morning about one of them dying rang in his head. He knew the danger was real.

"Jake," Lancaster called out. "Surveillance called. Allison left the house and he's following."

Jake's cell vibrated. "Austin."

"This is Paul Kincaid."

"How did you get this number?"

"Allison gave it to me. I just hung up with her. She's going to meet the killer."

Jake's heart plummeted. The vision came back in full clarity. "Where?"

"Commercial Street. Where the fish factories are located. The fourth building at eleven thirty. I'm heading out there."

"No, you stay put. I don't need you getting in the way. I'll handle it."

Jake slammed the phone shut. "Allison arranged to meet the Surgeon." He pulled his Glock from its holster and checked the magazine.

"Where are we going?" Lancaster asked as Jake flew out the door.

"I'll tell you on the way."

CHAPTER THIRTY-SIX

Allison didn't want to think about what would happen when she got to the rendezvous, so she sang on the drive to meet her adversary. No matter what song she started with it turned into the melody that had been playing in her head since this nightmare began.

The killer had to be stopped.

Allison parked close to the building. Fear kept her hands frozen to the steering wheel. *Breathe*.

The plan was perfect. Calling Jake herself would have only ended in him ordering the officer outside to detain her. Nick would have stopped her too. Paul was the only choice. She knew he called Jake the minute she hung up.

Jake would arrive in time. "He'd better."

Allison exited the car and walked slowly toward the side door. With a creak it opened. The lights were dim and the smell of fish overwhelmed the interior of the warehouse. Terrified, but determined, Allison advanced. "Hello?"

No response.

"Hello?" she called.

"Hello, Allison." The Surgeon's smooth, seductive voice echoed through the vast building. She couldn't tell from which direction it came.

"Move farther into the room. Over to that chair."

A metal chair sat by a small floor lamp. He'd obviously arranged things to his advantage. She approached the chair, but didn't sit. A sudden change in the climate warned her to be ready. A current of energy fizzled and he was there.

"I'm humbled. You dressed up for me."

The killer's breath warmed her neck. Allison didn't speak for fear her voice would betray how scared she was.

One hand trailed down her arm leaving chills in its wake. The other snaked around her waist, pulling her stiff body against him. No evidence of flab in his midsection and rock hard thighs pressed against her legs. He wrapped her long hair around one hand and jerked, causing pain.

She winced.

"I knew you were mine the minute I felt you. Long ago, do you remember?"

The hand around her waist slid down pausing above the apex of her thighs. Teasingly, one finger made circles through the thin clothing.

Allison tried to yank free. "Stop."

"It's a shame you didn't wait."

"For what?"

"For me to take you."

The words threatened and his finger pressed harder against her slit.

"Did you think I wouldn't know Jake dipped his cock in you?" Furiously the killer's mouth trekked her shoulder where he bit, leaving indentations, and sending painful awareness through the muscle. "I felt every shiver and climax when he was inside you. I watched everything."

His cold voice scraped her nerves. "It was entertaining." He bit her shoulder again. "No matter. I shall have you."

The killer's hands weaved around under the blouse and grasped her breasts.

Allison inhaled sharply. The roughened pads of his fingers scraped her skin. His touch was firm but light. Gorge rose in her throat.

"You're not wearing a wire, are you?"

"I'm not."

He shoved her toward a table in the center of the room

covered with long stemmed roses in a myriad of colors. "Put your hands on the table," he ordered.

Allison complied. Fighting now would only make him angrier. She needed to occupy him as long as possible.

"Lean forward."

She tried to turn, but from out of the shadows he produced a gun and held it to her neck.

"I borrowed this from one of the officers searching the Commons. Another ploy by Jake to keep me busy."

Allison's heartbeat accelerated to a mad rhythm. Adrenaline.

"Don't move." The killer pressed the barrel of the gun against her cheek for emphasis. His free hand skimmed her body, resting on one buttock and squeezing. "Nice ass. I'll examine it more closely when I have you naked."

Allison stiffened.

He grabbed the skirt dragging it up to rest on her backside. She worried that he'd find the dagger attached to her thigh. Maybe he already knew it was there.

The killer laid the gun on the table within reach, and used both hands to massage her flesh. Anxiety kicked in when the petite underwear

fabric breached the crack of her ass. "Very nice ass, Allison. I'm going to enjoy it."

She shifted her gaze to the gun. Could she reach it?

He swiped a single rose off the table and used the soft petals to intimately caress her. Taut, the muscles in her bottom tightened. "I'm definitely going to enjoy this."

"And you'll keep your word?" she asked desperately.

"About?"

"About the killing."

"Ah, yes. The killing. And, there was something about Jake too."

"Leave him out of it."

"Right. Leave him out." The killer sneered.

"Well?" Allison straightened and tried to face her tormentor, but he halted her with his thighs.

"You have to stay with me and do whatever I want." He rubbed his erection against her. "Whenever I want, and wherever I want." The sultry voice heated her skin.

Jaw clenched, she said. "Fine."

"Close your eyes," he whispered close to her ear.

She did.

"Now, very slowly, turn around."

Allison turned, wanting to open her eyes but too afraid. He tugged her hands and placed them on his shoulders. He was a good six inches taller. "What—"

A finger lay against her lips. "Shhh." He moved in close. Then his lips were there gliding, coaxing, tasting.

Allison still didn't open her eyes. She felt ill. Needing to break the moment, she bit his tongue.

Furious, the killer slapped her hard. "Bitch."

She fell to the floor.

He spat blood and hauled her up by the hair, forcibly twisting her head. "I'm not done yet." He ran his tongue roughly across her split lip. "Kiss me again."

She hesitated. Where were the police? They should have been here by now.

Her hesitation fueled his temper. With bruising force he dominated her mouth. The kiss was a testament to his control. The killer threw her across the table. "I'll bet your pussy feels good. Shall I tease you until you're dripping wet?"

Her mind screamed.

His lean body rubbed sexually against her bared flesh. Hot, ragged breath brushed her spine. "I'll fuck you with my fingers, my tongue, and when you're screaming for more, my cock will drive so deep you won't want me to stop."

A gun fired. "Enough!"

The killer stilled. "It looks like I won't be keeping part of our bargain." He snaked an arm around in an intimate hug, plastering her backside to the front of him so she could feel his erection "Hello, Jake."

Jake waited, poised, slightly in the shadows with his gun raised.

"I was getting ready to plunge my fingers into that tight pussy."

Allison cringed.

"Let her go." Jake ordered.

"You know I can't do that. I've been waiting for another chance with Allison." He licked her cheek.

"Only you ever thought you had anything to prove," Jake said.

"Everyone's golden boy. Made the parents proud. The heir apparent, and me just a rerun of the original."

"That's a lie and you know it."

The killer reached under Allison's skirt and pulled the dagger from its hiding place. He admired it. "Impressive piece." Slowly, he ran the blade down her cheek and lower to rest under her breast. "Just like its owner."

Jake kept his eyes on her.

"Again, you're playing the hero. But you blew it when you fucked her. That pissed me off, but you knew it would. I don't like sloppy seconds."

The killer ripped Allison's blouse rending the fabric down the front. Taking the sharp blade, he cut a bra strap to reveal a smooth breast. Without blinking, he sliced a thin line in her flesh.

Allison didn't make a sound but her eyes filled with tears.

"Is that why you did it?" The tip of the dagger lowered and gently ran across her stomach.

Unable to endure anymore, Allison screamed and jammed her elbow into his ribs. The killer grunted and let go, but recovered quickly. Grabbing her hair, he twined it until she butted against him. The dagger pricked her throat.

Jake bolted forward. "Jared, no."

"Stop, Jake, or the next one is across her throat," the killer yelled and moved the dagger to Allison's ear.

"You sonofabitch," Jake growled.

"As I've told you all along, we aren't so very different. You would kill me to save her."

"We're not the same. You kill to be in control—to hurt."

The killer's laugh filled the emptiness. Allison felt faint and closed her eyes. The laughter that haunted her dreams now played in her ears.

Jake's voice was hard with emotion. "Jared, let her go. We'll do this, you and I."

"And a good match it would be, Jake, but not as much fun."

"You know the place is surrounded."

Allison watched Jake's cold eyes fix on the killer. "You're not getting out of here unless I take you."

"I knew she'd tell you." He roughly bit down on Allison's earlobe.

She shrank back.

"I always have a backup plan. I could use her as a shield. No one would fire a shot for fear of hitting our dear, sweet Allison."

He poked the tip of the blade through her skin below the jaw bone.

She whimpered.

Jake balled his right hand into a fist while keeping the gun trained on the target with his left.

"Tell me. Was her mouth all hot and tight when she sucked your cock?" The killer licked the trail of blood up Allison's neck. "She tastes sweet. I'll give you that, but I want to feel her tighten around me."

The killer yanked Allison's hair and made her face him. "Unzip my pants."

Allison couldn't look at him. She was falling apart inside. "No."

He tightened the grip in her hair and wrenched it hard to make his point.

She yelped.

"Do it."

"No," she screamed. Her tear-filled eyes finally glared at him. Shock, disbelief and confusion.

"Surprise," the killer sneered. Fury was evident on his face. A face that she recognized, that she'd sketched.

"Loyal, yet foolish." The dagger moved under her chin as the killer leaned in to whisper. "You knew. One way or another it would end here tonight. But, that's why you sought me out."

"Please don't do this," Allison said.

For an instant a flicker of honest emotion appeared in the depths of his blue eyes. Sorrow. The killer released her hair, kissed her, then shoved her away. "Get out."

"Go, Allison," Jake yelled.

Allison stepped back and studied the two men, similar, yet different. Her heart torn between the one she loved and the one she pitied. Jake's stormy green eyes silently pleaded with her to leave.

Turning to the killer, Allison lowered her shields and pushed hard with her mind. If she could break through, maybe coax him into giving up, he would let Jake take him into custody.

"Why do you continue this useless quest?" Allison said. "You knew it would lead to your death."

"Or Jake's."

"Allison," Jake said.

"If you really wanted him dead, you would have killed him long ago."

The killer rubbed his forehead as she spoke. Hope kindled in Allison so she pressed on. *Surrender. It's over.*

"Allison," Jake warned.

The killer held up a hand. "No, Jake. She's fascinating. Even at a young age she had so much undeveloped power.

Allison's heart missed a beat.

"Do you think you can save me, Allison?" He laughed and grabbed her arms.

Jake inched forward. The killer raised the dagger to her throat again. "Don't do it. I still hold her life in my hands."

"Like hell you do," she countered.

"I've been seriously enjoying our match." He looked pointedly at Jake. "I finally found something I'm good at."

The next few minutes happened quickly, and yet, seemed to play in slow motion through Allison's eyes.

Jake bolted toward them. The killer threw her to the ground. He catapulted through the air, landing on top of Jake, and they fought. The dagger clanged to the floor. Each one got in good punches and a couple of kicks. Lancaster and the rest of Jake's team appeared out of the shadows with guns drawn. No one attempted to shoot.

The killer used his feet and threw Jake over his head. He landed hard against the concrete floor. The killer jumped up and pulled the gun from his waistband, leveling the site on Jake who was rising slowly.

Allison called forth her abilities. Several bulbs in the uncovered light fixtures blew. *Control. Direct it.*

The killer pulled the trigger.

It sounded like a sonic boom to Allison's ears and Jake went down. She screamed and rose to her knees. Several gunshots fired. Allison flung her arms out releasing an incredible force which tossed the killer through the air and into a nearby wall.

"Jared." Jake half crawled, half dragged his bleeding body to the motionless one. "Why'd you do it? I could have helped you. We would have worked it out together."

The killer coughed, spitting up blood. "There was never any hope for me."

Holding the ripped bloused tinged with blood Allison knelt beside Jake.

The killer looked at her. "Take care of our Allison, Jake. Even when we were kids I knew she was special. She's more than I ever deserved."

"Hang on," Allison said. "An ambulance is on the way."

"No more time." Blood trickled down his chin. "We all knew," he coughed. "One of us would die tonight. Looks like it's me." He took one more ragged breath.

Jake lowered his head to the killer's forehead.

"You okay? Peter asked, squatting next to Jake who rolled to his back. He ripped Jake's shirt open to look at the wound.

Jake nodded and hissed when Peter put pressure on the stomach wound.

Peter looked at her. "Care to explain?"

"I used my mind to throw him." She smiled weakly.

"Oh." Peter shook his head.

An officer handed her a jacket. "I'm still learning." She scooted closer to Jake.

Sirens sounded in the distance.

"Keep the pressure here," Peter said. He pressed her hand on the site. "I'll get the paramedics."

Allison was numb. Under her breath, she begged, "Yanni, please help me keep him alive."

Her hands began to glow with a soft light that settled around Jake's wound. Some kind of energy filled her body and radiated through her hands. A weird sensation that lasted only seconds.

Jake opened his eyes. "Have I died and gone to heaven?" he whispered and lost consciousness.

CHAPTER THIRTY-SEVEN

Allison lay in the ER.

"It is over." Yanni said.

"I hope so." Allison looked at Yanni. "Thank you for helping Jake."

"I did not."

"But I called for you to help him then it glowed around his wound and his eyes opened."

"It was your abilities that saved him."

"How?"

Yanni shook her head. "There is much to learn about your heritage. You are special."

Those were the killer's words too. It saddened her that they could be so wrong.

A male voice echoed through the emergency room. "Allison? Allison?"

She heard someone yelp and a nurse frantically arguing with someone. "Nick," she called.

The curtain flew back and Nick all but trampled the little nurse rushing to her bedside. "Oh my God, are you all right? The police came to the house told me they brought you here because there had been a shooting." He held her hand between his.

"I'm okay." She placed a hand on his cheek. "Jake got shot.

They took him into surgery."

****

Still a little groggy, Jake stared at the wall, contemplating how his life had gotten so fucked up. Peter knew the truth and said he'd put in a good word, but the report had to be filed.

He knew the minute Allison entered the room. She had bandages where she'd been cut. Jake closed his eyes reliving those moments and cursing himself for ever letting it get that far.

"Are you awake?"

"Hi," he said.

"I hear the operation went well."

"The doctor told me my wound had been cauterized. I thought you might know something about that."

She bowed her head. "I don't know what you're talking about."

He stared at her then looked away. "Someday you'll have to tell me more about your abilities."

"Someday?"

He nodded. "But first I need to tell you some things."

"Jake. You don't—"

"Yes, I do."

"Okay," she said in a soft voice.

"In case you hadn't guessed, Jared was my twin."

Her eyes fixed on his.

"Being a twin, you almost never have a thought of your own. At least that's how Jared and I were."

"You were close."

He made a face. "Yes and no. Jared had trouble with people, but he was brilliant. I didn't have a problem with people."

"You mean before you showed up here with your scowls and threats, you were actually pleasant?"

The truth of the telling took a lot out of him, but she deserved the whole truth. "Jared brought out the worst in me. He was a constant frustration." He sighed. "It took its toll on my folks too."

Jake ran hands through his hair. "There's no plausible reason for what Jared did. I tried thinking through all of them."

"You feel guilt, pain, like somehow you're responsible."

"Are you reading me?"

She shrugged. "The vibes you're sending are hard to miss. You can't blame yourself for his actions."

"Jared's IQ was high. He'd sit for hours working mathematical equations in his head, writing theories, but he struggled with the simple things in life. I took things as they came, embraced it, and advanced. In school, sports, girls."

Allison grabbed his hand.

"Jared went to college, the same one I attended, and studied to be a doctor. We were happy, hoping things had finally turned around for him."

Jake quieted, remembering.

"After several months Jared met a girl, Claire." Jake closed his hand around Allison's. "She wore her long hair in a ponytail and when she smiled, it would light up a room. They started dating and Jared settled down, happier than he'd ever been.

He stopped speaking and swallowed. "It turned out Claire started seeing Jared to get close to me. I had no idea," he said defensively. "One night, I came back from the library and found Claire lying naked in my bed. I threw her out immediately."

"Jared had been coming to see me and when I opened the door for her to leave, he saw Claire buttoning her pants."

Jake took a deep breath. "Jared didn't say a word, but the look in his eyes spoke volumes. He punched me in the face and walked away. I never saw him again until I got here."

Jake released Allison's hand. "Strange things began happening around campus. Animals found mutilated, graffiti then Claire was murdered."

Allison's hands flew to her mouth. "Murdered?"

"I eventually graduated and became a cop. In the back of my mind I suspected Jared had killed her, but had no evidence. I never knew for sure until now."

"So you joined the FBI," she said.

"Part of me hoped that I'd never hear from him again."

"You weren't responsible for what happened to Claire."

"Jared was right. We aren't that different, two parts of the same bad seed."

"Stop it," she yelled. "You stop it right now. Jared had mental problems, wiring gone wrong. You are not the same, dammit."

"Allison."

She rose and moved away. "I sensed something in him that kindled hope. He wanted to stop. His plan that night was death."

"Deep down, I knew that."

Tears flowed. "I'm sorry."

"Me too." His gaze followed her walk around the room. "There's more."

Allison froze. "More?"

"I'm afraid so. Come sit down."

She wandered to the chair.

"Did you ever wonder how you connected to Jared? Why?"

With a deep sigh she said, "I know why. There's something I didn't tell you either. I knew him a long time ago when we were teenagers. We met in our dreams every night." Her eyes got a dreamy look. "I thought I loved him, but then my parents died, and I shut down my abilities. I never contacted him again."

"You're wrong."

"Generally, about a lot of things." She huffed.

"No, I mean about Jared being Alex."

"How did you—" She narrowed her eyes at him. "I never told you his name was Alex."

"I had some identity problems back then. One night I discovered that I could create a dream world. A beautiful girl visited me there. I fell in love with her."

"But—"

"My middle name is Alexander."

"Why didn't I recognize you? I should have recognized you."

He shrugged. "For the same reason I didn't recognize you at first. I realized it the day I saw your mother's photograph." His gaze softened. "You pretended to be her in your dreams."

"Well, to look a little like her anyway." She smiled.

He grasped her hand. "I went to the island every night for weeks but you never came back. Finally, I gave up. I never wanted to feel that way again so I quit using my limited abilities and they disappeared."

"What about Jared though. How did he know me?"

"I've been thinking on that. Jared and I could link in our minds. We did it a lot when we were little. He probably watched us together."

Tears streaked down Allison's cheeks.

"Don't cry, angel."

She shook her head. "I'm sorry."

"Come here." He pulled her hand bringing her closer for his kiss.

"I'm sorry I hurt you like that. I had been so distraught I just—

"Don't." He put his finger to her lips.

"I need to ask you something."

Jake braced himself.

"I can't get this song out of my head and I want to know what it has to do with you."

He breathed a sigh. "What song?"

"I heard you playing it one night at your house."

"*House of the Rising Sun*. It was my favorite song in college. I played it all the time."

"Thank you. I needed a title."

"I love you, Allison."

She stared at him and blinked. He held his breath waiting to see what she would do or say this time.

"I love you too."

Allison leaned in to kiss him.

He trailed hot kisses down her neck and back up until their lips met. Visions of Allison's naked body wrapped around his and in various enticing positions played like a sensual love scene through his mind. Every nerve in his body crackled.

"Whoa. What was that?"

"I wanted to see if I could reach you so I sent a few images."

"It felt like a thousand volts."

"Did you see them?"

"Hell, yes. And when I get out of this hospital, I want to try them all."

Together in Darkness audiobook is now available at Audible.com

ABOUT THE BOOK

I have always been interested in the connection between twins. What makes one person do one thing and another person do another? The human mind is a fascinating piece of work and it intrigues me with the different facets.

When I started this book I asked the question what would happen if one twin had things easier than the other and how would that affect them, and their interaction with others. I researched profilers and how they approach each job. Then asked what if the killer was a twin?

The story catapulted down a darker road.

I have been a lover of the paranormal since about the time I could walk. It drew me long before it became a popular fiction genre. With psychics, again the mind comes into play. Since we only use approximately 10% of our brains, what would happen if we could use 50%? What amazing things could be accomplished? I've only shown bits and pieces in this book. Still, it's a thought-provoking question.

I hope you enjoyed the characters. I felt rather close to them myself.

Thank you to all the readers with whom I can share my obsessions.

~Sloan

The Perfect Storm by Sebastian Junger.

House of the Rising Sun by The Animals (1964)

Dear Readers,

I hope you enjoyed my paranormal romance, **Together in Darkness**, and would be kind enough to write an honest review on Goodreads, or whatever platform you frequent. Your time is much appreciated.

Thank you.

Sloan McBride

See next page for a glimpse of *The Fury*

Available at Amazon, iBooks, Barnes & Noble,
Google Play, Kobo and Audible.

Praises for The Fury

Rating: 4.5 Nymphs   "...the pacing for this story is perfect, leading the reader on a rollercoaster thrill ride of demon fighting, cultural understanding and the blossoming of new and forbidden love...And in great secondary characters, and you have all the things needed to propel this wonderful series into the future. I look forward to the next release. Read and enjoy!

~ Mystical Nymph, Literary Nymphs Reviews

Rating: 85   "...The Fury is a cleanly written and enjoyable story..., the emotion component in the romance is presented well enough for me to accept that there is more between the main characters than merely hormones going wild, and the last few pages are really romantic to read indeed..."

~ Mrs. Giggles

Rating: 5 Hearts   "Fight/action scenes add some tense and thrilling moments. The love scenes were arousing and incredibly sexy. The dialogue was well-written and flowed smoothly. It had me laughing on more than one occasion. This is a superb and thoroughly entertaining start to what looks to be an awesome series. It grabbed me and held me from the first to last page..."

~ Abi, The Romance Studio

Rating: 4 Hearts   "...THE FURY is the first book of a wonderful new series from author Sloan McBride called Time Walker. Full of intriguing characters, fast paced storyline and simmering sexual tension, this is an author who leaves you on the cusp of something wonderful with each page until the climatic ending is revealed..."

~ Dawn, Love Romances & More Reviews

THE FURY
A Time Walker Novel
By
Sloan McBride

The next couple of seconds happened quickly. She pushed him against the back quarter panel of the car, jumped in the driver's seat, and threw the car in gear. He only had an instant to move before she ran over his foot.

He growled his frustration. With a flick of his wrist, a sudden gale-force wind exploded, swirling the snow into a blinding tornado. Dagan held his hand out and said, "Hold." The car screeched to a halt. He could hear Reese gunning the motor as she pressed on the gas, still attempting to get away. Wincing, he bent over to retrieve his coat and silently cursed the blue-eyed vixen. Calmly, he strolled to the car, opened the passenger door and got in. The wind disappeared as quickly as it had erupted and the snow went back to falling lazily to the ground.

"Get out of my car!" she yelled.

His dark brow lifted. He'd never understand humans. Her life was in mortal danger. Kur would be drawn to Reese because of her ancestry, an ancient bloodline from Kur's most hated enemy, Enki.

Dagan's oath and duty required that he protect her whether she wanted it or not, and by the gods, he planned to keep her alive. Whispering the obedience spell in the old language, Dagan smiled when her eyes glazed over. The sprinkle of freckles on her nose and cheeks were light but gave her an impish look. Her brows were thin and perfectly arched over enigmatic blue eyes clouded with confusion. She put the car in gear and started driving.

"Where are we going?" Reese turned the knob so the air coming out of the vents got warmer.

"Drive out of the city. We'll find a cheap motel to stay for the night."

"I'll go out of the city, but only so far as my house," she countered.

Dagan gave her a penetrating stare. "You'll do as I say."

She growled. "I could go to the police station so they can arrest your ass for kidnapping."

He couldn't help but laugh. She had a feisty streak. And, for some reason, she had been able to subvert the spell. This warranted some serious investigation.

"You think this is funny?" She frowned. "You fly out of nowhere, knocking me down and bruising my..." He glanced over at her. "Never mind." She sighed. "I only have your word that those people were actually after me."

She had a point.

Dagan took a minute to study her before saying, "They shot the *melari* dart at you before I appeared."

The truth of his words registered on her face as she absorbed what he'd said.

"I'm an archeologist. I don't know anything important or top secret. My job actually bores most people, unless they love digging around in dirt to find pieces of ancient civilizations. Why would I be in danger?"

"It's not what you know but who you are that puts you in jeopardy."

"You make no sense."

He gently trailed his fingertips down the sleeve of her coat. He used his mental powers of persuasion to calm her nerves and minimize her fear.

"I can't be sure those demons are not following us. They may already know where you live and could be waiting." He felt her fear escalating again, and a glimpse of her disappointment had him saying, "I'll give you ten minutes at your place to grab some things." Maybe having some of her personal belongings would make this ordeal a little easier, if that were possible. "Then we'll find a motel. Once I'm sure you're safe, I will answer your questions."

Reese frowned, her brows dipping between her eyes. Waves of uncertainty coming off her battered him.

"Did you say demons just then? Demons, like in horror movies?"

"Not exactly like the movies, but demons they are."

"Have you visited a psychiatrist lately? I know a good one. I can give you her card," she offered dryly.

"I'm not crazy."

She gave him a yeah-right look, but said nothing more.

About the Author

Sloan McBride is a multi-published romance author who lives in the paranormal. Her current otherworldly fascination is the Time Walkers. These stories blend Sumerian Mythology with the past, present and future. This army of warriors battles the King of the Underworld, demons, and some fallen gods. Book 1 —*The Fury*, and Book 2 —*The Treasure* are available now.

Sloan currently has five books in the making, three of which are for a new trilogy. These heroes are sexy daredevils, who will steal your heart and leave you breathless. Check out Book 1 of the Men of Fire Trilogy —*Dangerous Heat* available now.

She belongs to a critique group with two other writers, A.J. Brower and Melanie Carroll. They are known as the Sassy Scribes.

She lives in the Midwest with her husband of 35 years, two grown children and one princess girly dog name Oakley.

Connect with Sloan online:
Website: http://www.sloanmcbride.com
Facebook: https://www.facebook.com/sloan.mcbride
Pinterest: https://www.pinterest.com/sloanmcbride/
Twitter: https://twitter.com/SloanMcBride1

CPSIA information can be obtained
at www.ICGtesting.com
Printed in the USA
BVHW01s0123051018
529374BV00014B/93/P

9 780988 403390